The Long Water

Also by Stef Penney

The Tenderness of Wolves
The Invisible Ones
Under a Pole Star
The Beasts of Paris

The Long Water

STEF PENNEY

QUERCUS

First published in Great Britain in 2024 by

QUERCUS

Quercus Editions Ltd
Carmelite House
50 Victoria Embankment
London EC4Y 0DZ

An Hachette UK company

A CIP catalogue record for this book is available
from the British Library

HB ISBN 978 1 52942 567 3
TPB ISBN 978 1 52942 568 0
EBOOK ISBN 978 1 52942 569 7

1

Typeset in Cambria by CC Book Production
Printed and bound in Great Britain by Clays Ltd, Elcograf S.p.A.

Papers used by Quercus are from well-managed forests and other responsible sources.

For Mags

Prologue

In Nordland (pronounced 'Noor-lan'), in the north of Norway, there is first of all the sea. The county is the longest, thinnest segment of a long, thin country, its coast fretted like a saw blade, teeth bared to the chilly ocean, which is so thickly sprinkled with islands it looks like the aftermath of some gigantic shipwreck. North of the Arctic Circle, life thrives along the coast, because the deep waters and clashing currents give rise to an abundance of nutritious silver treasure. Also along the coast, there are pockets and strips of flat, fertile land: at the foot of mountains, at the end of fjords, sheltered from icy storms. The largest towns are on the coast, because why would you want to live anywhere else? Even in the depths of winter, the Norwegian Sea never freezes, whereas, inland, temperatures are several degrees colder, and the lakes become fields of ice.

From the city on the coast, a crooked finger of sea pokes into the slender waist of Norway, as though trying to nip the country in two. The fjord is so squeezed between mountains and islands that it produces one of the strongest currents in the world – Saltstraumen: a boil of raging waters and whirlpools. The inner fjord – the one the sea is in such a hurry to get into, before it changes its mind and can't wait to leave – is the first of a chain of lakes and rivers. They are flung across the map like a necklace of misshapen pearls: Nervatnet, Øvervatnet, the sinuous ribbon of a river known as Langvasselva – the river of the Long Water – and then the lakes Langvatnet, Lomivatnet and Muorkkejávrre. The names of the outer lakes are prosaic: Nervatnet means the Lower Lake; Øvervatnet, the Upper Lake; Langvatnet – can you guess? – is the Long Lake. There is no road beyond the Long Lake. If you want to go further into the mountains, you have to walk, or hire a helicopter. By the time you've trudged all the way up to the small, peaceful lake called Muorkkejávrre, which abuts the border with Sweden, the language of the coast has given up its right to name things. The last name is Sámi, and it means the lake where you can drag your boat over the land, from when that was the only way to get around.

This far inland, the mountains are quite unlike the mountains that guard the coast. Those island mountains – you'll know them: they're the ones on the cover of those enticing cruise brochures – rise out of the sea like teeth; a landscape from the brain of a Romantic painter with tertiary syphilis: fanged, sheer and improbable. Cruise liners creep along at their feet, tourists lining the decks to film their grandeur. The island mountains are awe-inspiring: giants that block out the sun; walls of a prison of silver light. But there are also cute villages that hide luxury hotels; restaurants with amazing dishes; galleries where you can buy expensive souvenirs; erstwhile fishing stations that are retreats for artists; as well as whales and eagles and plenty of akvavit to take the edge off all that sublimity. Those mountains are much photographed and justly famous.

Inland, the mountains shun such attention. They seem older than the mountains of the coast – smoothed and worn down as they are by the grinding of ancient ice, traces of which remain – although they are not older, they're just more patient and quiet. They do not seek fame. Their lower slopes are furred with birch and willow, and in summer the ground is boggy, tangled with mosses and ferns and braided with waterfalls that stain the bare rocks red. In winter, the constant sound of water vanishes; everything is hushed and stilled by snow.

Some way inland, then, much nearer Sweden than the coast, on the northern shore of the Long Lake, at the foot of the modest mountains, sits the little town of Sulitjelma, known to all and sundry as Sulis. There is a narrow strip of land along the shore where the houses congregate; and the road, the hotel, the supermarket, the middle school, the white, spired church – everything you need, really, as long as you're not too demanding. You certainly can't complain about the quality of the air, which is clean and bracing, although it was not always so.

Before 1975, there wasn't even a road. It was too remote and useless a place for anyone to have reason to go there. For many centuries, the place was known only to Sámi herders who took their reindeer to breed in the sheltered valley. Things changed when a Sámi farmer, who had for years noticed veins of rust in the mountains and around the waterfalls, found a chunk of yellow, glittering mineral. He took it to a merchant in the town down on the fjord, who determined that it was not gold, but copper ore. Still valuable. Still worth a bit of effort, but nothing happened fast; it was the middle of the nineteenth century, and this was the remote Arctic, so it was decades before someone bought the mineral rights and built a railway to link the new mine to a landing stage on the fjord. It was the first in northern Norway, and Norway wasn't even an independent country, still being united with Sweden. The mining company followed the seams of ore further into the mountains, and people flocked there to work. They dug out iron, sulphur and copper, even silver and gold, and, by the end of the century, Sulis had become something of a boom town.

But, like everything else that comes from the earth, a mine has a lifespan. There were the good decades, when the population of the valley topped three thousand. Production from the Sulis mines reached a grisly zenith during the Second World War, when the occupying German army squeezed ore from the mountains and used prisoners of war to build the roads and railways which were to supply the troops on the northern front. Did you know that Hitler intended to move his new Reich's capital to Norway after the war? Trondheim, to be precise. Fortunately, they ran out of time before this grand, mad vision was carried out, but not before thousands of prisoners had died. The stretch of the E6 north of Rognan is still called the Blood Road.

In the 1950s, to shorten the journey to the coast, tunnels were blasted through the mountains. In the early seventies, when the ore became too awkward and expensive to pursue further, the railway was torn up and replaced with a road. The mountains were insulted with yet more dynamite as the tunnels were rebuilt, or re-blasted – whatever it is that they do to tunnels to make them more . . . modern. God knows what they were like before, because even today the tunnels are wormholes: narrow and low, no bigger than they need be, with rough, rock-hewn walls. From outside, they look like small, surprised mouths in the mountainside. I hasten to add that there is nothing at all unusual about these tunnels.

Despite these improvements, the mines of Sulis were increasingly unprofitable. From the late 1960s, there were decades of closures as, one after another, the mines were abandoned, and the last one was put out of its misery in the 1990s. The inland mountains could at last go back to being patient and quiet – or so the mountains might have been forgiven for thinking. In fact, the old workings were turned into a museum and the derelict buildings marketed as a tourist attraction – what else could you do with them? Well, doing nothing is always an option, isn't it? But nothing was not good enough. The miners' houses on the mountain were picturesque, and, painted in Nordic primary colours – ochre yellow, rust red, you know the sort of thing – they have become a resort for hikers and skiers. Remoteness, beauty, snow: it turned out these could be sold, just as the fish and the ore had been.

So, get on with it, you're probably thinking. Why are we here, of all places?

I shall tell you.

One night in May, when already it hardly grows dark, four senior pupils at the high school in Fauske went on some sort of expedition in the mountains near Sulis. They had been going to look for something – maybe gold. There have always been rumours that there is still gold up there, waiting to be unearthed. Or they were going to climb a summit to enjoy the view and keep vigil through the soft twilight of a spring night, to get drunk and hold their childhoods once more in their hands before they buckled down to final exams and then spun off in various directions, to national service and university degrees, to live their separate lives. Accounts of their purpose and even of their whereabouts on the night differed, but one thing was certain: only three of them came back.

One

My name is Svea. That's an unusual name, you might think, for a Norwegian of my vintage. Basically, it means 'Swedish', although I could argue that it is a version of the masculine Sverre, from the Old Norse *sverrir*, meaning 'wild, swinging'. That's rather more exciting, but take your pick: swinging, or Swedish; I don't care. Svea Hustoft. In town, I get called both Miss Hustoft and Mrs Hustoft. Both are equally meaningless. At one point in my life, I was called Svea Øvergaard, but I didn't like that. Not that Hustoft is any great shakes, but at least it doesn't have such unpleasant associations. Anyway – what is my vintage? I'm seventy-nine, if you must know, although I think it's rather rude of you to ask. No, I don't look it, do I? Don't think you can get round me with flattery. It's too late for that. Really, people these days – no manners at all.

I live in a house on the edge of town. From the south-facing rooms upstairs – in other words, my bedroom and the room I never know what to do with, so it is full of stuff that doesn't matter – there is a view of the fjord that people rave about, if they are allowed that far into my house. I live alone with Asta, who is a puffin hound, and more intelligent than most people. I cannot think of her as 'my dog', as that is beyond insulting. She is no more mine than I am hers. Without her, I don't know what I would do. Well, I suppose I could get another dog, though I still miss my last companion, Tommy, who died eight years ago, at the good age of fifteen – rest in peace, dear Tommy. I was heartbroken – that's what it felt like – as though the thing I needed to keep me going was *kaputt*. I had serious misgivings about getting another dog after losing Tommy, as to do so implied that he was replaceable, which he was not, but Odd Emil kept urging me to do it. I couldn't retort that he didn't know what he was talking about, as he had recently lost his wife. Anyway, I'm glad he persisted. Asta is seven now, and she may well outlive me. Though, it wouldn't be fair – would it? – to leave her alone when I am all she's ever known. I suppose she could go and live with Odd Emil, if he hasn't already fallen off his perch (he may be four years younger than me, but he is a man, and somewhat plump – need I say more?). Perhaps Asta and I will have a suicide pact, and we'll go together when the time comes. Would I tell you if I had planned this? You're entitled to ask a question, but it doesn't mean you deserve an answer.

I've never much cared for this house. For as long as I can remember, I dreamt of living in the middle of nowhere, at the end of a very long track, in an impenetrable forest. As far as I could get from the sea. I suppose I could have done it, but, when you have to work in an office and you're bringing up your daughter on your own, you need to think about practicalities like getting to work in winter and taking her to school, and access to doctors and play dates and dance classes and so on. I dreamt about it, but I never did it. When I finally retired from the power company – they had to practically throw me out of the building, as well as pay me off handsomely, because I threatened them with an age-discrimination suit – and Klara had, obviously, left home long before, the need to live in town was no longer so pressing. But, by then, well, I suppose I had lost my nerve.

So, here I am, living in this characterless but efficient house, in a very penetrable cul-de-sac. On the edge of this little town that looks, from afar, as though someone has chucked a bucket of sugar cubes on to the ground. Like so many towns in the Arctic. We have the Germans to thank for that – or, rather, a combination of the German occupation and Allied bombing. During the Second World War, we (and, by 'we', I mean the whole of northern Norway) were in the unenviable position of being occupied, bombed, blown up, set alight, you name it – by both sides. That's why we have hardly any buildings that were built before the war. Razed. We were erased. Almost.

Nowadays, the house is bigger than I need, but being on the edge of town makes it handy for walking Asta. Although, increasingly, I tend not to walk her in the woods; rather, I turn the other way and go into town. Why is that? In case I fall and break a hip. I'm joking. Partly. There are too many people who run in the woods now, pounding past, radiating the smugness of the physically fit, or – worse – riding those fat-wheeled bikes and pinging their bells to make me hurl myself out of the way. Your operating radius shrinks in inverse proportion to your awareness of frailty, but I do what I can. When I was younger, Tommy and I would take long hikes together. Our favourite place was on the spit of land beyond Finneid, between the fjord and Nervatnet. I would park by the campsite and we'd walk through the woods, past the marble quarry and down to the water. That's the small quarry, not the big one up the hill, but the stone from there is uniquely beautiful: you see cut faces layered with peach, carmine, ivory, charcoal, all in perfect stripes, like a silk curtain, or one of those French opera cakes. Years ago, I stole a particularly satisfying chunk and lugged it all the way back to the car. It sits on my hearth, where its stripes glow a radiant pink when hit by the sun. It's not just iron and copper that hide under the ground here. I couldn't do that now – steal something that weighs eleven kilos. As of last year, I'm not really supposed to drive, but, without the car, my radius would be very small indeed.

So, we don't go far. But, also, I stay in town so that I will see my best friend. What? I have friends – did you think I was the scary old witch whom everybody hates? I'm the scary old witch whom some people hate, but that says more about them than it says about me.

Today, the fjord is the intense blue of lapis lazuli. It's late April and the sun is low enough, at midday, to strike right through the living room like a sword of truth. I made the mistake of opening the curtains with thoughtless abandon, and had to recoil like a vampire, swearing. With the new eye drops Sunny has given me, it takes a long time for my vision to return to something like normal. She tells me I should get those glasses that darken in bright light, to protect my eyes from further damage, but so far I haven't capitulated; I don't want to look like a South American drug lord. You're probably laughing now – you're thinking, Don't be silly; South American drug lords don't look like white-haired old ladies. Well. Shows how much you know.

Now I have to take Asta out. Things to do.

We take the road down towards the waterfront. Asta scampers along happily, in the prime of life, tugging at the leash as she investigates the delicious aromas of dogs' piss and last night's vomit. I, on the other hand, have to walk carefully, as any sudden movements can cause a sharp pain to shoot through my hips. That is the price one pays for not dying young. We follow our usual circuit. Past the stadium, past Eivind Arnesen's hunting shop, where they are, as always, having a sale – shooting things being a great Norwegian tradition – and down to the waterside, where we walk along the front. This way takes us to my favourite café, where we will stop in for coffee and *møsbrømlefse*. My granddaughter tells me it's unhealthy to eat *lefse* so often, consisting as it does of flour, sugar and butter: three things I am, apparently, not supposed to eat. That's before you've added the brown cheese and sour cream. I don't have that many pleasures in life, I could have replied. Or I could have said, I've got to the age of seventy-nine and who cares what happens next? But I couldn't be bothered, as Elin is annoying enough before you try to argue with her. She's a vegan and will go on at great length about the cruel horrors of dairy farming. Those horrors don't seem that bad to me, but she is sixteen and has the eyes of a fanatic. The young are so righteous, these days. Quick to take offence, quick to judge, quick to condemn. I think it's because they are terrified, and, with the way the world is now, who can blame them? The other reason we walk into town, apart from a good helping of all the delicious things that are going to kill me, is to see Odd Emil, who is often the only person I speak to in a day – that is, apart from Asta, if you count her as a person, which I most certainly do.

By the way, I'm not being rude about my friend. 'Odd' is an Old Norse name that means 'point of a weapon'. Odd Emil is not a particularly sharp person, but we have these names that hearken back to our Viking past, especially in the older generation. My sisters were christened Magny and Nordis, which mean 'strength' and 'north goddess', respectively. A lot more impressive than being named after someone else's country, I think you'll agree, but then, I drew the short straw in a lot of ways.

We get to the café after two. It's a good time to come – after the lunchtime rush has died down and before the schoolkids pile in. But, today, annoyingly, one of the booths is occupied by a pair of giggling girls in ugly red overalls; although, surely they should be in school this afternoon? They have shrugged off the tops of their overalls to reveal tight, too-short white T-shirts, even though it's nippy outside and snowdrifts still lurk on the north side of every building.

I take a table at the back, as far away from them as I can get. Katrin is behind the counter. She knows me well enough to know what my order will be, and she brings a bowl of water for Asta and strokes her head.

'Hello, girl. It's nice to see you both. How are you today?' asks Katrin.

'Surviving,' I say, which is the only honest answer you can give when you are my age.

'I'm glad to hear it. The usual?'

I nod and grunt in reply. She's a nice girl, Katrin. Nice woman, rather, I suppose, since she has two girls of her own. I have to be careful what I say to her, as, given the slightest encouragement, she will go on and on about the kids. When I was bringing up Klara, I didn't bang on about her all the time, and certainly not to people who hadn't met her. Why can't more people be like that?

As I wait, I'm trying to ignore the schoolgirls, but their voices are unnecessarily loud; they emit high-pitched bursts of laughter, toss their long hair around and talk without looking at each other, eyes glued to their phones as though the screens are the umbilical cord that connects them to all life. They seem detached from their surroundings, yet also to be performing – for whom? I do not flatter myself that it is for my benefit. For Katrin? For some invisible audience out in the æther, or just each other? Perhaps they are rehearsing being their best selves on the off chance that they will encounter some male persons worth the display.

I hardly ever see kids this age on their own, but, if they are, they are invariably communing with their electronic companion. I worry about them, I really do. When I was eighteen, I was alert and attentive to the people around me. I spoke quietly and didn't call attention to myself. But then, when I was eighteen, I was already working, supporting myself and living on my own. People became adults earlier, in those days. Nowadays, teenagers, and even adults, seem to act like irresponsible children until – well, sometimes, they never stop.

It isn't long before Odd Emil comes in. First, he greets Katrin and asks after her kids. That takes a good five minutes. Then he politely asks if he may join me. He always asks, even though we have done this three times a week, for . . . oh, the last eight years.

The first time I saw him come in here, it was January – one of those spirit-sapping days that make you believe winter will never end, when you fantasise, once again, about moving south. Old age and Arctic cold are not the best of friends. The light outside, even in the middle of the day, was a listless, grey twilight. I was sitting at the back, as usual, and Asta's predecessor, dear Tommy, was lying under my chair. My mood was as dark as the sky; I was trying to push from my mind the knowledge that Tommy was on his last legs. He had been diagnosed with liver cancer, prognosis not good. I'd been putting off taking him to the vet, but I knew I'd have to do it. It took more and more effort just to get him out of the house. Once he'd made it to the café – and sometimes he didn't – he could only flop on to the floor in exhaustion. He would gaze at me with his patient brown eyes – not pleading, just waiting for me to be ready. 'I know,' I told him, 'I know.' It wasn't fair to hang on to him just because I couldn't bear the prospect of life without him.

The opening door sent a blast of cold air rolling through the café. I blotted my eyes and looked up from Tommy to see the damp, bulky figure of Odd Emil Holmen. Like everyone around here, I knew that he spent his days looking after his terminally ill wife – he was devoted to her, everyone said. That is the sort of knowledge you absorb through the air of a small town, where people live in uninterested proximity for decades. We weren't friends. Up till this point, we had exchanged greetings perhaps a dozen times over the years, although we'd known of each other all our lives. We grew up in the same fishing village, but he is, as I have said, four years younger than me, and, when you are children, that is a huge gulf, although he went to school with one of my sisters, and, in fact, he dated my other sister for a while. But all that is a very long time ago. He moved away and married someone else, and so on and so forth. Until we both, via different roads, ended up here.

Even when young, Odd Emil had been awkward. He was a large, cumbersome boy, who became a large, cumbersome man. He moved slowly, as if worried he was about to knock over something or someone smaller than himself. It came across as a physical expression of his shyness. But, on that day in January, it was something else. He dragged himself through the door with extreme weariness. His face was sagging, his eyes almost hidden behind loose folds of skin. When he pulled off his cap, I saw that he needed a haircut. He looked utterly worn out. I

13

guessed that it was near the end for Ann-Karin. Perhaps we had that dread in common. Somehow, our eyes snagged in the middle of the room and, instead of quickly moving on, our gaze held and something odd happened. The only way I can describe it is to say that I felt something give inside me, something vast and cold, just as, once in a blue moon, a glacier will shift by whole inches and a crack will appear on the surface, letting in the light.

'Mrs Hustoft. Hello. May I join you?'

I wasn't taken aback by the question, as it already seemed inevitable. I nodded to the chair opposite, and he sat down, and I began to tell him about Tommy; I said things I had never said to anyone else. We'd known of each other's existence as long as I could remember, but that was the beginning of our friendship.

I only ever see Odd Emil in the café. We're like a pair of elderly, clandestine lovers who rendezvous in secret. Except that we're not lovers, and the café is hardly a private place, so . . . not really like that at all. There was a time when he seemed to be hoping for something more. About a year after Ann-Karin died, he invited me over to his house for dinner a couple of times, and once or twice even tried to tempt me along to a Holmen family gathering, but that prospect repelled me. I didn't want to be Ann-Karin's replacement, which was rather too much what it felt like. I think marriage is a habit for some people, but it's not a habit I ever acquired. So, I declined anything that felt like a date, and now he no longer asks. It has, occasionally, occurred to me to wonder if he might be seeing someone else in that way, but I don't know, and I suppose I don't want to. I keep my nose out of other people's personal business, for their sakes as well as mine. I don't know about you, but, generally, the more I know about someone's private life, the more I hate them.

I make the mistake of glancing towards the young girls, and the dark one catches my eye, leans forward and mutters something to her friend. They both shriek with laughter. The noise seems to grate the inside of my skull.

'Why do they have to talk so damn loudly? They're right next to each other.'

'They're happy, that's all.'

Odd Emil is more tolerant of young people than I am. I suspect he actually likes them. Whenever he talks about his five grandchildren, his face softens into a foolish smile.

'Is your Elin excited about the russ time?'

'I shouldn't think so. She won't be russ for another two years.'

The russ time is our tradition for graduating high-school seniors. Why it consists of weeks of drinking and partying, dressing up in brightly coloured overalls and carrying out humiliating pranks – all just before their final exams – I couldn't tell you.

'But they all get involved in the parties, don't they? Daniel is loving it.'

Daniel is his eldest grandchild, set to graduate this summer. Although Daniel and Elin are two years apart, Odd Emil likes to tease me that our grandchildren will become best friends and may even – who knows! – get married. He hasn't met Elin, so he doesn't appreciate how unlikely that is. My granddaughter is a bit of an oddball, to put it politely, while Daniel is handsome and popular: in every way the perfect grandson. I saw a picture of him in the paper once when his ski team won some competition.

'But you hear these awful stories, especially around the russ

15

time – young girls like that getting so drunk they don't know what they're doing, getting taken advantage of.'

'Oh, I don't think that happens much. Not now. I know you hear stories, but that's just –' he waves his arm vaguely – 'down south. Not here. They're good kids.'

'And the way they dress!' I glance over at the two girls. 'Showing everything off. They're so careless.'

Odd Emil says, 'They're carefree.'

I don't really know what aspect of the russ time upsets me more: the absurd waste of money, or the loutish behaviour of the youth. The young girls – like these two: navels out, giggling over their phones – seem to believe that, however wantonly they behave, nothing bad will ever happen to them.

Two

Elin Torstensen is slumped in the back seat of Marylen Sundfær's Volvo, because it's that time of the morning. Beside her is her best friend Benny Iversen, their backpacks forming a damp bulwark between them. They are both sixteen and in their first year of high school, and, as the school is in Fauske and they live nearly an hour's drive away, up the valley of the Long Water, they have a ride-share arrangement. Marylen teaches at the school, and she lives near Benny and his mum, further up the valley, by Nilsbakken, while Elin lives in Sulis proper, by the church, with her dad. The arrangement is convenient for everyone. Benny's mum teaches yoga most mornings, and Elin's dad is too busy to spend hours a day driving to and fro from the school. To return the favour, Benny's mum lets Marylen come to her yoga classes – the ones that take place at the hotel in Sulis or at the gym in Fauske – for free. Elin isn't sure what her father offers in return for the lifts, but he is the vicar of Sulis church, so maybe everyone, even teachers, feels the need to keep on his good side. Or perhaps he pays her.

The car snakes along the road that follows the shore of Langvatnet, while rain rattles on the roof and the wipers swish back and forth.

It's like being inside a drum. Dense packets of rain are swept down the valley from the mountains. Each new gust claws the surface of the lake, making it shudder like the skin of an animal.

Elin pushes the hair out of her eyes; she's still getting used to her new, short haircut that won't tie back in a ponytail. She ran from the house to the car with her hood up, but she got soaked all the same. Elin is taller than Benny – she is taller than most people – and her legs are jammed into the well behind the passenger seat at an awkward angle. This morning, her nerves are more than usually on edge. She knew she would feel like this, but over breakfast is always the safest time to broach a difficult subject with her dad: there's a guaranteed escape after ten minutes, and there's nothing he can do. And it had worked out according to plan, in that she had screwed up her courage to make her statement while staring at her porridge, and her dad responded in his usual way. Then she got up and left.

'So, how're you guys today?' says Marylen, from the driver's seat.

In chorus, they both mutter, 'Fine.'

@VelociTazz:
—So, huh, told my dad this morning!
—Biting-lip emoji

@Supertwink3000:
—Wow, how'd it go?

—Scream emoji
—How'd you think?
—Breakfast apocalypse!
—Head-exploding emoji

—What did he say?

—He says he wants to understand, but
then he won't listen.

—I'm sure it'll be fine. he just needs time.

—*Kiss emoji*

—Hmmm

—*Confused-face emoji*

—How'd you leave it?

—He's pissed off/disappointed/thinks I'm
an idiot

—The usual basically.

—What – after only ten minutes?!?

—*Groucho Marx emoji*

—????

—I mean it'll take a while for him to get it.
Different generation, religious etc . . .

—But he will. It'll be ok.

—I hope so

—Of course it will. I promise.

—*Heart emoji x3*

Elin stares out of the window at grey sky, grey water, grey mountain. They leave the shore of Langvatnet behind and the road begins to wind through the valley of the Langvasselva. The slopes are covered with forest, the hilltops invisible under heavy cloud. She feels her throat closing up.

@Supertwink3000:
—You okay?

19

@VelociTazz:

—He makes me feel stupid and small

—You know you're not stupid

—Or small!

—I know

—But – it's like he thinks someone must
  have made me feel like this

—Or that something bad happened

—He can't believe it's who I am.

—I get it.

—He asked if I'm a ledbaim!

—. . . lesbian!

—NOOOOO! Not that! Anything but that!

—*Drooling emoji, Peach emoji*

—Nice Freudian slip btw!!!

—*Laughing emoji*

—Are you a ledbaim, btw?

—Can't tell you, that's private!

—*Laughing emoji x 3*

—He needs time to get used to it. Maybe
he could do some googling!? It'll be okay.

—*Crying emoji*

—I promise hon *Heart emoji x 3*

—Seriously – *Groucho Marx emoji*???

—Errrr . . . confused old man??

—I was under pressure!

—Don't judge me!

—*Laughing emoji*

Benny reaches around the backpacks and takes Elin's hand, rubbing it with his thumb in a gesture which she loves and can hardly stand in equal measure. Mrs Sundfær can't see, not that she's looking. She's squinting through the windscreen, complaining about the rain and how it's going to mess up her hair. While messaging Elin, Benny has been making sympathetic *I'm listening* noises, which seem to satisfy her. He's good at that – making people feel at ease. Benny is good at pretty much everything Elin finds difficult: dealing with other people; being liked; school stuff – which also seems to be life stuff. Benny sails through every subject, thinks of witty things to say at the right moment and manages the trick of being gay and popular at the same time. It helps that he has a cute, impish face and curly dark hair. Even the morons generally leave him alone, as they realise that picking on him would hurt their chances of making out with the top-tier girls, who all adore Benny.

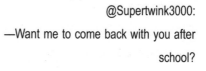

@Supertwink3000:
—Want me to come back with you after school?

@VelociTazz:
—Idk . . . I'll have to face him sometime.
—Thanks tho

—Might be better than you think??
—Why don't you send him some links?
—*Thumb-up emoji*
—*Heart emoji x 3*

It's been like this since they were eight years old and were sat side by side in primary school. Benny calms her down. He makes her feel

21

normal. She wishes he was her brother. She wishes she were him, basically. The fact that Benny will one day go away and do wonderful things and leave her here alone is too awful to contemplate.

The Volvo passes the scatter of buildings at the head of Øvervatnet and dives into the first of the three tunnels that bypass its precipitous shoreline. The noise around them switches from rain rattle to echoing engine drone: the sound of being in a confined space. As always, Elin finds herself holding her breath in response to plunging into this black maw. A stream of dim lights swoops overhead. Elin hates the tunnels; they don't seem big enough. Or reinforced enough. They're just naked rock tubes, dank and oppressive. When you pass a vehicle coming the other way, you can feel the car fight the force of its passing. After a bit, she has to breathe in – it takes too long to drive through on one breath, and, of course, it's fine. It's just a tunnel.

The three-kilometre tunnel takes two minutes to drive through, and then there is a short, rainy respite. Elin cracks open the window to replenish oxygen levels before they plunge into the next one. Once the middle tunnel releases them (open window, deep breaths), there is just the Grønnlifjell tunnel to go. It's as long as the Sjønståfjell tunnel, but worse, because she can't prevent herself from seeing in her head the pictures of the tunnel when it was flooded by heavy rains and they had to close it. Tons of earth and gravel were washed down the mountainside into the narrow tube. They keep talking about improving the drainage, but the tunnels are too small for the required machinery. So. It wasn't closed for long, but she is hyper-aware that this road is the only way in and out of her valley, so, if the tunnel closes, they are trapped. For some reason, no one else seems very bothered about this.

The Grønnlifjell tunnel widens its dark jaws and swallows them.

Benny is absorbed in his phone. Elin flicks on her timer. When she was little, and her family was still together, her mum and dad used to make-believe that they were driving into the belly of a dragon. Into its gaping mouth, down its gullet, into its gut. Oda, her big sister, loved it; she would shriek with delighted laughter. Elin did not.

'What the hell are those idiots doing?'

Mrs Sundfær has swung into the car park behind the high school and reverses into her teacher's spot.

A couple of students are standing in the car park, filming something on their phones. Two of this year's russ seniors have bound themselves together so tightly that they can hardly move. The three-legged entity is trying to get out of a car, to the accompaniment of swearing, jeering and yelling. Lorentz Jentoft eventually levers himself out, but he can't stay upright as Johnny Skarstein tries to keep up. Gaffer tape is wrapped around the entire length of their legs – one left, one right – and torsos. They collapse on the ground, shouting with laughter. Daniel Fjordholm gets out of the driver's seat, holds up his phone and films them writhing in a puddle as he backs away, ignoring their demands for help and flipping them the finger.

Mrs Sundfær sighs. 'I hate this time of year.'

It is well known that, last year, on the final night of the russ celebrations, some seniors climbed on to the roof of the head teacher's house and covered it with toilet paper. It rained and the paper turned into pink paste that took days to remove. Elin and Benny are juniors, so they have two more years before they will be expected to behave in a like manner. They all watch as the sodden pair struggle to their feet and begin to shuffle into the school building, bellowing with laughter.

'Dickheads,' says Benny. 'Sorry, but, you know.'

Lorentz is Elin's second cousin – well, second half-cousin. Half second-cousin? Whichever. They're not close.

'No, they are. Lorentz is worse than any of them.'

'Them' refers to the most notorious russ group in the school. Self-appointed party lions, these boys have named their group the 'Hellraisers' in a clear statement of intent – that of becoming legends for attention-grabbing stunts and hardcore partying. Membership of their group was the most sought after in the year, as the founding members are sporty and successful – generally seen as desirable dating material. The unofficial leaders are Lorentz Jentoft and Daniel Fjordholm. Lorentz rarely deigns to speak to Elin, either in school or outside. At (fairly rare) family gatherings, he either ignores her or teases her for being a) tall and b) weird. She has no response to this. It was Lorentz who first came up with the idea of calling her E.T. – which are, admittedly, her initials – but that's not why it stuck. It stuck because she is gangly, with a shock of pale hair and an arrangement of features that give her a resting expression of profound alarm. Elin tells herself that she likes it.

They get out of the car, pulling up their hoods, although the rain has almost stopped.

'Thanks for the lift,' says Benny.

'I've got a meeting till five thirty – will you wait for me?'

Elin nods vigorously.

'Yeah, sure,' says Benny. 'I've got piano, anyway.'

'And you, Elin?'

'Yes. I've got swimming.'

'Okay, then.'

She opens the boot to collect her briefcase and several bags full of papers.

'Do you want a hand with those?'

'No thanks, Benny. I've got it.'

Benny and Elin trail towards the entrance and Jamila Khan Kleve, a girl in their year, falls into step beside them. Elin listens as Benny and Jamila chat, marvelling at how easily they do it – this talking about nothing, skipping from topic to topic, from school gossip to a TV programme to homework and back. She can't follow the logic of it. Jamila mentions the big party at the weekend – is Benny going? Benny says, um, maybe, but he might have to work and he won't know until later in the week. Jamila, who is a kind, polite girl, then asks Elin – what about her? Elin shrugs, looks away and says she doesn't know. Jamila looks cross. She turns back to Benny and asks him about their homework. When they reach the door, she smiles at Benny but not at Elin. Elin has the sense that Jamila is upset with her, but isn't sure what she has done to cause this. She and Benny agreed they wouldn't tell anyone their plan, and saying she doesn't know is easier than coming up with a lie. She's bad at lying, which is okay, because lying is bad. But she often feels like this – as if she has missed some vital signal and, as a result, people don't seem to like her.

She is thinking about her father again, worrying, wondering now whether she should have just written him an email telling him that she identifies as genderfluid, instead of bringing it up over breakfast – why didn't she think of that? She could have asked him to write down his response, along with any questions he might have. It would then be easier to answer point by point or refer him to relevant material, instead of trying to interpret his troubled (appalled?) expression, as he said, 'But what does that actually *mean*?'

She gets out her phone and messages her dad some links, hoping that he will do some research before she gets home. That way, maybe she won't have to discuss it, ever again.

Three

As of two weeks ago, all the senior-year students are dressed in the same baggy overalls – as though they have succumbed to mass brain-washing and joined a cult. Marylen has never been comfortable around uniforms – a mass of people all wearing the same thing has never presaged anything good: soldiers, riot police, prisoners. But these bright, primary colours – the upper year is a sea of scarlet, with a few islands of blue and black – also make them look like giant toddlers in romper suits. And they are still children – just about – so why shouldn't they make the most of it?

Marylen hoists her armful of books and marking higher and tries to open the staffroom door with her backside. It doesn't move. She sighs. She's good at not swearing in school. She makes up for it at home, where no one cares. The door gives and a tall, blond youth is smiling at her, holding the door open.

'There you go, Marylen.'

'Thank you, Daniel. That your good deed for the day?'

He just laughs and rejoins his friends, and she feels a little mean. Daniel Fjordholm is a nice boy – one of the good ones. As a teacher, she is not supposed to have favourites, but of course she does, and

Daniel is a favourite of many. It's not always a question of outstanding talent – sometimes a young person just radiates some indefinably attractive quality: charm, openness, kindness ... Daniel has all of those, yes, but they don't quite capture it; the word that comes closest to describing him is 'good'. Despite that, Daniel is part of the most annoying russ group, the Hellraisers, and seems to be something of a leader, even though he's not academic, like Tobias Mero, or a champion skier, like Lorentz Jentoft, or too handsome for his own good, like Johnny Skarstein. There are other members in their group, but these four have special status; they are the ones that the girls cluster round, hoping to be chosen.

In the staffroom, Helene Shirani-Lund and Erik Lindqvist are already there, bitching and drinking coffee. Marylen goes over to the machine and pours herself a mug. Erik is repeating a rumour that his daughter Edny has heard – a rumour that some of the russ groups have made a secret list of dares, things that are unpalatable, even illegal. More unpalatable, that is, than drinking a whole bottle of wine in fifteen minutes or eating a kebab without using your hands – that sort of thing is standard. Russ celebrations have changed since she was at school; it was always about daft pranks and letting your hair down, but, since then (many years ago, now), a whole sector has grown up to cater for it, selling overalls, caps and cards ... all manner of stuff that the students dutifully buy. Then there are the sound systems for buses, the DJs making horrible electronic dance music, and the event companies that host parties and raves. Colossal quantities of alcohol are consumed, and doubtless other, less legal substances. It's a profitable juggernaut that everyone goes along with, even the police, although her old friend Hanne Duli, a senior officer at the local police department, rolls her eyes whenever she talks about it. For the police, this is a busy time of year.

Marylen has heard the rumour about illegal dares, since it crops up every year, and has discounted it as urban myth. It's true that, in the past, awful things have happened when celebrations got out of hand – the things that tend to occur when competitive alcohol consumption meets immaturity and toxic masculinity – but they haven't, generally, happened here; not in the past few years, what with increased awareness and the mandatory lectures on consent.

Erik is still going on about the things some teenagers get up to – what about the craze for naked sea swimming, extra points for going in before the first of May? He thinks it's only a matter of time before a hitherto unsuspected heart defect makes itself felt and someone drops dead ...

Helene says crisply, 'There are always rumours, Erik; they always turn out to be rubbish.'

'Edny swears a second-year from Bodø she knows of was drugged at a party last weekend. Luckily, her friends were around and took her to A & E.'

'Yeah, but it's difficult to tell the difference between being spiked, taking something you don't want to admit to, and being stupidly drunk. Were the police involved?'

'I don't know. She was very sure about it.'

Marylen says, 'The police are quite good on that, though, aren't they? And there are stewards and so on.'

'There can't be stewards in every house.' Erik looks at her through his rather daring new spectacle frames, the ones he's so proud of. Everyone else agrees they make him look like a serial killer. He says,

'Is it true the Hellraisers have a jacuzzi in their bus? Have you heard that? How on earth can they afford it?'

'The Jentofts have plenty of money.'

Lorentz Jentoft's grandfather is a local legend; from the poorest of fishing backgrounds after the war, he built a fish-farming business, then sold it at a huge profit. Consensus in the staffroom is that Lorentz is a spoilt brat.

Helene says, 'What I don't get is why Tobias Mero wastes his time running around with that lot.'

Tobias is a bit of a project for Helene. The Mero family arrived in Fauske from Syria, and are on the verge of applying for permanent residency. From his first year, Tobias has been a model student, winning prizes and getting his name on the honour roll. He has even been interviewed on local television: 'Boy who Lost Everything is now a Winner' – that sort of thing. The school is duly proud.

Marylen says, 'They're his friends. I mean, I know Lorentz and Johnny can be a pain, but it's nice, the way they've stuck together since he arrived.'

Helene harrumphs. 'To pick his brains, probably.'

The school bell rings to call them into lessons.

Erik sighs and shakes his head. 'I suppose I'll be volunteering to keep a lookout when it's Edny's turn.'

Helene says, 'They're eighteen, they're not babies. They have to learn to negotiate risk. At least what they get up to out of school isn't my problem, thank God.'

She sweeps out. Helene is the deputy head and has more than enough to worry about.

Erik snorts. 'She wouldn't say that if she had a daughter.'

Marylen watches his face change with comic slowness as he realises what he has said to her. 'God, sorry, Marylen, I didn't mean—'

'It's all right, Erik. Got to go. First-years.'

Erik, blushing, makes an elaborate show of tidying the coffee cups.

Marylen is always telling people it's all right when they put their foot in it about her daughter, because what else is she going to say?

Her phone buzzes as she walks along the corridor. She takes it out to read the message. Her heart rate increases.

It says:

—Hi! How are you? Would really like to talk
  sometime – when can you manage it?

The texts are always polite. Always properly spelled, with the correct punctuation. She texts back, despite the ban on texting in school corridors:

—I'll try and call you tonight
  Heart emoji x3

She thinks, Calm down, that's too much. She deletes two of the heart emojis. Pause. Then she deletes the third one.

The unadorned message flies away with a soft pop.

Then, as always, she deletes both messages in their entirety, before putting on her game face and entering the first-years' classroom.

Four

By evening, the rain has stopped and a low sun paints the white buildings with buttery light. The wind has dropped too, and the air in Sulis feels soft and springlike. Some days are like this – you can pass from one season to another in the space of a few hours. Mrs Sundfær drops Elin off at the house by the church. Benny watches Elin trudge up to the front door with shoulders slumped. He hopes things will be okay with her dad. He hopes he'll be kind and non-judgemental, but it's not a given. Benny spends a lot of his time worrying about other people – usually about Elin or, if not Elin, then his mum.

Elin's dad isn't a bad person, but he's a vicar and quite traditional in certain obvious ways. He's always been decent enough to Benny; at least, he's never seemed judgemental of Benny's sexuality – not that they have discussed it (Ha! Just imagine . . .). Benny tends to bring up the fact that he's gay if he thinks someone might not have noticed; once everyone is on the same page, then he knows where he stands; until then, there is always, for him, an element of tension. But Reverend Torstensen is rather intimidating. A while ago, Benny wondered if, as the vicar has known Benny since he was a kid, the fact that he's gay has just never occurred to him. When he brought it up with Elin, asked her if her dad knew, she said, 'Yeah, of course – he's not an idiot.' Then he asked her if he minded, and she paused, with her typical deliberation, before saying she didn't think so. It shouldn't matter in the slightest, of course (it's the third decade of the twenty-first century, FFS), and usually it doesn't, not at all – until, sometimes, it does.

He messages Elin to wish her luck. And a *Raised-fist emoji*, for courage. A *Heart emoji*, for love.

His own coming out to his mum, Toril, was fine. He hadn't really had to come out at all. When he'd told her, ages ago, that he had a crush on someone at school, she asked carefully, 'What's their name?' and, when he told her their name was Filip, she said she hoped he was nice. She told him she loved him, and they hugged. He was laughing and crying at the same time. Which made her laugh and cry too. Neither was surprised. It has been just the two of them for years and he thinks she's actually rather proud of having a gay son, as though it makes her somehow cooler. She is pretty cool, anyway; she's a ceramic artist and yoga teacher, and into lots of alternative things. She listens to him and rarely passes judgement on anyone. Basically, he is that gay cliché – his mum is his biggest cheerleader. No battle scars to parade. When he came out to his dad, he was staying with him in Stavanger, where his dad is some big oil executive. That was more nerve-racking, but his dad had, after a second or two, just hugged him – rather awkwardly – and said, 'As long as you're happy, Bendik, that's all that matters. I love you – you know that, don't you?'

That was his fourth (or fifth, or sixth?) coming out. The thing about being queer is, you don't just come out once and then it's over. Whenever you meet someone new, you have to balance the pros and cons of saying something or dropping a hint – or not doing so. You do a cost–benefit analysis every single time, and it takes an awful lot of energy – straight people don't realise. The morning Benny told his father, he was so nervous that he threw up in the basin while cleaning his teeth, but afterwards it turned out okay: you wind yourself up, then you say it, then (hopefully) cry and hug and experience a tsunami of emotions. Then you collapse with exhaustion. Rinse and repeat. Actually, when he told his dad, it was an anticlimax of a different kind: his father is so busy with his high-powered job and his high-powered girlfriend and their twins, whatever Benny says or does doesn't seem to matter a great deal.

Benny is used to it – his dad left when he was three, so he doesn't remember what living in a two-parent family was like. Things could be worse. He could be like Elin, whose mum also left, but she took Elin's older sister with her. That must have really hurt. Elin says it was because her mum couldn't cope – her mum was 'too fragile', as her father put it. But taking one kid and leaving the other? Wow. And the parent Elin was left with isn't exactly warm. Benny doesn't think Reverend Torstensen really understands his younger daughter, and some of the time he doesn't even seem to like her very much.

Benny and his mother live in the valley of Balmielva, nearly as far up as the Nilsbakken ski resort. For every few metres they climb in altitude, there is more snow lying on the ground and the temperature drops. Spring comes late to the valley – it's not only the altitude, but because it sits on a north-facing slope. When Sulis is already basking in spring sunlight, Nilsbakken is in winter shade. They live up here partly because Toril likes being surrounded by wilderness, and partly (the bigger part) because it's cheap. She holds regular yoga classes in Sulis and in Fauske, but her most lucrative gig is teaching the tourists and giving massages at the resort.

Now, in late April, there are fewer tourists staying in the old mining houses. It's too early in the year to hunt, and a bit late, this year, for really good skiing. But the Fagerheims, who run it, are canny, and have built a reputation for hosting corporate groups for wilderness activities and strengthening company bonds. They hire in chefs and organise fishing trips and guided hikes and visits to the local caves – as well as yoga and spa treatments and Sámi cultural encounters. They've even installed a helipad, so that guests can hire a helicopter to fly them over the Saltstraumen whirlpools and, maybe, spot sea eagles and humpback whales frolicking in the water below. It all looks great on Instagram.

Benny also works at the resort when he can, at weekends and in the holidays. He cleans rooms, does odd jobs and serves at table when there is a group dinner. Say what you like about the tourists (and everyone does), they do bring in a lot of work. His mum couldn't survive without that income – that and selling them the occasional bowl she throws in her garden studio. Benny fears that their existence here isn't really sustainable. His mum relies on child support from his dad to make ends meet, but that will end when he's eighteen – less than two years away – and he worries about what she will do then.

When he gets home, Benny shouts a greeting to Toril, but runs up to his room before she can detain him. Earlier today, he got a message, and he has been savouring the prospect of replying to it. Replying properly, that is – he messaged back straight away, saying:

—Skype later? I'm in school!
  Books emoji . . .

because he knew how much the recipient would love it.

'Dinner in half an hour!' shouts Toril.

'Okay,' he shouts back, firing up his computer with one hand and undoing his belt with the other.

During the Easter holiday, a group of investment-fund managers from Oslo spent a week at Nilsbakken. They spent the days skiing, dog sledding, visiting the local sights and, presumably, strengthening their bonds. It was a swanky affair and the whole thing must have cost a small fortune. The Fagerheims flew in an award-winning chef who cooked amazing meals, and the work was intense. Benny was there from morning till night – cleaning and helping Eva Julie Fagerheim in the office during the day, then waiting table and clearing up in the evening. The fund managers were mostly men in their twenties and thirties, expensively dressed, with gym-honed bodies and a seemingly relentless will to compete. Benny was initially repelled by the testosterone-fuelled teasing that ricocheted around the dining table, then he realised that they didn't know each other all that well and were jockeying for position in the pecking order. Even the women took part in the competitive banter. It reminded him, in a depressing way, of school.

One morning, he was carrying a load of sheets to the laundry room when he came across one of the guests loitering under the eaves, having a cigarette. Guests didn't usually come round here, and it was unusual to see any of them alone. Benny had noticed this man, as he was sexy, with a hooked nose and sensual mouth, buzz-cut hair and deep, hazel eyes. He also seemed a bit quieter than the rest of them.

'Hey,' he said, causing Benny to almost drop the sheets. 'Sorry, I didn't mean to startle you.'

'No, it's okay. Aren't you . . . ? I mean, isn't it the trip to the Marble Cave today?'

'Yeah. I didn't fancy it. Being stuck underground isn't my thing. I didn't want to have a panic attack in front of everyone.'

Benny was charmed that he would volunteer this sign of vulnerability. 'It's not that bad. I went last year. Most of it is huge – not claustrophobic at all. There's even a glacier in the cave. It's pretty amazing – you have these swirls of pink marble and then swirls of blue ice . . .'

'Then I expect there'll be lots of pictures.'

Benny grinned. 'Oh. That's for sure.'

When the man smiled, dimples appeared under his stubble. He held out his cigarette packet. 'It's Benny, isn't it? David. Can I tempt you?'

'Oh, I . . .'

He meant to say that he didn't smoke, that he was working, that he had a long list of tasks to check off that he had barely begun. Instead, he glanced around to see if anyone was watching.

David said, 'Are you still at school? How old are you?'

Without even blinking, Benny said, 'Eighteen.'

That first encounter – consummated in the windowless equipment store amid racks of skis – was now four weeks ago. Benny was so happy, he thought he would burst – it was the sickening excitement of every childhood Christmas rolled into one. David was the first man with whom he had done more than kissing, and he felt turned inside out. David was so impressive – handsome, clever, worldly. It seemed incredible that he could be interested in someone like Benny, but he'd even feigned a slight illness so they could meet in private. Benny told himself he would not become too attached, that he would take this in his stride, but he barely slept or ate for the rest of that week, and lay awake at nights fantasising about their blissful, shared future . . .

At the end of the week, they had made a rushed goodbye in the laundry room, pressed against a warm, churning washing machine.

David said, 'I've had a great time.'

Benny pushed him away, trying to say something that would be enticing yet cool. 'I really like you,' was not it, but that's what he said.

'I like you too.'

'So . . .'

'I've got your number. Keep in touch, yeah?'

Even then, Benny tried not to expect too much, but, astonishingly, wonderfully, David did keep in touch. In practice, what this meant was hooking up over his dodgy home internet connection, if and when David felt like it, which was hardly ever. He was very busy, of course, doing his mysterious, highly paid, fund-manager thing. Benny occasionally messaged David, but he was scared of appearing clingy and naive. He might be naive, and he wanted to cling, but he had a hunch that would not be welcome.

Neither his employers nor Toril noticed anything untoward – and his mother, after initially worrying that Eva Julie was overworking him ('No, I love working there!'), was pleased that Benny had added a tidy sum to his travel fund. In one week, Benny made nearly seven thousand kroner – including some generous tips. The most generous of these had come from David. He hadn't found it until he was putting on his coat at the end of the last day and he felt something foreign in the pocket. He pulled out an envelope, nonplussed, then excited. The envelope was blank. Checking that no one could see him, he tore it open with fingers that trembled. The contents of the envelope puzzled and, at first, upset him. Inside were two brand-new, thousand-kroner notes and a piece of paper that just said, *For a rainy day*. A drawn heart. And a *D*.

It was the first time he hadn't told Elin everything. He did tell her that he'd met someone, one of the guests at the resort, and that they'd 'had a thing'. Elin asked Benny if he was in love. He laughed, and said, 'Of course not – it was just . . . just something that was nice. But . . . David lives in Oslo, so . . .' He shrugged. He didn't want to tell her about the infrequent Skype sessions (three in four weeks, not that he's counting) that leave him feeling sated and depressed in equal measure. He also didn't tell her that David is more than twice his age. He told himself there was no need, and, anyway, where's the harm? And, obviously, he didn't tell her about the money. Others in the group had been generous with tips. He tries not to think about the difference between a tip of two hundred kroner, and one that is ten times as much.

Benny refreshes his screen for the twentieth time, but David is not replying. Okay, no. Too early. That's just the way it is. Maybe later – but there are no guarantees that later will happen. Basically, he has no power in this. He tells himself that he is a free agent, that this is casual, sophisticated, adult fun. It's exciting . . . it's great! He tells himself that David has no power either, but somehow that doesn't feel like the truth.

Five

I remember everything about the day my sister Nordis was born. I was five, although this seems odd to me now, as I recall how grown-up I felt. Things at home were chaotic; by then, my mother was already dealing with two young children: Magny, who was a toddler, and me. My stepfather was not helpful around the house, but this was not long after the war and men weren't expected to lift a finger indoors, so that wasn't unusual. Not that we'd have known if his behaviour had been considered beyond the pale: at that age, your life is just your life. We lived in a small coastal village a few hours to the north of here, and he spent his days fishing or working on someone's boat. I suppose we were poorer rather than richer, compared to other people in the village, although this was Before Oil, when those distinctions were very different from what they would be now. There were no foreign holidays in those days (no holidays at all, for us), no car, no television. Norway as a whole didn't get television until the 1960s – the same decade it reached Madagascar, Mongolia and Antarctica – and my parents didn't buy a set until the moon landings, long after I'd left home. Anyway, my stepfather was a shadowy, frightening presence. I suppose I thought of him then as my dad, since, at the time, I didn't know he wasn't.

I remember Mum disappearing for a while, and a woman – I can't remember who – coming to look after us, whereupon everyone behaved rather better than normal. Then Mum came home with a new baby girl, a third daughter, which we realised was a disappointing outcome for all concerned. In a fishing and farming community, a clutch of three daughters was a liability. Disappointing for everyone, that is, except Magny and me. Even as a baby, there was something unique and wonderful about Nordis; I adored her from the moment I laid eyes on her, and I know Magny was equally captivated. She seemed to be of a higher order of being than the rest of us crappy Øvergaards – an emissary from a better place. She had a way of looking at me with her wise, watchful eyes that made me feel calm and happy, no matter the chaos raging around us.

I remember certain times – like that one – vividly, but there are gaps in my childhood where I don't seem able to remember anything at all. The first five years of life, for example, is an empty blank; or what my stepfather was like when he was sober. Certainly, by the time my brother Karl arrived, five years after Nordis, Erling was a hopeless alcoholic, and, as I was then ten years old, I was rather more clued up, and aware that not everyone's house was as insane as ours. If that sounds extreme, well, 'insane' is the only word that really describes it. I suppose one of the things that I find relaxing about Odd Emil's company is that he knew my family, so I don't have to explain. He knows better than to talk about it. The Holmen family lived in the same village as us, but his parents kept the general store and were relatively well-to-do. Mr Holmen had the first car in the village – the sight of him driving it along the single dirt road and honking its horn is another event I remember as if it were yesterday. As children, Odd Emil and I weren't friends (I think I said this before), as I was four years older than him, but the family as a whole were always kind to us. Magny and he were about the same age, so she sometimes went to their house after school and, when she came back, she reported that it was lovely and peaceful. No one yelled or belted you. No one lay on the settle and snored during the day – at least, I highly doubt it.

My poor mother. I know I should feel some sympathy for her. She had a hard time of it, being married to Erling Øvergaard and everything that went before, but that doesn't mean I can forgive her.

I'm sorry, but I can't.

I freely admit I have done things in my life that were not good. And I'm not saying that my shortcomings were all the fault of my mother and stepfather, but it seems to me that what goes around, comes around. All my life I've had a somewhat problematic relationship with alcohol, by which I mean I know that I drink too much. I drink too much now; I always have. I drank throughout Klara's childhood because it made me less lonely and less angry. I never got *drunk*. I haven't been truly, embarrassingly drunk since I was about thirteen . . . (Actually, I know exactly when it was – I was thirteen and had very good cause.) Drinking every day, when Klara came home from school and I'd had a long day dealing with idiots at the power company, well, it smoothed the rough edges and made her whining less annoying, but there were less beneficial side effects.

Who was Klara's father, you ask? More to the point, where was he? Well, that's another story. Klara's father was one of the magical, vanishing men in my life. His name was Thomas Anstruther. Such an exotic, English-sounding name, like some ancient lord living in a castle, but, in reality, Tommo was an intense, Tasmanian hippy I met while I was living in a commune. That was in Thailand, in the 1970s. Weren't expecting that, were you? It wasn't so unusual at the time. There's a sentence you hear a lot, these days: 'Things were different then.' It's generally used to excuse reprehensible behaviour, like the sexual abuse of minors: 'But things were different then.' They weren't that different. But, in the seventies, living in a commune, in a handily warm, cheap part of the world, and practising what we called 'free love' was an idealistic experiment. We practised, but we never got very good at it. Tommo didn't want to be 'tied down' – not to me, anyway. I know, it's not an original story. I didn't want to turn into my mother, so I wasn't going to do any of the dumb things she did, like marrying the dregs from the bottom of the barrel. I was going to be bold and brave and different.

So, how did that work out? I hear you ask. Well, as you can probably tell, like many idealistic experiments, it didn't live up to its initial promise.

From the conservatory on the western side of my house, I can see the peninsula curving south and west into Skjerstadfjord, and the bay it shelters in its embrace. The road to Bodø follows the curve of the bay, and it's a pretty place, with meadows and birch woods. A good place to walk your dog. I can also see the lights from the campsite on the shore, and that is where, late on Saturday afternoon, the godawful noise begins. Some sort of festival is taking place, with thumping music and flashing lights. The road is a stream of crawling lights from miles of backed-up traffic, much of it emitting its own jittery noise – the kind of so-called 'music' that makes me want to bang my head against a wall until I go deaf.

The doorbell rings. Elin's father rang earlier in the week to ask if Elin and her friend could use my house to get ready for the party, and then stay the night. I suppose Eskil doesn't want to be put to the trouble of scooping up his child early on a Sunday morning, before he goes to work telling other people how to behave. Actually, I don't mind. I've been quite looking forward to it. I don't see her that often. We're not a close family, did I mention that already?

Elin kisses me on the cheek in her offhand way. It is one of her peculiarities that, when you look her in the eye, her eyes skitter away and she looks at the ground. She does it now – the brief glance, then down. A sketched smile. She has got better at this, over the years.

'Hi, *Bestemor*.'

'Hello, Elin. I like your hair this way.'

Like all the young girls, Elin used to have long hair that fell down her back. Now, she has chopped it all off, and it's as short as a boy's. I'm heartened by this sign of independent thinking. The short, almost white hair fluffs around her face like feathers, and enhances her resemblance to a startled bird. She's not a conventionally pretty girl, but she cuts a striking figure.

The friend she has brought with her is someone I don't know – a boy with curling, dark hair and a sweet, open face. He sticks out his hand, projecting a quiet certainty that he will be liked.

'Hi! I'm Bendik Iversen. Benny. I've heard Elin talk about you. It's nice to meet you.'

He looks as though he means it and I take to him immediately. I wonder if he's her boyfriend, but almost as quickly as the question pops into my mind, I dismiss it. That is not what is going on here.

They both have large bags with them, as they are going to change into their costumes for the party, and the results have to be a surprise to everyone. Despite myself, I'm curious about the event. I don't want to appear too interested in their teenage doings, as that would be undignified, so I make some coffee and leave them in the sitting room to get on with it, while I retire to the conservatory, where I sit with Asta, surrounded by my seedlings and my beautiful grapevine, now coming into tender leaf. Like most cultivated varieties, it is a hermaphrodite and self-pollinates, although, if I'm being honest, I don't get many grapes – probably barely enough to fill a couple of bottles. Did you know we now have actual vineyards in Norway? Yes, in Vestlandet, on the south-facing slopes. Shocking, really. But, you're right, this is not Vestlandet, and I wouldn't try to grow a vine outside here. Despite my habits and the exorbitant prices, I have not yet been reduced to making my own alcohol.

The conservatory was my present to myself a few years ago, once I accepted that I was never going to move to the impenetrable forest. That fantasy – like most fantasies, I suspect – was probably best kept as such. I spent more money building the conservatory than I have ever spent on anything, other than the house itself. The biggest drawback to living in the Arctic – I'm speaking for myself, here – is the short growing season. Not the climate per se – there's nothing wrong with the cold and the dark, and anyone who tells you otherwise has no imagination; they have been brainwashed by those clichés of what constitutes 'paradise': hot sun, turquoise sea, balmy nights and so on. In the Arctic, we do enjoy hot sun, periodically (increasingly, of late), and endless light in summer. Now and then, we have beautiful turquoise seas. Occasionally, nights are balmy. But it is contrast that gives piquancy and flavour to these things, and I should know – after a couple of years in Thailand, I couldn't stand it any longer. Every day the same: the heat like a suffocating blanket; the sun that doesn't caress the land at flattering angles, but crashes down on your head like a sledgehammer; and always that awful, life-sapping humidity, enlivened by the occasional mad deluge. Here, we have bracing contrasts, which I appreciate, but there is just not enough time to watch things grow and flourish. I needed to make more time. So, I had my conservatory built and insulated with the most expensive triple glazing I could find, so that I could grow a vine that provides me with dappled shade in summer, and a few sweet grapes, and I can propagate the sort of flowers that I like to have in my little garden. The conservatory is on the side of the house that faces west, so, when the days begin to shrink, I can sit out here, without putting on too many extra layers, watching the sun make its long goodbye.

Part of the wall and the floor is tiled with the local marble that has been quarried here for over a century. Long summer evenings are when it really comes into its own: sunlight refracted through atmospheric pollution brings out the glowing pinks which give it its name – Norwegian rose. There are islands of pink in swirls of ivory, outlined with a delicate tracery of grey-green, almost olive. It's a stunning stone – like a captured sunrise – if you like it. Alternatively, it reminds some people of a coarse, fatty terrine; I believe the French call it 'head cheese'. Personally, I love it – the marble, that is. Sitting here in the sun, I can imagine I am transported to antiquity, enjoying a Roman sunset surrounded by glowing pink marble and green leaves.

The conservatory is more or less my only luxury, but I do enjoy it. Asta likes it, too. She snoozes in a corner in the sun, where her white and russet fur blends into the colours of the tiles and turns her into a marble dog.

There's a noise behind me.

'Don't look, *Bestemor*! Can you come into the living room in ten minutes' time – and not before!'

Elin has barely poked her head round the kitchen door before she's gone. It's rather sweet, like when Klara used to perform plays to me and an audience of her teddy bears. So, in ten minutes – I time it – Asta and I go back to the sitting room and knock on the door.

'Come in!' say two excited voices.

I go in and stop in confusion. I'm honestly shocked. Elin and her friend have gone; two strangers are there in their place. Not strangers, of course: my granddaughter, wearing a man's black suit, with her hair slicked back, and Benny in a glittery dress and pale blue wig. It takes me several seconds to be sure of who is who. Yes, Elin is dressed as a man, complete with some sort of beard and moustache, although these are sparkly and pink and look solid. Benny's transformation is even more startling – he has disappeared into the skin of a beautiful girl. I spent the greater part of the 1960s drawing a black flick on my eyelids, and I recognise an expert hand when I see one. Elin, unusually for her, has her chin up and shoulders back. She even smiles at me, as far as she can with that stuff stuck to her face.

'What do you think?'

'We're not finished yet,' says Benny. 'I told her we wouldn't be.'

'I think you look immaculate. So, this is a cross-dressing party?'

'No. Not really,' says Benny.

Elin says, 'It's a political protest.'

'Well, I'm sure you will get a lot of attention. What are you pro-
testing against?'

'The russ,' says Elin. 'Heteronormative bullshit.'

'Excuse me? What's that?'

'Traditional gender roles. Women being subservient. You know.'

Huh, I think. I've protested against traditional gender roles my whole
life. Much good it's done me. But then, it never occurred to me to
wear a pink beard.

'Ah,' I say, although that doesn't seem to be enough. Then, as nothing
else comes to mind, I say, 'Well, I think this calls for a drink.'

I open a bottle of wine (Italian, not Norwegian – I'm not crazy)
and sit on the sofa, watching as Benny puts the finishing touches to
both of their faces. He is obviously in charge. He applies more eye
shadow to Elin's face: pink, to match her beard, until it forms a solid
stripe across her eyes. Petroleum jelly and glitter is added to eyes and
cheeks and even Elin's hair, turning it into a smooth, sparkling helmet.

Benny intrigues me. At sixteen, he not only radiates a winning confidence on meeting a stranger (me), he is confident enough to dress
up in drag and confront his whole school. Things have changed so
much since I was young, and almost all for the better.

Elin blurts out suddenly – obviously, she has been storing this up –
'Actually, *Bestemor*, I'm genderfluid.'

'Oh?' I say politely. I think I've heard this term. 'Right. What does
that mean?'

'It means that I don't identify as a girl, and I don't identify as a
boy. I'm fluid.'

'Oh. That sounds nice. Your life will be so uncomplicated.'

'Exactly!' Elin looks pleased. 'I can't get Dad to understand that.'

'Well, I'm sure he'll . . . come around,' I say doubtfully. I would like to have been a fly on the wall during that conversation. Eskil Torstensen is the very epitome of a man with a stick up his arse. I always knew Klara's marrying him would end badly, although my opinion on that subject was neither sought nor given.

Benny says, 'That's what I said.'

'Are you, er, "fluid" as well?' I ask him.

He considers the question. 'No, I think I'm a gay man. Who likes make-up.' He shrugs, focusing on the mirror over the mantelpiece, where he's making imperceptible adjustments to his false eyelashes.

'It's wonderful that you're so confident at this age.'

He flashes me a glance. 'I'm not really confident. I'm just pretending. You know: "Fake it till you make it."' He says this in English, rather self-consciously.

'Well, it's very convincing.'

Elin – poor kid – she wants to be like him, I can see it. I understand. I want to be like him too. Why would anyone want to be a woman? I know – *of course* I know – that feeling of outrage at coping with the leaky, vulnerable body you have been dealt. Elin has her own special difficulty on top of that, too, the one an angrily sobbing Klara told me about all those years ago (implicit in her rage was that Elin's condition was, of course, my fault) – although, at this moment, I can't remember what it's called.

Words. People are so keen to put themselves in a box and stick a label on it. A pre-emptive strike, I suppose, against others putting you in a box and choosing a label you don't like. When I was young, we also invented or found or borrowed words to differentiate ourselves from those who didn't understand us: hippy, mod, beatnik . . . I was first a mod, as soon as I could conceive of being anything other than my parents' bugbear. When I left Norway, I reinvented myself as a hippy, and then I became . . . well, anyway.

Genderfluid: now, that's an interesting term, if rather nebulous, or perhaps that's the point. Fluid things are soft, they flex and split and reconstitute themselves without damage. Fluid things can't be broken. That must be nice.

I am this. I am not that. I identify as a person who is not responsible for the harm I have caused. Trouble is, whatever words you use, it's not that easy to leave the flesh behind. Or the past.

The face-painting, and the excitement, make me think of the squat in Amsterdam – the time in my life when, I suppose, I had the most fun. That was before Thailand and Klara. I was another person then. I don't tell the kids, but I'm thrilled that she has shared this with me, rather than . . . although, maybe they didn't have another option. I suppose they couldn't have done this transformation at her father's house – I can't imagine Reverend Eskil smiling benevolently at this cross-dressing – and Benny lives even further out of town. But they could have done it at a school friend's, say. Although, this, I gather, is the point: no one can know what they are doing until they arrive. What I know, of course, doesn't matter, as I am old. I drink my wine and try not to feel envious. The kids drink glasses of wine too, becoming more flushed and sparkling as the bottle empties. Benny puts on a terrifying pair of high-heeled shoes that make him taller than Elin. He applies finishing touches to his glittery lips. They are so pleased with themselves they are almost bursting.

'You can't walk there in those shoes; you'll break your ankle.'

Benny shrugs and says he's been practising.

'I'm going to call you a taxi – my treat. You can't go to all this effort and then not make a proper entrance.'

A few minutes later and the children have gone, giggling and glittering. They were sweetly effusive in their thanks, but already their minds were racing elsewhere. I am left with an almost empty bottle of Grillo and this dull ache in my chest. Sixteen years old, and all that freedom. I know there are difficulties these days, for the young: worries about the future; fears for the planet; wars and forest fires; the trolls that now lurk in the æther, instead of in the forest . . . But, oh, just imagine it! When I was sixteen, it was 1961 – before we had television, or the pill. Before the oil money. Only sixteen years since the end of the war.

One of the consequences of a five-year enemy occupation is that local girls and women will inevitably form relationships with occupying soldiers, and my mother, Ingvild Hustoft, was one of them. She was a *tyskertøs* – a not nice word that means 'German slut'. She wasn't a collaborator or anything like that, just a girl who fell in love. Otto Behmer was a guard at the local prisoner-of-war camp, and he was in love with her, too. That's what I was told by my mother, when I was a teenager. I realise that perhaps she was eager to paint the relationship in the best possible light, but, for all I know, it's true. Anyway, when the Germans were forced to retreat in the autumn of 1944, Otto left, leaving Ingvild bereft. She was only eighteen. She was also pregnant. As I wasn't born until the following April, it's quite likely that he didn't even know. In the chaos at the end of the war, it was next to impossible to communicate with a defeated enemy.

51

Ingvild wrote letter after letter, not knowing if they ever reached him. She never had a reply.

I used to wonder what my life might have been like if she had given me up for adoption. Some of the *krigsbarn* were sent to Germany; I might have been German. I had to believe that Ingvild kept me because she hoped that Otto would come back, and that somewhere in the whole sorry tale there was a kernel of goodness, of love. It would be nice to believe that. Anyway, after two years of silence, Ingvild gave up waiting and married a fisherman called Erling Øvergaard, who was seventeen years older than her. He was poor and ill-respected, and he wasn't a nice man – he *had* been a collaborator – so he was certainly not much of a catch, but I think she believed that no one else would take on a *tyskertøs* and her *naziyngel* – 'Nazi spawn' – which is what he used to call us when he was drunk.

They had three more children. I think my mother became an alcoholic only after she married Erling. He was already a drunk – not unusual, in that period, especially in the Arctic, where people's lives and homes had been destroyed, or, at the very least, turned upside down. When I realised that this drunken bully was not my father, I clung to this fact as to a lifeline. I dreamt of getting out. I didn't feel a lot of solidarity with Ingvild. Living with her was like living on a volcano. She screamed, she lost her temper in the blink of an eye, she lashed out with her hand or whatever happened to be in her hand. She seemed angry about everything, all the time, boiling with fury and resentment at the unfairness of life – much of which, as I was made all too aware, was my fault. I was always scared that I might make her so angry she would have a stroke – this seemed quite likely – and then her death would be on my conscience as well. She hated cooking, used to bang the dinner plates on to the table, hissing, 'Well, it's ruined!' Then she would drop into her chair and rest her forehead on one hand while, with the other, she poured herself another glass of akvavit.

When I was old enough and brave enough to ask about my real father, she shut me down. Either she would not answer at all, or she would say she couldn't remember, which, at the time, I accepted (how would I know better? Perhaps the getting of children was such a forgettable, regrettable thing). Then, when I was sixteen, she told me that she had fallen head over heels in love with my father, and he – handsome, dark-eyed Otto – was the love of her life. Oh, she had been a wild girl, she said, with a wistful yet coy smile that, I am sorry to say, made me want to slap her. Her parents could do nothing with her. And now, look at her! Now she was paying the price. Clearly, I was the price. I decided then that I would one day find my father.

I cherished the idea of this handsome man, who just had the misfortune to be born on the wrong side of the Nazi / non-Nazi divide. Not even that – many Germans did not agree with Hitler's ideology, and of course he would be one of them. But, in the late sixties, when I went to Germany to try to find my father, and I wrote to Ingvild asking for as many details as she could supply, she was dismissive and unhelpful. She said she had never known his date of birth and couldn't remember where he was from. She seemed to take my wanting to find him as a slight against her. I realise she felt bitter and hard done by. I know she felt that I'd abandoned her, just as Otto had, but even so . . . Thinking of it all these years later – it makes me so angry, I get a headache. I have to remind myself that it was a long time ago, and everyone involved is dead, except me, and you – that is, I – cannot continue to live in the past.

Asta whines and pushes her nose into my hand, and I fondle her velvety ears.

'Yes, I know. I know. We'll go out. In a minute, my girl. There's my good girl.'

I might just have another drink first.

Six

Benny has almost definitely decided that the Saturday of the russ party is going to mark the end of the thing with David. If, that is, it hasn't already died of natural causes, which he fears is the case. He's had enough of waiting on tenterhooks for the next message, of feeling as though he is being dangled at the end of a very long, thin thread. It's tremendously exciting, but, with so much uncertainty and disappointment, is it really worth it? Whether he will actually take decisive action to end things, he still hasn't decided. It would be pathetic to break up with someone who had already forgotten you, but he might have to, for his own peace of mind. This is as far as his thoughts have gone by the time he and Elin go to the russ party.

As Saturday approached, Benny wound himself up to an intense pitch of nervous excitement. Dragging up in public is something he has wanted to do for ages, but he is scared, too, all too aware that there might be negative reactions. They might be laughed at, jeered at, or worse. But he reassured himself: he is going with Elin and she always makes him feel confident. For all her quirks and anxieties, in certain, marvellous ways, Elin doesn't give a fuck.

'Your grandmother is cool,' he says, when they are in the taxi for the short journey down the road to the campsite, hearing the throb of bass and chatter of treble grow louder.

'Mm. Kind of,' says Elin, anxiously pressing her cardboard beard. 'Dad says she made Mum crazy, and that's why she left.'

'Don't fiddle with it. It's fine. What do you mean, made her crazy?'

'I don't know. Just, you know, she was mean to her growing up. It feels like it's coming loose.'

'It isn't. Leave it alone.'

Benny holds up his phone and takes another selfie of the two of them, posing on the back seat. He shows Elin the results. She is entranced – they both are. They look fantastic. Benny is pleased that the required level of excellence has been achieved. People might mock, or jeer, but – and this is important – they won't be able to say it's badly done.

The anti-russ protest goes better than he ever imagined, although it feels less like a political statement, and more that they have become, briefly, popular. They may have set out to subvert the russ and its conventional stereotypes, but the russ – in its hedonistic, party mood – just opens its arms and absorbs them into itself. Seniors he has never spoken to come up to him and tell him he looks amazing. He loses count of the number of photos they pose for.

As evening lengthens, the sun creeping along the fjord and fading into the lilac twilight, Benny and Elin are invited into pimped-out buses and drinking circles. Neither of them has ever been so feted. Benny is drinking too much, but he is in that delightful state where, although a voice in his head is telling him to slow down, he chooses not to listen. He's been keeping half an eye on Elin, although she seems to be fine, and he has begun to relax his vigilance. He'd wondered how she would cope with the attention. At school, she often hangs her head and slouches, as if trying to disguise her height and all the things that make the meaner students call her 'E.T.', but tonight she walks tall, her chin held high.

At some point – after he finally stops taking selfies, as Elin's beard has fallen off and even his carefully monitored paint is losing the battle against the night – he takes out his phone to add the number of Jonas, a boy from Bodø, and sees that he has a message. From David. He feels shock. He tries not to read it right away – thinks, tomorrow is soon enough to be officially dumped, he doesn't want to spoil this evening – but can't help himself. There is no acknowledgement of the long radio silence (perhaps he hasn't even noticed?); there is only this: David is flying back up to Nilsbakken next weekend! Hopes Benny will be around??

He is so stunned by the message, he doesn't notice at first that Elin is nowhere to be seen, nor can he remember when she was last there. He tells himself she's fine. She's having a great time, and, if she isn't, she'll come and find him – and he's pretty hard to miss. She's been chatting with a couple of girls, although he doesn't even know who Elin might be interested in sexually. She doesn't seem to have made up her mind – which is totally cool, of course.

'Good news?' asks the boy from Bodø, a slight edge in his voice, put out that he seems to have slipped down Benny's list of priorities.

'Oh. Yeah. Just a friend.'

But he can't keep the grin off his face. Not that it changes anything, he tells himself. He taps Jonas's number into his phone, smiles at him and gestures to the empty bottle he has been toying with for the past ten minutes.

'You need another one? Let me see what I can do.' He looks around and spots a familiar logo: the words *Hellraisers* and *Ride or Die* are spray-painted in huge letters on the side of a bus; pulsing lights flicker from the open door. 'Come on.'

The Hellraisers' bus is every bit as luxurious as gossip has indicated, with the exception that there is not actually a jacuzzi inside. But there are sofas lining the walls, a fridge, lights that pulse with the sound system. The sofas are packed with bodies pressed close together in the dimness.

'Hey, Johnny,' says Benny. 'Got a couple of beers?'

Johnny Skarstein is crouching by the fridge. He turns to look at them, and the fridge light throws his cheekbones into sharp relief.

'Well, well.' His eyes take in Benny's face and his body in the tight blue dress. 'My little friend. Look at you. Have you come back for more?'

They are not friends, but, a few weeks ago, there was an incident at a party where someone dared Johnny to kiss Benny – because making out with someone of the same sex is a perennially popular russ dare. And Benny hadn't exactly minded. Kissing Johnny Skarstein was something that he – along with half the school – had fantasised about. Although, in practice, it was a let-down – kissing someone for a dare, however good-looking they are (and, when you are that close, it hardly matters what they look like), is not a turn-on.

'No. We need some beers.'

'Oh? And what do I get if I give you some of our beers?'

'I got you your russ knot, remember? I think you owe me.'

'I didn't realise I had to pay for it. Thought you enjoyed it.' Johnny gives him his famous fuck-me look.

Jonas looks from him to Benny, unsure what is going on.

Benny says, 'You get good karma. That's always worth having.'

Johnny grins. 'I'm pretty good on the karma front.'

Tobias Mero turns from where he is talking to Emmy Fu. He stares at Johnny. 'Come on, man – give the kid some beers.'

'Your make-up,' says Emmy, focusing on Benny, 'is so awesome. Where did you learn to do that?'

Benny shrugs, pleased. Emmy Fu is officially gorgeous, as well as being all set to go to Harvard or somewhere fancy like that.

'YouTube. You know.'

'I can never get my eyeliner like that. I always end up with a smoky eye!'

'Yeah, happens,' says Benny, and they grin at each other.

Tobias and Johnny exchange a look. Johnny shrugs and takes two beers out of the fridge, handing them to Benny.

'Thanks,' Benny says coolly, and smiles at Tobias and Emmy.

Tobias nods at him and holds out a bottle opener. 'No worries.' He doesn't smile, but then he rarely smiles. Emmy puts her hand on his arm, looking as though she's planning on changing that.

Benny opens the bottles and hands one to Jonas. They drink, then Jonas fixes on something in the corner and he nudges Benny with a meaningful look. Benny turns to see that among the bodies entwined on one of the sofas are two boys. The quiver of recognition slides into another: slick fair hair ... one of the boys is Elin. Disappointment, and something else. It's weird enough to see Elin making out with someone, but what gives Benny a peculiar feeling is that the body she is pressed up against is that of Daniel Fjordholm.

'Oh. My mistake,' says Jonas, pulling a face.

Benny says, 'Let's go outside. Too noisy here.'

Seven

Elin hates it when her dad is angry with her. She wants to shrivel up and crawl into a hole. Normally, she would never tell lies, but last Saturday she'd found it easy to lie by omission. She'd wanted to wear the black suit so badly, she pretended it wasn't stealing. It was borrowing – just without asking. Stupidly, she hadn't realised, smuggling the suit back into his wardrobe while he was at church, that it stank of cigarette smoke, but, of course, he noticed. He was shocked. Disgusted. At first, he blamed Benny, so she had to tell him that she had worn the suit. He was furious, and made it very clear that this was unacceptable behaviour. He made out that it was because of the taking without consent, but she thinks the whole her-wearing-a-man's-suit thing hadn't helped. The result is, she is grounded for two weeks, and the dry-cleaning bill is coming out of her allowance. She hadn't asked his permission because she was afraid he would refuse, or, at the very least, he would have asked what she wanted it for, and that was a conversation she couldn't imagine getting through in one piece.

In a small way, she's relieved to be grounded. At the party, she had the best night of her life, but, for all the things that were wonderful about it, there were others that were alarming. People are generally

60

confusing, but the party took things to a whole new level. She had never felt so seen, or so desired, as though Elin Torstensen was a person that people wanted to be with: a new and intoxicating feeling. But, though the attention was delicious, it was confusing because she was in drag – almost in disguise – so now she can't be sure whether the thing that people liked was really her, or only the drag.

She shifts her laptop to a more comfortable position and types into the search bar, in English, *Am I trans ftm?* Dozens of quizzes come up. Every so often there are new ones. It's not the first time she has done this, but each time her heart is in her mouth. By typing in the words, the internet will know the truth about her. She clicks through to the first quiz. There are fifteen questions, which doesn't seem that many for such a big decision, and the questions themselves are ridiculously simple, like: what gender clothes does she like to wear, and what toys did she like to play with?

Question: What sort of movies does she like? a) Action/adventure, b) Horror, c) Romantic comedy . . . (Seriously?)

Question: Does she feel comfortable in her body? (No, but she doesn't know anyone who does.)

Question: Does she park backwards? (WTF?)

She wondered if the experiences of Saturday night would change her answers. At the end of the quiz, the internet fairies announce, *You are probably trans.* Elin goes back to the search engine, clicks on the page for another quiz and fills it in. This one is more circumspect. It suggests that she might be non-binary. Another – she is genderfluid. Is it a spectrum? Can you be all three?

Can internet quizzes be wrong?

@VelociTazz:

—The internet thinks I'm trans and

  nonbinary AND genderfluid!

—Can u b all 3?

—At the same time?

—*Shrugging emoji*

                                          @Supertwink3000:

                                          —Internet is full of idiots

—I know

                                          —Does the word really matter?

—IDK!!!

—*Scream emoji*

—Ppl seem so sure

                                          —They aren't tho

                                          —Internet removes nuance

                                          —Also ppl lie!

                                          —I like that ur not sure

—*Dotted-line-face emoji*

                                          —Elin = *Stars-in-eyes emoji*

—*Heart emoji x 3*

—*Head-exploding emoji*

                                          —*Kiss emoji x 3*

—What u doing?

                                          —Ha ha guess . . .

                                          —Ninja Wipeout!!!

—Sooo predictable!!

                                          —*Grimacing emoji*

—Enjoy *Ninja emoji, Splash emoji*

—*Aubergine emoji*

                                        —*Tongue-out emoji, Winking emoji*

—*Vomiting emoji*

She sends the vomiting emoji not because she is truly nauseated, but because it makes her laugh. It's probably her favourite one. Either that, or dotted-line face, which looks like a person who is dissolving into thin air. She can relate.

Benny is obsessed with all things Japanese. He watches endless reruns of *Ninja Wipeout* on YouTube – a sadistic gameshow in which terrifyingly lean and muscular Japanese men throw themselves over a giant obstacle course and, inevitably, fall into the lake below. Benny falls in love with every contestant, so much so that he is planning to study Japanese at Bergen University (making him, claims the website, 'eminently suitable for work in areas such as tourism and fish exports'). Benny isn't interested in fish exports. He'll be in Tokyo, or Osaka, trying to catch wet ninjas.

In the past, Elin has wondered if the love she feels for Benny means that she is *in love* with him. Then, she wondered, if she was fluid enough, or non-binary (and she isn't entirely sure of the distinction), or if she was trans . . . would that make enough of a difference? Benny loves her, she knows that, but he doesn't want to have sex with her. She knows that too, because she asked him.

Since Easter, Elin has had the feeling that Benny is keeping something from her. She knows that he lost his virginity with a tourist at Nilsbakken – an actual grown-up person, with a job and an apartment. That was shocking enough. Telling her what happened, he made light of it, said it was not that big a deal – but his face betrayed him. The excitement came off him in waves. When she asked if he was in love, he'd shaken his head, laughed, flushed a little, and said it was really nice, but now it was over. But, ever since, there has been something different about him. He has seemed preoccupied, or is it bored? When they message, the icons and the words are the same as ever – hearts and stars and kisses – but in person, *IRL*, it hasn't felt the same.

What scares her is the thought that, now he has gained this momentous experience that she has not, he has grown bored with *her*.

Since Saturday night, her worries about Benny have been swamped by another set of feelings that came out of nowhere. She cannot stop thinking about Daniel Fjordholm. Before Saturday, she had never fantasised about him, she didn't *like* him – he was, apart from being friends with her horrible cousin Lorentz, just another senior: popular and conventional, barely on her radar. Now, the images and sensations of Saturday play on a loop in her brain. Does that mean she is in love with him? The thought is both painful and addictive – like pushing her tongue against a wobbly tooth. Daniel has always seemed the epitome of regular and straight, and half the girls in the school fancy him – therefore, she is just like everyone else. Not original. Not interesting. She had got kind of a strange vibe from Benny after the party, as they trailed back to her grandmother's for what remained of the night. She knew he'd seen her and Daniel kissing; she saw him looking – so why didn't he mention it? Was he disappointed in her? She is a little disappointed in herself. The following day, he *had* brought it up and asked if she thought they would hook up again. Elin said no, she didn't think so. And, since that somewhat blurred encounter on Saturday night, she and Daniel have not exchanged so much as a glance.

64

She was enjoying herself at the party, bathing in the novelty of being looked at with admiration. She was drinking beer, which was pretty safe because no one can slip anything into a bottle if you're holding it, and, also, she doesn't like the taste, but at some point she found herself holding a cup of sweet red liquid that was delicious, and she drank it without even worrying what it was. She thought it came from a girl called Sofie, who told her she looked hot and asked if she could touch her beard. They had giggled a lot. Elin didn't know if they were flirting, but, with hindsight, it very much seems like it. By then, she had lost track of Benny. Sofie went off to meet her friends, though Elin knows she didn't imagine their conversation, as Sofie's number is in her phone, and there is, as of Monday, also a text from her:

—Sat night was sooo crazy!! Loved
  meeting you! *Stars-in-eyes emoji*

She hasn't, as yet, replied.

After that, she was surrounded by the Hellraisers, and, to her surprise, they invited her into their bus. In her new persona, she felt invincible. Lorentz was there, being nice to her, for once. He even told her she looked good. She had never exchanged more than a couple of words with any of the other Hellraisers. She's only a first-year, and not pretty or especially noteworthy. The Hellraisers tend to hook up with senior girls, or with girls from other schools, and there is no shortage of candidates. Johnny Skarstein is notorious for the number of girls he has been with. Lorentz is the only one with a serious girl-friend: pretty third-year Solgunn Ingebrigtsen. Elin didn't recognise many people inside the bus – but it was dim and crowded, and the music was very loud. It was the sort of sensory overload she would normally hate, but somehow, that night, she didn't hate it. Instead of feeling battered by lights and noise, she felt porous; the music flowed through her like water through a net. Someone pressed a beautifully cold bottle of beer into her hand. She looked round to see Daniel Fjordholm. Her eyes were exactly on a level with his. Inside the bus, you had to be really close to someone if you wanted to hear what they were saying, and she could feel his warm breath on her ear. It was amazing – he didn't just leave, but kept talking, looking into her eyes, and touching her cheek as they talked, brushing at the crumbs of sparkly glue left behind by the beard. And she didn't mind. Daniel Fjordholm, the russ leader, the boy everybody likes, looking into her eyes and flirting with her – it was like a dream.

Then they were on one of the sofas and they were kissing, and she was so surprised, she didn't know what to think. She can't recall the steps in between drinking beer with him and having Daniel's arms around her, but that's where they ended up – on a sofa at the back of the bus, so close she felt his solid heat all the way from shoulder to knee. She felt as though she was made of wax. Her bones were softening and she could hardly move. When they broke apart to breathe, Daniel looked at her, smiling.

'You're such a cool girl. I mean, look at you – you get it, don't you? Everyone here is so conventional.'

'Yeah, I know what you mean.'

Elin would never have imagined Daniel, who seems like one of the straightest people in the school, saying such a thing. She remembered she was genderfluid, and wondered if she should correct him, but she couldn't quite bring herself to do it. He seemed to like her in the suit, anyway, so . . .

They had stopped kissing and he was saying something that didn't make a lot of sense to her. Something about inner journeys being more important than outer journeys. He looked suddenly grave. And then Lorentz came over and said something in his ear. They made some peculiar bro-gesture, slapping their hands together, and Daniel brightened.

'I'm talking crap. Sorry, I'm . . .' He laughed. 'Let's go outside.'

The sky was finally dark; the only light came from the strings of fairy lights and flashing windows. Competing rhythms spilled from the buses. Away from the lights, under some trees, Daniel took something out of his pocket – something he carefully halved with his thumbnail. He held out his hand: two tiny white semicircles were just visible in the dim light. Her heart felt like it was climbing up her throat.

'Wanna get fucked up?'

The way he said it made it sound really good. A part of her wanted to say yes – yes, *of course* she did, because this was *Daniel Fjordholm*, and she had never in her life felt so chosen. But another part, the stubborn thing that always holds her back, that she hates because it means she can never really be like other people – that part grabbed the wheel and slammed on the brakes.

'Uh . . . No. Thanks. I'm good,' she muttered.

Daniel shrugged, withdrawing the hand and the offer, and the shivery warmth that had been between them drained away into the shadows.

'Sorry, I, um . . .' she murmured, and was crushed.

'No. Okay. S'cool.'

He smiled without looking at her, and, in a flash of movement, his hand went to his mouth, he took a swig of beer, swallowed and gazed over her shoulder, into the darkness.

Since then, in school, she has caught glimpses of Daniel, in the distance, disappearing down the corridor, always surrounded by the other Hellraisers. These glimpses plunge her into a state of sick disappointment, but what did she expect? They hadn't exchanged phone numbers. Saturday night meant nothing to him, which, in retrospect, doesn't surprise her. So why can't she stop thinking about him? She feels as though she is going mad. She would give anything to go back in time to the moment when he had held out his hand, and answer, instead, *Yes*.

She looks at Sofie's text and wishes it was from him. She's so stupid. If Daniel really liked her, he would have taken her number, done something. She looks at the matter objectively. It's absurd to think that someone like Daniel Fjordholm would be interested in someone like her. It's probably on the Hellraisers' list of dares: *No. 37 – Make out with a girl dressed as a boy*. She's being everything she despises, mooning over a popular boy. And how can she claim to be genderfluid if she's just going to fall for the straight boy that everyone likes? Then she's not different, or special. Is it just something she has made up to make Benny like her?

Her phone vibrates.

@Supertwink3000:

—R u awake?

@VelociTazz:

—Yes

—Can I ask you something?

—Sure

—Talk?

—*Thumb-up emoji*

Elin switches her phone to silent, so her dad won't hear it ring.

'Hey.'

'Sorry it's so late.'

'No, it's fine. Is everything okay?'

'Yeah. No. Just . . . Can I ask you a favour?'

There is something unusual in Benny's voice – something urgent and alive.

'Okay – what?'

'I need your help. On Saturday night – this Saturday, I mean . . .'

'I'm grounded. I'm not allowed to go out.'

'No, I know, but . . . um, can I say that I'm going to spend the night at your house?'

'You want to spend the night here?'

'No, I just want to tell my mum that I'm spending the night at yours. As an alibi.'

'For what?'

'Well . . . so, David's coming back at the weekend. To Nilsbakken.'

Elin hears the excitement in his voice.

'I thought that was over.'

'So did I . . . but, please, Elin. I really want this. I'll owe you. I thought I could say we're going to watch horror films, like that other time.'

'What if your mum talks to my dad?'

'That's not very likely, is it?'

This is true. Elin's dad has never really hit it off with Benny's mum, whose spiritual interests are everything her father most disapproves of. It's not as though she'll be in church on Sunday. The only time Benny and his mum set foot in church is at Christmas, and then only because Toril likes singing carols.

'Don't worry. If you don't feel comfortable, I'll think of something else.'

'No, it's fine. I probably won't need to say anything to anyone. I mean, obviously I'm not going to tell my dad.'

'No, no. It's just for my mum, in case . . . Are you sure? God, you're a lifesaver. I really appreciate it. Thank you!'

'So, you really like him?'

'Well . . . I don't know! It's . . . I don't know.'

But there it is again, the vibration of suppressed thrill that even Elin, over the phone, cannot miss.

'Well. Okay. I'd better go to sleep.'

'Yeah. Thank you, El. Love you. Night.'

'Bye.'

She closes the lid of her computer, and then the only glow is from her phone, which lights up again.

@Supertwink3000:
—You're the best!
—*Prayer-hands emoji*
—*Heart emoji x 3*

@VelociTazz:
—*Thumb-up emoji*

Pause.

She isn't going to leave him hanging, is she?

—*Heart emoji*

Eight

At last, the longest week of his life is over, and it is Saturday once again, and Benny has lied to his mother. He feels bad about this, but he can't imagine telling her the truth. It's not that she would object to him having a boyfriend, but that should be a boy his own age, someone he could bring home to meet her, who she could ask about his hobbies and his family – someone like Jonas, in fact. But that's not what David is. He doesn't know how to describe their relationship (wrong word, but anyway . . .) to her. He can't describe it to himself in a way that doesn't make him slightly uncomfortable. He really had been going to draw a line under the whole experience, until the sight of David's name on his phone changed everything. He was coming back to Nilsbakken and he didn't have to – so, therefore, it was because he wanted to. He said he was going to do some hiking, so, of course, there is that – but he could hike anywhere . . . yet he chose here.

On Saturday afternoon, he showers and dresses carefully, and pulls up the hood of his jacket before cycling to Nilsbakken. He hopes he won't encounter anyone who knows him, and he is lucky – there are hardly any cars on the road. He loops round the back of the buildings to the cabin where David is staying, and hides his bike in the bushes.

He sends him a message. The whole thing is so clandestine, he feels like a spy, or as though he is doing something wrong. But all the subterfuge is worth it – isn't it? To experience this churning, almost unbearable excitement. Jonas was nice, and Benny had liked flirting with him, but he seems very young and gauche in comparison with this. The door of the cabin opens, and David is grinning at him – God, he has the sexiest eyes Benny has ever seen. He isn't sure what to expect. Although it was David's suggestion that he come over in the evening, he doesn't even know if he is expected to stay the night. The schedule for the evening has not been specified.

He is enchanted when David sets about making dinner. So: it's like an actual date. Benny sits at the table in the kitchen, trying not to drink his wine too quickly. He is thrilled, but he also feels somehow younger and shyer than when the ground was covered in snow and they made out in the laundry room. At Easter, he'd had as much right to be here as David; now, his presence is by invitation only. Also, it's surprising how many things you need to say while eating, just to keep a conversation going. He hasn't read the books David has read, or seen the films he has seen. He doesn't want to ask if David watches *Ninja Wipeout*. He also has to remember that he's supposed to be a russ, and finds himself telling David about last weekend, when he and Elin were queen and king of the party. David is silent.

'This is really good,' Benny says, again, of the dish David has rustled up with effortless aplomb. He's never tasted anything like it: it's Lebanese, apparently. David is good at so many things – another sign of his worldly superiority.

David pours them both more wine. 'Thanks.' He looks away, preoccupied for the first time. 'So, do you do that often?'

73

'What? Dress up in drag? No. It's the first time. Well – to go out like that, anyway.'

David doesn't meet his eye.

'Why? Is there something wrong with it?'

David shrugs. 'No. It's fine.'

It doesn't seem fine. The atmosphere in the kitchen isn't the same as before.

Benny feels guilty and obscurely angry. So, David is one of those masc. on masc. guys you see on the apps? Not that Benny has used any apps, he hasn't the nerve, but he has glided through, a saucer-eyed phantom. The silence lengthens awkwardly; it's all going wrong. He supposes that, if their relationship (wrong word! Again!) hadn't died before, it probably will now. He takes a sip of wine and his swallowing sounds incredibly loud.

'Um . . . You seem weird. Do you want me to go?'

'God, no!' David reaches over the table and takes Benny's hand. 'Sorry – of course not. I just had a bad experience, once, that's all – with a queen.'

'I'm not . . . It was just a party.'

David looks him in the eye, and smiles again, and it feels, if not great, then at least better.

The nights are so short, now: the sun has barely set down the valley before it is peeking round the mountains behind them. When they went to bed, David pulled down the blackout blind, all but a crack, so they could sleep, but Benny can't sleep. He has so looked forward to this: spending the night with David. Having sex with him, of course, but also, and almost as much, being in bed with him, lying next to

74

him, listening to him breathe. But it isn't the way he'd imagined it. After sex, there is no spooning, or cuddling, just David rolling over, putting on his eye mask and apparently falling asleep. Benny tries not to mind. He should be happy; this is what he wants, isn't it? But, for a long while afterwards, he lies there and his throat feels suspiciously tight. He wonders whether he should get up and cycle home, but that seems too much an admission of failure.

He thinks about Elin, wonders if she's awake and fretting about the lie she's telling so that he can be here. Or perhaps she's fretting about Daniel Fjordholm. She seemed rather bowled over by him, although she said she knew it meant nothing. But Elin has never had a boy- or girlfriend, and little experience of making out with anyone, so it's not surprising that it had an impact on her. That they had hooked up at all had been surprising, to say the least, and Benny's first reaction to seeing them had been a stab of jealousy. Even though they are best friends, it was a shock to see her favoured with Daniel's attention. Benny knows Daniel is straight, but, at the same party where he had made out with Johnny, he had also made out with Daniel. It was no big deal. Again, it was in front of people, simply for the dare, but it had felt entirely different from kissing Johnny. Daniel was cool, and nice, and didn't try too hard to show off. He kissed Benny as though he enjoyed it, and, on that night, it had made drunk Benny think that, maybe, just maybe, he was in with a chance. But, later that same night, he saw Daniel with his tongue in Rebekka Arnesen's mouth, so he squashed that idea down for good.

As he lies facing the window, watching the line of light under the blind grow brighter and brighter, he hears a sound that makes his heart flip-flop with fear. A car is drawing into the parking space beside the hut, tyres crunching on gravel, right outside their window. He starts up, and a second car draws in next to the first. Surely, someone else can't be staying in the hut? Or has David . . . ? He shakes his shoulder; a murmur.

He whispers urgently, 'David! There's someone here!'

David is awake and pulls up his mask. 'What?'

'There are cars outside – right outside!'

'Well, so what? Ignore them.' He pulls the mask down again and rolls away from him.

'You're not expecting anyone?'

'No.' He sounds irritated. 'Of course not.'

Benny sits there, frozen, waiting for something to happen.

David mumbles, 'For God's sake, they'll be hikers.'

Benny's heart begins to slow. He's right, of course: hikers. To the Fagerheims' annoyance, people often use Nilsbakken as a car park when they go hiking in the mountains. Now, he's embarrassed by his reaction, but still he peers through the crack under the blind. Two men get out of one of the cars, and Benny's heart clenches again, painfully, because he knows them. They're wearing hoodies, but the sun has risen and he recognises Tobias Mero and Johnny Skarstein, two of the Hellraisers. They're speaking, but in low voices, and whatever they're saying is muffled by the thick glazing. He clutches David's arm.

'I know them! They're from my school!'

David sighs and sits up again, alert now, and they listen.

Benny looks at him, scared. 'Is the door locked?'

It is. David lives in Oslo and doesn't take risks. But the boys just get into the other car and close the doors. Benny sees that the driver of the second car is Elin's cousin, Lorentz Jentoft. He thinks the first car belongs to Daniel – usually, when you see these three, he's not far away – but Daniel doesn't seem to be around. Although, to be fair, Benny knows next to nothing about cars, so he could be wrong. He has a mad fear that they know he's here and are about to inflict some horrible homophobic prank on him. They can't know that he's here, surely, and, even if they did, they can't do anything, can they? But the second car is already turning around, and then it has gone, leaving Daniel's empty vehicle tucked behind the cabin. The noise of the engine trails away into the morning.

He waits for his heart to go back to its normal rhythm.

'Wonder what they're doing.'

David lies down again. 'It'll be for a hike. They're leaving a car at the end point.'

This is a sane and reasonable explanation. Benny takes a deep breath and sighs it out.

'Sorry. I thought they might have come to play a prank on me.'

'How would they know you're here?' David's voice is sharp.

'They couldn't. No one knows! I haven't said a thing.'

'Well, then . . .'

'But – it's russ, you know, and the group they belong to – they're called the Hellraisers – they're supposed to have a secret "blacklist" of russ dares – illegal stuff . . . extreme, you know? So—'

'You believe that? You know there's always a group, in every school, that's supposed to have a "blacklist" of dares, since, like, forever. That one's as old as the hills.'

Benny shrugs, embarrassed. He had half-believed it. And then there was the strange, woozily remembered encounter with Johnny last weekend, when Johnny had made those odd comments in front of

Jonas, which had weirded Jonas out because it came across as though Johnny was jealous . . . But how could that be, from arch-player Johnny? Yet, Benny had definitely got a vibe. And you hear those stories about supposed straight men who are into trans girls, but then they can't cope with it. And God knows how *that* might rebound on him.

'I made out with one of them, for a dare.'

David laughs. 'God! I'd have been beaten senseless if I'd done that at school.'

Benny feels emboldened. He traces a finger down David's arm. 'That's awful.'

He smiles, feels foolish for his previous panic.

David is properly awake now and takes off his mask. 'Come and tell me about it. Which one was it?'

Nine

It's Sunday afternoon, and Marylen is on her own at last, walking the path beside the stream that runs down from the mountain. She's parked her car up by the old mines, so it's not far to walk to the lake. This will give her enough time to stay there for a few minutes, before turning round and coming back. When she was younger, she roamed all over these mountains. Once, she would have thought nothing of circling Lomivatnet, would probably have gone on to complete the circuit of Muorkkejávrre and wander over the border into Sweden. But she doesn't have the time for proper hikes nowadays; a stack of marking is sitting on her desk, awaiting her when she gets home. Her body used to be hard and lean; now, it . . . isn't. All the same, it's good to feel the little platelets of ice crackle under her boots, hear the gurgle of water between still-snowy banks, feel the cool breeze from the mountain breathe its mighty calm in her face.

Marylen has lived in the valley most of her life. Her father worked for Sulitjelma Gruber for years, when the mine was still operating and the company was at the centre of everything in the valley. You either worked for it or were related to someone who did. Marylen herself never set foot inside a mine: highly dangerous to young girls, her father said, which made her worry about him going down there in the wagon lift and riding the underground train that carried the miners deep beneath the earth. At school, she'd heard stories about cables snapping and horrible injuries, but somehow her father survived it all. In those days, when you went for a walk on the mountain, you knew not to drink the water from the streams, because it might be contaminated with toxic run-off. There were places where a thick yellow fluid seeped from the earth like pus. And dominating the head of the valley was the smelting plant, pouring out smoke that, on windless days, blanketed the village in a malodorous cloud. Marylen hated it, couldn't wait to leave and see the world, and, when she was qualified, she sought out teaching posts in places that were as different from Nordland as she could imagine. After a few years, she grew homesick for the midnight sun and the snow – if not for the pollution. But by then the mines had closed down and the air had recovered. Too late for her father, who, like a lot of former miners, suffered from pneumoconiosis – that was another reason she decided to come home, to be near him in his declining years. She met Petter Sundfær when they were both working in Syria, and he came home with her. She once thought she was lucky to have a man like that, one who would subordinate his dreams to hers. Lucky also to come from this beautiful, wild place whose wounds were healing – the heaps of reddish spoil were veiled with birch trees, and the streams, at least those higher up the mountain, now ran clear.

This morning, Marylen asked Petter if he wanted to come for a walk, but he said he was too tired. He's always too tired. Being tired is a symptom of his depression, which has barely budged over the years despite all the medications and therapies he's tried. Or, the medications, anyway; she has never been successful in getting him to commit to seeing a counsellor regularly. He did try. A few times, he agreed to see someone, but each time he went once or twice, then stopped, because he 'knew it wouldn't help'. He's a clever man who always believes he is the smartest person in the room. He's usually right, but the fact hasn't helped him.

Yesterday, as they do every Saturday, she and Petter made the three-hour round trip to visit their grown-up daughter, Nora, and, after spending several hours inside the residential facility, as she had a cold and couldn't go outdoors, they drove home in exhausted silence. Nora had been moody and difficult. The staff in the facility are wonderful, and put her bad temper down to her not feeling well. But Marylen still feels that they are being punished (or, more specifically, *she* is) for leaving her there. Of course, she is to blame; she is the mother. She wouldn't give up everything to take care of her disabled daughter for the rest of her days: guilty, guilty, guilty. After lunch, Nora threw a box of crayons at her. Marylen's face ached from smiling. Afterwards, she drove them home. The simplest remark went unanswered. She didn't have the energy to try to lift him out of it. After a day spent with their daughter, she doesn't have any left.

Now, a flash of movement over the water catches her eye and she stops. It's a white-throated dipper, bobbing on an ice-glazed rock. There's something so cheerful and resolute about a dipper: compact and round, with its jaunty tail. She's heard snatches of its sweet, bubbling song, but this is the first one she has seen today. Marylen watches. The little bird is so close, she risks taking out her phone to try to sneak a photo, but, just as she does so, it rings, and her left boot breaks through some hidden ice and sinks arch-deep in freezing water.

She's been expecting the call. In fact, she is here on her solitary hike, knowing Petter wouldn't come, for precisely this reason, and she's been continually checking her phone to make sure she hasn't wandered out of range. Her heart speeds up when she sees it's him – a cocktail of arousal and guilt. It's annoying to react like this, but she wouldn't be without it. This – a frail, almost disembodied thrill – is pretty much the only excitement in her humdrum life.

'Hi!'

'Hello. Where are you?'

'On the path just below Lomivatnet. Alone.'

'Oh. Nice.'

'Yeah. It is. It's really quiet. Why don't you come up here?'

A sigh. 'I wish I could, but . . .'

This is his chorus; the regular punctuation to their conversations; their – whatever this is – it's not a relationship, is it? Nothing so definite. Certainly not an affair.

He wishes he could, but he can't.

She wishes she could tell him to go and jump in a lake, put a stop to it, because this is so . . . so paltry, it isn't even anything – but she can't, because then she would be left with less than that, with nothing.

So she says, 'What's up?'

'Oh . . . the usual. How was Nora yesterday?'

He always asks after Nora, so she tells him, briefly. It clears the way for him to moan about his own daughter – although, in her opinion, he has little to moan about.

'How are things with you?'

'Er, fine. Well, there was something I wanted to talk to you about. I'm at a loss to know what to do with Elin.'

'Oh? Why?'

He goes on to tell her that his daughter, Elin, who recently announced she is genderfluid, has started stealing his clothes. Is this a sinister development?

'I wouldn't worry about it, Eskil. Quite a few kids at school are genderfluid or non-binary. It's no big deal.'

'Oh? But she went to a party last weekend and wore my suit ... It's the deception I worry about. It's not like her.'

'How does she seem to you, generally? Is she different from usual? Quieter? More withdrawn?'

'Not that I've noticed. Have you noticed anything at school, or in the car? Has she said anything to you?'

'No. Not at all.'

'Elin is Elin, you know. She doesn't really confide in me.'

'It sounds as though she has confided something that is important to her. That's a good thing, don't you think?'

'I just don't know what it means. I mean, it's literally nonsense! I don't even know if I should be worried or not.'

'It means what she says. Elin's fine. There are kids in school I worry about, but not Elin.'

'But ... I don't know what I'm supposed to *do*.'

'Is she changing her name? Has she asked you to use different pronouns?'

'What? She hasn't said so ... Good God!'

'Then you don't need to do anything special. If she asks you to use different pronouns, then try to do so. But otherwise treat her the same as always. She's your child.'

'Right. Okay. So, you think – I just have to go along with it?'

'The alternative being what? Of course! She's sixteen. She's exploring, finding out who she is – who they are, whatever.'

'So, you think it's a phase?' His voice sounds wistful.

Marylen sighs. Why is everything always her problem?

'I don't know. But, for heaven's sake, don't suggest that to her!'

'No. That's what they say. On the, er, web.'

Marylen smiles. 'You've looked? Well, good for you.'

'She sent me some links.'

'Commendably efficient!'

'Are you taking this seriously?'

'Yes, Eskil. This is me taking it seriously. Because I don't think it's a big deal.'

A loud sigh comes from the phone. 'What if it leads to something more?'

'There's no reason to think it will. The main thing is that she's happy, isn't it? A lot of kids aren't.'

And a lot of adults, too.

'It's just that I worry because she's – you know – different.'

'She's not that different. A lot of kids at the school have a diagnosis of some sort. Honestly, I think she's doing very well.'

Another sigh. 'Thank you. It's such a relief to hear you say that. I don't know who else to talk to.'

That, right there, is a large part of the problem. Eskil's wife moved to Oslo years ago, when Elin was little, taking their elder daughter with her. It was a mental-health issue, that's as much as she knows. Eskil doesn't seem to have close friends that he can discuss parenting problems with – other than, presumably, God – and confidante seems to be the role she has fallen into – the comforting ear, the sympathetic shoulder – which is not the part she wanted, at all.

'Sure,' she says. 'Any time.'

They have kissed precisely twice. Once in church, scandalously, after the service, when Marylen wanted to have a word about the autumn festival (which was last *year*), and once in her car, after a parents' evening, cloaked by darkness – and even that was in winter, months ago. Since then, they've been ringing each other every few days, having awkward, hesitant conversations and, perhaps, making guarded reference to their mutual affection, the impossibility of doing more. Occasionally, they run into each other in the Co-op, whereupon Marylen goes hot and cold with longing – and he says he feels the same. But she is married to Petter and they have a disabled daughter, so she can't, can she? Not to mention his reputation as vicar of the local church.

He wishes he could, but he can't.

Marylen told him that she has no intimate relationship with her husband and hasn't done for longer than she cares to remember. They have separate bedrooms and can go for days without exchanging words. Petter is on medical leave from his job – and this situation has been dragging on for years. She would divorce him, only his suffering from clinical depression makes the prospect seem insurmountably cruel. When she said this, Eskil didn't disagree with her, which was annoying.

'Eskil, listen,' she interrupts him, and turns to face the river. 'Come and meet me, now. Come to the hiking hut at Lomivatnet.'

'What? Um . . .'

'What are you doing?'

'Well, just . . . nothing, really, but Elin's here.'

85

'Elin's sixteen. You can leave her alone in the house. We have to talk. I'm going mad. If you don't . . . I don't know what I will do.'

A pause. 'Well . . . all right.'

She pockets her phone and resumes her walk to the lake. She's breathing hard, as though she has been running. The lake will calm her down. She's not one for melodrama – has always despised it. But somehow it felt necessary to put her foot down.

A cloud drifts in front of the sun and the air feels colder. She tramps on up to Lomivatnet and stands looking at it. The lake is an old friend, one she has known all her life. Often dark and sullen, today it has put on its spring finery. The lake is revealing itself again: the membrane of ice that sealed it all winter is melting and breaking up, and the water is a milky turquoise. The sun reappears, casting its angled light across the lake: dazzling white, turquoise, blue; flecks of gold and green from buttercups and buds of cotton grass on the shore. The water will soon be clear of ice, but there will be patches of snow on the slopes until July. Her foot aches from its encounter with the hidden puddle. A dipper (the same one?) darts past her, and she watches it land and dive under the icy water. After a few seconds, it bounces up like a cork and hops on to a flake of rotten ice. It looks around, waddles a few steps, then plunges back into the water. It doesn't seem to find anything, but it keeps going. It's an optimist, like her.

For these few weeks in spring, third-year classes are always less productive than usual. In every lesson, at least one student spends the entire forty-five minutes crouching under their desk, or refuses to speak, or answers questions by reading out porn. Marylen doesn't know which she hates the most. There is no point trying to enforce

normal discipline during russ time – to do so would be unpatri-
otic, practically treason. There have been efforts in recent years
to remove the most problematic dares, such as those that involve
filming their peers having sex, or extreme alcohol abuse, but there
will always be students who push the boundaries. And, anyway, how
do you set restrictions on a tradition that is all about taking risks
and testing boundaries? There was that awful incident a couple of
years ago, where a girl was sexually assaulted by two boys wearing
No Means No badges. What must she have thought? In Norway, generally, they are safe and comfortable – so much so that the young
need to manufacture risks to prove themselves. Marylen, who spent
years teaching in the Middle East, often has to bite her tongue. She
reminds herself that they're still kids, and kids are allowed to be
idiots. The russ is a wearisome trial that happens every year, and
there's no point making a fuss. At least her students know better
than to ask her for a kiss – kissing a teacher or police officer being
a perennial favourite.

So, she is surprised by how quiet the third-year classroom is this
Monday morning. Going in, she finds it oddly empty. Half the boys
seem to be missing. Last Monday, most of the seniors were hung-
over after an epic party that had lasted more than twenty-four hours.
Today, they haven't even bothered to turn up. She doesn't repress a
sigh of annoyance.

'Where is everybody?' she asks of the room.

Silent glances criss-cross the space. Shrugs and head shaking.

Rebekka Arnesen says, '*We*'re here, Marylen.'

'So I see, Rebekka, thank you. Let me rephrase, then. Where are . . .
Tobias Mero, Daniel Fjordholm, Johnny Skarstein and Lorentz Jentoft?

Is there a virus going around? Or is it the aftermath of another party? Anyone?'

'We don't know.'

This is from Solgunn Ingebrigtsen, who is dating Lorentz. She likes to flaunt the fact that she is going out with a Hellraiser, so it must be galling to admit that she doesn't know what her boyfriend is up to.

'Solgunn, you don't know why Lorentz isn't here? Is he ill?'

Solgunn shakes her head. 'I haven't heard anything.'

It's the four main Hellraisers who are absent. They've garnered a reputation for hard partying – except for Tobias, who doesn't drink. But he, despite being the best student in the class and the most diligent, isn't here either.

'Well, anyone who isn't here will have to make up this module within the week, because, without it, we can't move on. So, if any of you are speaking to them, will you let them know? I will assume that those who are absent have all come down with the same highly contagious russ virus. Let's hope it only lasts as long as the party you were at last weekend.'

Rueful glances. Some smirks, quickly smothered.

'I know it's the russ time, but your final exams are only a few weeks away. You don't want to waste all your hard work, do you?'

Solgunn has her head down, illegally texting behind her desk. Presumably to her absent boyfriend. For once, Marylen decides to let it go.

Her annoyance about the Hellraisers doesn't last. At lunch, Erik Lindqvist notices her mood and says, 'Well, looks like someone had a good weekend!'

She says, 'It was all right, thanks.'

No one will know what is making her smile. They will not know that Eskil Torstensen did come and meet her yesterday, and she had the key to the Trekking Association cabin in her pocket. And at last, at last – one thing led to another . . . His desire for her was intoxicating. It took her breath away. Even his self-torment is sexy. When she laughed at him, for the way he was obsessively checking the bunk mattress for traces of Sin, he laughed too. He can be pompous at times, but he has enough self-awareness to appreciate the absurdity of the situation – and that she gets to see both sides of him makes her heart full.

On the way to her next lesson, she spots Eskil's daughter, Elin, for whom she feels a new, secret tenderness. Elin scuffles along with her head down, headphones on – she has a special dispensation to wear them – eyes on the ground. Staying in her own head. She seems very much like a kid who needs both parents, but apparently there isn't much of a relationship with her mother. Eskil has been open about the fact that he doesn't know how to talk to Elin, but how many single fathers do know how to cope with the complexities of teenage girldom? Marylen was intrigued by the story of the drag outing, and calmed him down on the issue of the suit, telling him that cross-dressing is so common these days as to barely raise an eyebrow, but Elin has made no mention of genderfluidity at school – and rumours go through the school like wildfire, so she is sure she would have heard something. Coming out in public must be a daunting prospect for someone as shy as Elin. On their rides to and from school, Marylen leaves her (them?) and Benny alone, unless they want to talk. School is exhausting enough – for teachers as well as pupils – and the last thing they need is one of their teachers grilling them on the way home. The kids mostly spend their car time with their heads down, glued to their phones – messaging each other, she guesses, from the syncopated giggling. Benny Iversen, by any measure a great kid, does talk to her as well, although he also has the tact to know when to be quiet. Elin rarely makes eye contact, and barely speaks at all.

Marylen wishes she could take Elin to one side and talk to her: tell her that life gets easier as you grow older (at least, it becomes less excruciating); give her some much-needed confidence, as that is not Eskil's forte. She wants to give the girl – the person – a hug. But of course she doesn't do that, because she isn't supposed to know.

Ten

This morning, I have to go to the pharmacy to refill my prescriptions. The pharmacist is a small, lively woman called Sunny. Sunny likes to talk to everyone, but even she has given up trying to draw me out of my shell. She no longer attempts to engage me in conversation, but she always gives me her warm smile. Occasionally, I have wondered about her indomitable niceness. People like her throw me off balance. They do not conform to the laws of the world as I understand them. I always think there must be an ulterior motive behind it, or it is bogus. Anyway, I don't trust it.

'How are you, Mrs Hustoft?'

Sunny is one of the people who persist in giving me this courtesy title.

'Oh, surviving, thank you.'

'It's worrying news, isn't it?' says Sunny, with more than her usual degree of sympathetic energy. I can tell that she is excited about something. She hasn't even said good morning to Asta, which is unusual for her.

'Usually it is, yes, but to what are you referring in particular?'

'Oh, you haven't heard?'

'Apparently not.'

'About the boys? From the high school? One of the seniors has gone missing. At first, everyone thought they had gone camping and got drunk and lost track of time, but they all came back except for one of them. It's been three days, now.'

'Oh. I hadn't heard that. But three days isn't really that long, at this time of year.'

'No, I suppose not – but his poor parents. I feel for them. I mean, I'm sure he'll turn up. After all, he'll be eighteen – a young man, really . . . He must be at the school with your granddaughter.'

'My granddaughter's sixteen.'

'Oh, yes. Of course. But they all know each other, don't they, at that school?'

'I really don't know.'

'Well – we'll have to hope for the best, won't we? Take care of yourself, Mrs Hustoft.'

I take the bulging bag of blister packs and sprays that Sunny hands to me, which has grown larger and heavier over the years, and mutter my rudimentary thanks. I don't think much about the gossip at first – a few years ago, a senior from the high school went missing and it turned out he had run off with one of his teachers – but, gradually, a bad feeling creeps over me, like a cloud swallowing the sun. My unease intensifies as Asta and I walk to the café. It's one of our regular days, but Odd Emil isn't there. I order and drink some coffee, but the minutes tick past and he doesn't come. It's unlike him not to turn up without letting me know in advance. When I get home, I try ringing him. There's no answer at his house, so I call his mobile. By then, I have convinced myself that the missing boy is his grandson Daniel, despite telling myself to stop being silly, but, when I hear his voice, the bad feeling crystallises into something cold and sharp.

'Odd Emil? I missed you at the café. Is everything all right?'

A sigh. He's whispering, as though he doesn't want to be overheard. 'Oh, Svea. Uh, no – that is, I'm fine. It's Daniel. He's—'

Why couldn't I have been wrong?

Odd Emil is at his daughter's house – Daniel's mum, Maria, who married Arne Fjordholm, although I don't think they're together anymore.

'I know it's probably nothing, but Maria's in a bit of a state, so I've come over for moral support.'

He tells me what he knows, which isn't much. Daniel went out with his friends on Saturday afternoon, and told Maria that he was going to stay out all night – not an unusual occurrence, in summer. So, Maria didn't think anything of it until the Sunday afternoon. Even then, she was more irritated at his thoughtlessness than anything. Daniel is a young man, an experienced hiker and skier; he knows what he's doing. She rang him and left a message. It went straight to voicemail; phone reception is often bad in the mountains and she assumed his phone was out of range. She carried on with her day, but by evening she was worried enough to call the Jentoft house. She spoke to Lorentz, who told her that Daniel had gone hiking on his own on Saturday evening. He was planning to stay up and watch the sunrise from one of the fells behind Nilsbakken – Vássjátjåhkkå, he thought. From there, at this time of year, you can watch the sun rise over the Padjelanta wilderness in Sweden. Staying awake for twenty-four hours is a common russ-time dare, and Daniel loves wild camping, so she wasn't surprised that he would choose to do it on a mountain. He had taken outdoor clothing and a backpack, so probably he was just staying out a bit longer than planned. Perhaps he couldn't get a phone signal or had run out of battery. She thought, Well, so . . . okay. Inconsiderate of him. She'll have to have words.

But also, even in summer, accidents can happen. Maria is not a nervous person, but late on Sunday night she phoned Odd Emil, in tears. Then she phoned Daniel's dad, who, since the divorce, lives in Bodø. He hadn't heard from him either, but he reassured her: Daniel is eighteen; he was sure there was no need to panic.

That was Sunday. On Monday, Maria rang the police station and spoke to her friend there, one of the senior officers, Hanne Duli Bodøgaard. Hanne Duli was sympathetic but reassuring: there wasn't a particular time that Daniel had failed to come home by, so she couldn't make an official report, not yet. Technically, he had been gone for less than twenty-four hours. Hanne Duli told her to wait a bit longer, as he was sure to return, but, unofficially, she would make some enquiries. Odd Emil doesn't know what those enquiries were, but, another twenty-four hours later, there had still been no sign.

Now, it's Tuesday afternoon. A report has been filed, photographs have been handed over, an alert has gone out. Daniel Fjordholm is, officially, missing.

I don't know what to say. I know that, in similar circumstances, people often say something like, *Well, if there's anything I can do . . .* But, clearly, there is nothing I can do. Yet I feel something is expected of me.

'I'm sure he's all right,' I say, idiotically.

'Yes, yes, I expect so.'

'He's a champion skier, isn't he?'

'Yes.'

'So . . . well, ring me if you want to.'

'Yes. I will. Thanks, Svea.'

'Bye, then.'

He ends the call. I feel hopelessly inadequate. I wonder how I would feel if Elin had been missing for three days. Awful, I expect, even though we're not that close. That's what people say, isn't it – *not a close family*?

But, if a sixteen-year-old girl was gone for three days – that would be an altogether different kettle of fish, wouldn't it?

Eleven

On Tuesday, there are rumours. People whisper in corridors, look around furtively, like conspirators. Rebekka Arnesen is spotted weeping copiously, surrounded by her friends. On Wednesday, there is an announcement. The entire school gathers for a morning assembly, and Mrs Shirani-Lund stands up and says there is something they need to talk about. By then, everyone knows what it is.

Several senior girls are in tears. The Hellraisers look strained and pale. Rebekka Arnesen, who, as of yesterday, has been proclaiming that she and Daniel were practically an item, has cried so much that her eyelids are almost swollen shut. Stina Kristiansen, who was Daniel's girlfriend for part of last year, is also barely holding it together. It feels as though the two of them are vying to be queen mourner. Their respective girlfriends cluster jealously round them, handmaidens at the wake. Although – mourner . . . wake – it's a bit premature, isn't it? Because no one actually knows anything.

Mrs Shirani-Lund introduces two officers from the police investigation team: Hanne Duli Bodøgaard and Merete Nordheim. The presence of the officers makes things seem very real and serious. Hanne Duli, the senior officer, explains what they are doing, and how they need to hear from anyone who has information about Daniel's movements at the weekend.

'If there is anything that you can think of that might help us, if you know anything at all about Daniel's plans for Saturday or Sunday, or if you saw him at the weekend, or if he said anything, will you please come forward. You can imagine how worried his family are.'

She looks around the hall. She is a powerful-looking woman in her forties, familiar to many as a mother from PTA meetings. Her son has left school, but her daughter is a second-year. People sneak glances at Elizabeth Bodøgaard to see how she reacts to seeing her mum in this weird, professional role; or they pointedly don't look at her. In any case, she keeps her head down.

Benny also recognises the younger officer, Merete Nordheim, from Toril's yoga classes – a smiley, ponytailed presence. Only, now, she is wearing her uniform and not smiling, as she gives out information. There is a dedicated phone line they can call; everything will be treated in confidence; all they care about is finding Daniel as quickly as possible. The officers are a sober, steadying presence in the midst of this turbulent grief. Someone lets out a sort of impromptu shriek: it's almost funny. Indeed, someone snickers, but is firmly shushed. Tuts and murmurs of disapproval sweep around the room.

Mrs Shirani-Lund steps forward again.

'This news is very concerning, but of course we don't give up and assume the worst. There may be a simple explanation. We must maintain hope and be open to all outcomes.'

That makes it sound even worse, thinks Benny. How many outcomes can there be?

As they trail to their classroom afterwards, he puts his arm around Elin's shoulder.

'You okay?'

Elin nods. She hasn't cried, despite her make-out session with Daniel. She hardly ever cries. She looks stunned, but then, they all do. Benny feels on the verge of tears himself. He wasn't close to Daniel, but so what? You couldn't help but like him. Everyone liked him (*likes* him, he means). Likes him. And fancies him, either a little bit or a lot. Benny had that moment at the party, weeks ago, when he and Daniel kissed. Afterwards, they'd laughed. They were both drunk, of course, and it was for the dare, but Daniel had, Benny was sure, blushed a little bit.

For the hour following assembly, regular lessons have been cancelled and the time set aside for people to talk about what's happened, ask questions, discuss their feelings, and so on. Benny can't think it will help any of them. Mrs Sundfær doesn't know anything they don't, and he for one doesn't know what his feelings are – and isn't it too soon to have feelings? Everything is unknown, except that one of their number isn't where he is meant to be. He is haunted by the phrase 'all outcomes'. Previously (as in yesterday, when the rumours began), he'd assumed that Daniel was carrying out a dare to 'disappear' for days. Doing something a bit over the top was certainly a possibility with a member of the Hellraisers – they were rumoured to have been behind a suspicious fire in the local quarry. Probably, they would like nothing better than to go down in school history for having turned the town upside down.

If that is the case, then it's a stunt in very poor taste. Daniel's car is still sitting up at Nilsbakken, as the police had been notified yesterday by the Fagerheims. The wilderness beyond the resort is studded with hiking cabins, most of which are stocked with basic necessities. Daniel will be familiar with many of them, and, even if he doesn't have a key, he could get in without much difficulty. At worst, maybe he's broken an ankle and his phone's run out of juice. They'll find him, now that the police are out there with dogs. They're even doing a helicopter search of the area. Surely by now it can't be a stunt – he can't believe Daniel would be that inconsiderate. But Benny doesn't really know him, does he? Still, the phrase 'all outcomes' makes him think of awful things . . . Drowning in a lake – he wouldn't drown, would he? Not Daniel. Falling off a mountain? The fells at Nilsbakken aren't the sort of mountains you fall off. Or something worse . . . but what could be worse? Suicide? Kidnapping? Murder? That sort of 'outcome' is simply, completely absurd, and any student talking about such things is just attention-seeking in the worst possible way.

He is worried about Elin, because she told Benny she couldn't sleep for thinking about Daniel after the russ party. She also said she knew that it didn't mean anything, so that was that. It's hard to know how much Elin is feeling about a thing, because she doesn't give much away. When he asked her if she was upset by Daniel's silence in the days following the party, she just shrugged and said, 'No.'

Elin sits quietly in the class as other people talk and hug and cry. Jamila and a couple of the other girls look utterly devastated; perhaps they nursed a quiet crush on Daniel. Or they are just very empathetic.

For her part, Elin is trying not to speculate, because there is no point in speculating without information. Of course she feels weird, has felt weird since hearing the first rumours yesterday. She had never spoken to Daniel before the party, and since then – nothing. Her memories of that Saturday night seem ever more unreliable: did he really tell her she looked amazing, while he brushed at her chin with his thumb? Had they really sat on the sofa in the corner of the bus, pounding music blotting out the sounds of others nearby, kissing for what seemed a really long time? Despite the music and the surroundings and the unexpectedness of it all, she'd felt safe, a thing moulded from wax, softening in his radiant heat. Until he offered her that pill, and she'd been too scared to accept.

Increasingly hard to be sure. The Saturday before last was, perhaps, a literal lifetime ago, and it didn't mean anything, anyway.

Twelve

Like everyone else in town, I'm on edge. I carry on with my usual routine, walking Asta, doing my shopping, sitting in the conservatory, even going to the café, although Odd Emil doesn't come, hasn't come since. I called him again, the next morning, and he said, in a heavy, weary voice, 'I'll let you know as soon as we hear anything, I promise.' I don't dare call him again.

Time moves both fast and slowly. You think – Oh, by lunchtime today, I expect it will all be over. Lunchtime takes forever to arrive, but that is good, because that means there is more time in which to find him. Of *course* he'll be found by now – what with the helicopter searches going on up the valley, and the teams of police dogs and handlers, and all the locals who have turned out to help look. Any minute now: he's fine! Hungry, cold, broken leg or whatever . . . but fine. We can all move on with a sigh of relief. And then, suddenly, it's the end of the day, and there's been no news – and the sky gets a little darker, and the footsteps that pass in the street get a little heavier.

The police have removed Daniel's car from where it was parked up at Nilsbakken, taking it away to do whatever tests they do in such circumstances. I find myself using the phrase 'in such circumstances' a lot, at least when I'm speaking to someone, which isn't often. I don't know how else to describe it: the awfulness of not knowing. We both are and are not in a state of normality. We both are and are not in a state of tragedy. A place I have been before, because, once, it was my own sister who was missing. 'It's like Schrödinger's cat,' I overheard someone say yesterday, while I was in the Co-op Mega, buying dog food. They meant, I suppose, that Daniel is both alive and dead, as long as we have no proof. I don't think I agree; it seems the height of hubris to assume the state of a thing depends purely on one observer's perception of it – but I am not a quantum physicist, only a retired bookkeeper. Although, either way, the longer the cat is shut in the box, and the longer Daniel is out there, the bleaker the outlook, for both of them.

I've been thinking about what Sunny said – about all the kids at school knowing each other – and wondering if she's right, and Elin does know Daniel. If so, I realise that she might be quite upset.

Elin sounds surprised to hear my voice, because I don't call often, but that's because I don't want to intrude.

'Oh. Hey, *Bestemor.*'

'I was wondering how you were – what with all this going on – with, er, Daniel.'

'Oh. Yeah. I don't know. Okay.'

'Do you know him well?' I decided in advance I would use only the present tense.

'Um. No. Not really. He's a senior. You know.'

'Yes, of course. I know his grandfather, Odd Emil. It's very hard for the family.'

'Uh-huh. How do you know his grandfather?'

'Well ... gosh, we've known each other a long time. We're both from Gammelsøy.' I name the village up the coast, where I haven't set foot in decades.

'Oh. Yeah, it must be awful. I mean, Lorentz is really upset. They're, like, best friends.'

'I didn't know that. Yes, he must be.'

'He was one of the last people to see him.'

'Ah. I didn't realise.'

I'm slightly ashamed that I haven't yet considered Lorentz in all this. All I can say in my defence is that – as previously stated, Your Honour – we are not a close family, and I know nothing of Lorentz's social life. Elin, I feel a connection with, as she is my granddaughter and her mother is not around (yes, all my fault, I realise). Lorentz is only my great-nephew – and a half-great-nephew at that. He's the grandson of my younger brother Karl, whom I was never close to as a child, and now, although Karl lives not far away, in a huge fancy house outside Bodø, we often don't speak from one year's end to the next. Karl is the golden child: the one member of our family who has done well for himself. In the eighties and nineties, he built up a successful fish-farming business and sold out to a foreign buyer at an opportune moment. He's the only one of us who took after Erling in having anything to do with fish, but he has managed to avoid having much else in common with him. He's not an alcoholic, as far as I know, and he's certainly not poor. From a starting point of not being close as children – I left home when he was only seven – Karl decided, a long time ago, that he didn't want anything to do with me. He claims it was because I refused to visit Ingvild when she was in the nursing home, but I think, long before that, he decided I was not the sort of sister a man like him wanted to have around.

Neither Elin nor myself are at our sparkling best on the phone, so, after enquiring after her father – 'Fine' – and then her mother and sister – 'Fine . . . I think' – I wish her well and we say goodbye.

It is Friday afternoon. Daniel has been gone for nearly a week.

There have been too many missing people in my life. In my own family. I don't know how many is normal. In the natural course of things, the longer you live, the more people you encounter, and some of them will slip through the cracks. I can't count the number of people I have lost track of over the years – but they are not missing. People are only missing once you have tried and failed to find them. But there are enough of those that I have sometimes wondered if it is something to do with me – that I carry a curse. That is foolish, of course. I know I'm not that important. Perhaps it is a family curse – that's certainly more credible. To have mislaid a father *and* a sister – that, as someone once said, looks like carelessness. Anyway, the first missing person in my life was my father. Maybe I'll come back to my sister later. If I feel like it.

By now, you might have guessed that I never found him: Otto Behmer. Or perhaps you've forgotten all about him – or you don't care. Better off without him, the cheating Nazi – something like that. Or, if you are a different sort of reader, you've been thinking, Aha, there is some story here, and it'd better be good, when she finally gets around to it. Well, I'm sorry, but there isn't. Or, more accurately, his story, whatever it is, is unknown to me. Maybe I *have* been better off without him, but I'll never know, because he stayed forever out of my reach. He might have led a good life after the war and redeemed himself for whatever he did – or didn't do – in the POW camp outside Rognan. I might have had German half-sisters and -brothers. I might have been in line for some serious cash. (I'm joking, at least about the cash.) Then again, he might have been a nasty, embittered loner, forever unbalanced by the war. He might have been a criminal. He might have died before he even made it home.

When I was in my early twenties, I left my job at the mining company and moved to Germany to look for him. I had dreamt up all sorts of scenarios for our reunion: there wouldn't be a dry eye in the house. He would be overwhelmed with emotion at seeing me; his voice would break when he spoke Ingvild's name . . . except that part never really worked in my head, knowing my mother as I did. But I imagined half-siblings that I could love as much as I loved my sisters, but without the shared shadow of our upbringing. We would become best friends. And, to be completely honest, I did fantasise that there might be some money. So what? I'd never had any, so think about that for a minute before you judge me.

I was naive. I didn't speak German at first, and my clumsy forays into the thickets of German bureaucracy ran up against one dead end after another. For one thing, thousands, if not millions of civic records had been bombed into oblivion at the end of the war. I couldn't find any trace of him, but then, I didn't know when or where he was born. And if he'd come from what was then East Germany, I was stymied. My mother didn't know, couldn't remember. It was a long time ago, painful memory, etc., etc. Why was I even making her think about it? I saw the hopelessness of my position – my sole source of information was Ingvild, and I didn't have a lot of reasons to trust her. I began to wonder whether he was even called Otto Behmer. After a few weeks of trailing around town halls and records offices, sitting in waiting rooms and being glared at by German administration officials, I realised the futility of the whole endeavour, and more or less gave up.

I drifted to West Berlin, where I found a job in a bar. It was easy to find work, in those days; there was lots of it about and no one was too bothered about visas and documents. That was where I met Astrid Junger. She was at university, studying philosophy. She was clever, beautiful and accomplished: she spoke four languages and had immense, enviable self-belief. She was a year younger than me, but I felt like a child around her – all I knew about was bookkeeping and the transportation of iron ore, and how to avoid sleeping with your boss without getting fired. Astrid knew about art and philosophy and politics, and had opinions on all of them. I listened to her talk, squirrelling away fact after fact to be chewed over and digested later. I changed my look, ditched the heavy eyeliner and skirt suits that had been so daring at Sulitjelma Gruber HQ, and copied her thrown-together style. Astrid gave me scarves and bangles and a disgusting astrakhan coat that I loved. I still have one of the bangles she gave me – a chunky Lucite ring of bright orange. I have it in a drawer, somewhere, although I can no longer fit my arthritic hand into it. Looking back, I think that, to her, I was a kind of pet – this exotic Arctic peasant who could be remoulded in her image. One night, when I had known her a couple of weeks, I told her about my father – that he had been a German soldier, possibly a Nazi. I no longer knew if I wanted to find him. To my astonishment, her eyes filled with tears and she seized my hands.

'Svea, you and I are the same! My father was a Nazi politician. He's still alive. I don't speak to him. I will never speak to him again. We have to look to the future. You see it, don't you? We have to purge the past of its crimes; it's up to us.'

It was as though I had found another sister. I had never met anyone who could understand the shame in my blood. Astrid wasn't a hippy; she was a revolutionary. She showed me a way to cleanse the past and thus myself. I adored her. Perhaps, in some way, Astrid took the place of my father, for, after we discovered our common shame, the desire to find him left me altogether.

1969. An exciting time. I hadn't known Astrid and her circle for very long before I fell properly in love for the first time: he was a friend of hers, Rolf. I'm ashamed to say that I thought a man was the most important thing I could have, and soon Astrid and I drifted apart. She scolded me for being insufficiently serious and said some quite hurtful things: that I was a hausfrau who would spend my life cooking and cleaning. Of course, I didn't want that, but I was in love and I thought it was natural that I would spend most of my time with him. I began to avoid Astrid, but I missed her. One day, I went to her apartment in Kreuzberg and hammered on her door. I shouted and pleaded for her to forgive me. Eventually, an irritated neighbour appeared from across the hall and said that the young lady had gone, vanished overnight, leaving the place a tip and owing rent. I was devastated, because I understood that she had moved on, and I had been left behind.

Astrid Junger. I don't think I have ever met anyone who crackled with such a powerful charge. She reminded me in some ways of Nordis, although Astrid was bright sunlight to my sister's starshine. In the end, their glamour brought them to the same place. Some people make an impression on your life that is out of all proportion to the time you know them. They affect you like an asteroid that hits Earth with a blinding flash and disappears in the heat-shock of its own impact, but, afterwards, the climate is forever altered.

Thirteen

The Hellraisers are keeping their heads down. A week ago, they were the loudest, craziest, most visible people in the school; now, they are quiet and withdrawn. Tobias is often with Johnny, and Lorentz with Solgunn, or the three boys walk around together in gloomy solidarity; they are rarely alone. There is a kind of force field around them which other people do not dare penetrate; they are not approached with trivial questions about homework, or crass internet memes, and, of course, they are not involved in any more pranks. In the school, there have been emergency meetings about the russ, and it has been decided that this year's celebrations will be drastically curtailed. This is not a unanimous decision; there are those who grumble that it is unfair that, due to one person's . . . misfortune, everyone else's fun will be ruined. Years of planning and fundraising have gone into it. A great deal of money has been spent. But that is the decision. Everyone is free to go to parties in the surrounding area, but, in this school, the dares and shenanigans have stopped.

Everyone treats the Hellraisers with kid gloves. The teachers give them special dispensation with their schoolwork, and, after Rebekka Arnesen complains, she gets a dispensation too. Then Solgunn

Ingebrigtsen complains – as Lorentz's girlfriend, she is just as affected, and spends a lot of her time giving him emotional support. The staff give in and allot extra time to the whole of the senior year.

For the pupils in every year, being at school is weird. There are pockets of normality, outbursts of boisterousness, just like at any other school, but then someone will suddenly remember and catch themselves, or they'll notice someone eying them with a mournful, accusing look, and the laughter quickly dies.

Elin tries praying. She doesn't usually pray, but her father is a vicar, so surely it's worth a go. She stopped going to church a couple of years ago, as soon as she could argue that her father could legally leave her alone in the house, but this Sunday she decides she's going. It's the least she can do. She asks Benny to go with her, and he is surprised, but agrees. In the end, a lot of people come to the Sunday-morning service in Sulis. The church hasn't been this full since Christmas – actually, not even then. Marylen Sundfær is there, with an overweight, silent man who must be Petter Sundfær; her husband is so rarely seen in the village that it causes comment. Elin sits with Benny and his mum. Elin's dad gives a really good sermon. She is impressed by him, even surprised. He manages to find just the right tone for this awful time: grave and heartfelt, serious but still allowing for hope. Afterwards, Elin shuts her eyes and begs God: *Please, please make Daniel be all right. I'll try to be a better person; I'll be nicer to Dad, I promise – even though I know what I do doesn't really matter. God, are you listening?*

As she prays, she has a sudden flashback to the party, when she was with Daniel, squashed together on a sofa in the bus. He had rambled a bit about inner voyages, or some nonsense like that. She didn't know what he was talking about, but they were both drunk, and he didn't

110

seem to mind that she wasn't answering with any enthusiasm. Then he had said, 'God, I can't wait to get out of this place.'

Her eyes snap open mid-prayer. Did he really say that? She hasn't thought of it again before now, so is she making it up? But she can picture his face, the way he cast his eyes to the roof of the bus, the way the pulsing lights were reflected in them. And his voice was ineffably weary. It sounded as though he was tired of everything.

After the service, Toril asks Eskil if Elin can go home with her and Benny for the rest of the day, and he agrees. He even smiles, as though he thinks it's a great idea. He seems to have forgotten that last week he grounded her – or, under the circumstances, he has decided to rescind it. Elin isn't going to bring it up.

'So, I guess you couldn't ask Lorentz about what happened last Saturday night?'

Benny has put some music on and shut the door of his bedroom.

'No. It just felt weird, asking right out like that.'

'No, I know.' He sighs. 'Sorry to ask. I should've done it, but I thought it would be more – I don't know – normal, coming from you.'

'So, why did you want me to ask? The police already talked to all of them.'

'Yeah, I know. That's just it.'

'What is? I don't understand.'

'Okay. Don't say anything to anyone else.'

Elin shakes her head vigorously.

'I'm not sure ... I don't know exactly what it was they said, so maybe this is all bullshit, but – I think they lied.'

'Who lied?'

'Lorentz and the others – Tobias and Johnny.'

'How do you know?'

'Well, it depends whether . . . What I heard was that Daniel was supposed to have driven up to Nilsbakken alone and left his car and gone hiking from there.'

'Yeah. I think so. So?'

'So, that must have been what they told the police, since they were the last people to see him.'

'I suppose.' She shrugs.

'Well, he didn't. I mean, that's not how it happened. The other three drove Daniel's car up there and parked it, and then they drove off in Lorentz's car. Daniel wasn't even there.'

'Who? Lorentz and Johnny and Tobias?'

'Yeah. I saw them parking his car at Nilsbakken on Sunday morning. It must have been around four o'clock.'

'You're sure?'

'Yeah, it was daylight. And they parked right next to the cabin we were in.'

'So . . . maybe they were leaving his car for him, and he'd already set off.'

'Yeah. Could be. Then why lie?'

'Maybe he was there, and you just didn't see him. That's possible, isn't it?'

'I suppose so, I just . . . I don't know. No, he wasn't there. There was something odd about it.'

'Odd, like how?'

Benny thinks. 'Like, I don't know, they were trying not to be seen. They were being really quiet.'

'It was the middle of the night. They didn't want to disturb anyone.'

'Yeah, but it seemed – I don't know – like they were up to something. I was scared. I thought for a minute they'd come to prank me.'

'How could they know? Did you tell anyone you were there?'

He shakes his head. 'No. I know. I was just being paranoid. But it was weird.'

'So . . . what difference does it make who drove his car up there?'

'I don't know.'

'I mean, why would they lie about it?'

He shrugs. 'Yeah, that's the whole point.'

Elin looks at the poster above Benny's bed. A shirtless Omar Rudberg looks down at her with melting brown eyes. For some reason, the sight of him makes her sad.

'I don't know if I should tell the police or not. I mean, like you say, it's probably nothing.'

'Well, yeah, of course you should tell them. It's a fact. Facts are important, right?'

'That's what I thought you'd say.'

'You can ring them up. There's a number. I took a picture of it.'

'Yeah. I'm just not sure what to say about why I was there. I'm scared I'll get David into trouble.'

'Why?' Elin asks. It's not like Benny to be coy.

'I'm trying to think of a way to say I was there on my own.'

'What does it matter? Who cares?'

'Because I'm sixteen, and he's . . . in his thirties. I told him I was eighteen.'

'Oh.'

Elin tries not to look shocked, but she is shocked. Also, the way Benny

113

says 'in his thirties' makes it sound like David is nearer thirty-nine than thirty-one. Which is kind of gross. She'd imagined the mysterious, alluring David to be more like . . . well – more like Omar.

'Okay. But it's not illegal, is it?'

'Not technically. But I lied . . .'

'Okay. Why don't you say that you went up there to . . . I don't know, smoke a blunt on your own.'

'I don't smoke! But, yeah, maybe that would work.'

'Can't you ring up and, you know, do it anonymously? Say you saw them, but don't give your name or anything.'

They look at each other.

Benny reads the number off her phone. He's already looked up how to hide his caller ID. Elin nods at him, encouraging. It's the right thing to do.

After a long time, the phone is answered. Benny says hi, and that he has some information that might be relevant to the Daniel Fjordholm case. There's lots of waiting, then talking at the other end. He says 'okay' and 'yes' a few times, then he mutes the phone.

'She's asking for my name!'

'Just say what you're going to say and hang up.'

Benny unmutes the phone and quickly gabbles his piece – Nilsbakken, the three boys, the two cars, 4 a.m. on Sunday morning. No sign of Daniel—

Then he cuts off the call and gives Elin an anguished look.

'She recognised my voice! She said, "Is that Benny Iversen? It's Hanne Duli Bodøgaard – Elizabeth's mum." Fuck! What do I do?'

Elin stares at him in horror. Fuck, indeed. 'It's okay. You haven't done anything wrong.'

'Christ. What do I do? Do I have to call back? She knows where I live.'

'Yeah, I think maybe you have to call back. You know, just . . . go with plan A, I guess.'

Benny rubs his face with his hands. 'Fuck!' He looks close to tears.

'And I think you need to tell your mum.'

Fourteen

Benny insists on Elin coming with them while he gives a statement to the police. His mum drives them down to Fauske, uncharacteristically silent and stern. Benny has a feeling that that won't last, not once Elin has gone home.

Hanne Duli greets Toril by name – of course, they know each other from the school, and from yoga classes, too, apparently. Toril gets around. At the school assembly, Hanne Duli came across as warm and approachable, but today she is businesslike, a deep little groove etched between her brows. Benny feels sick as he follows her into an office and she starts to take notes on her computer. He begged Toril not to come in with him, so she, still looking suspicious, has taken Elin around the corner to get cake. Elin kept telling him he has nothing to feel guilty about. Toril seemed less sure, but then, he has lied to her. Not once, but twice. He gave her the whole going-up-there-to-get-high story, and she has been frowning and looking worried ever since.

'So, Bendik, last Saturday evening, you cycled up to Nilsbakken, and you were in the southernmost cabin, on your own. How did you get into the cabin?'

'Um, I work for the Fagerheims, in the holidays. I knew it wouldn't be locked.'

'Okay . . . So, you went into the cabin – what time was this?'

'About . . . eight o'clock. And I just, you know, smoked and played games on my phone.'

'What made you go up there?'

He shrugs. 'I don't know. Just somewhere to be alone.'

'Did you see anyone else there, anything unusual?'

'I didn't see anyone. Not even the Fagerheims. I knew there weren't a lot of guests there, because of Mum— because of Toril, teaching there.'

'Okay. And then?'

'I just hung out, and then I fell asleep on one of the beds, and then the sound of cars woke me up – it was two cars, parking behind the cabin. I saw Tobias Mero and Johnny Skarstein get out of the first car, and get into the second car, which was driven by Lorentz Jentoft, and then that car drove away, leaving the first car – Daniel's car – parked there.'

'And what time was this?'

'The sun had risen; it was just before four. I looked at my phone.'

'Do you remember the colour of the cars?'

'The first one – Daniel's car – was dark blue, and the other – Lorentz's – was white. I've seen them at school.'

'How near were the cars to you?'

'I was just by the window, and the first car was maybe three metres away.'

'Did you hear them say anything?'

He shakes his head. 'The window was closed. They didn't seem to be talking much. It was quick. They just parked, then Johnny and

Tobias got out of Daniel's car and got into Lorentz's, and they drove off, leaving Daniel's car.'

'Who was driving Daniel's car?'

'Johnny.'

She types. 'Okay. And you were alone in the cabin?'

He nods, looking her in the eye and trying not to blink.

'And you didn't see anyone else there?'

'No. Daniel wasn't there. I'm pretty sure I would have seen him if he'd been in one of the cars, but he wasn't.'

'And you were there on your own.'

'Yeah.'

'Okay. I'm just wondering . . . I've been up to Nilsbakken and I saw where Daniel's car was parked, and we've actually spoken to the guest who rented the cabin that weekend. Er . . .' She makes a show of checking her notes. 'David Mæland.'

Benny thinks he is going to throw up. Is there a faint glimmer of satisfaction on her face? *Did you* really *think we don't know how to do our job?* He can't even speak.

'Bendik, were you there with Mr Mæland on Saturday night?'

Benny's throat works. What has David said? Fuck, fuck, fuck.

'It's okay if you were. You haven't done anything wrong. I'm really glad you've come forward with this information.'

To his horror, he feels a tear sliding down his face. 'I didn't want to get anyone into trouble.'

'There's no trouble. We're just interested in Daniel, at the moment. Anything you can tell us about that is super helpful.' She looks at him gravely. 'Is there anything else you can tell me?'

Benny tries to remember. Is there? He can't think of anything. The only suspicions he'd harboured at the time were of his own impending humiliation; he'd been worried about himself, not Daniel. If anything, the fact that Daniel wasn't there strengthened his paranoia, because he was sure Daniel wouldn't have taken part in a mean prank, whereas he wouldn't put anything past Johnny and Lorentz.

He shakes his head, and another tear spills down his cheek. 'That's all we saw – I saw. I mean, David didn't know who they were.'

'But you told him?'

Again, Benny finds it hard to speak – is this a trap? 'Um, I said I knew them from school. I was worried they'd somehow found out I was there and were going to prank me.'

'Had they done that before?'

He shakes his head. 'No. No. I was just . . . No.'

Her fingers are flying over the keyboard. The soft clicking is a less soothing sound than usual. He feels as though he is being skewered on to that computer screen, that he has said something that will haunt him for the rest of his life.

'Um . . . sorry . . . do you have to tell my mum?'

Hanne Duli looks up. 'Did you feel pressured into this relationship, Bendik?'

'God, no! I wanted— I went there because I wanted to.'

'Okay. Fine. Then I don't see any need to, at the moment.'

'Please don't – it wasn't his fault. Please, you have to believe me!'

'I believe you. It's just that Mr Mæland is quite a lot older than you.'

'I told him I was eighteen! It's not his fault.'

'Okay. Well, if you think of anything else, even if it doesn't seem relevant, please give me a call. Any time. Even really small things can make a difference, okay? All we want to do is find Daniel.'

He nods, and sniffs. Of course. It's not about him.

'I'm sorry I didn't tell you this before, but I only heard on Friday that, you know, he was supposed to have driven up there on his own, and I thought, Well, no, wait a minute . . . I mean, I don't suppose it matters—'

'Here's my number. If you think of anything else at all, Bendik, please give me a call. Don't hesitate.' She hands him a card. 'Kind of old-fashioned, isn't it, giving out cards? But that's what we do. You'd be surprised at the number of people who prefer it like that.'

He gives her a wan, expected smile.

'It's good that you've come forward with this now.'

'Is it?'

Hanne Duli looks at him, her face serious. 'Of course.'

He wants to, but doesn't, ask: *Why?*

She seems energised, which worries him. He'd been expecting her to say that his account is irrelevant, that what he saw doesn't make any difference. But she probably isn't allowed to say things like that, is she?

'I don't mind what you do, Benny, I'd just rather you were honest with me. If you want to smoke weed, you can do that here! I know what it's like being young. God, I sound . . . I don't know . . .'

Toril is upset, understandably so, and Benny hates being the one to make her that way. He has spent the drive home wrestling with the question of whether to tell her the truth. He and Elin messaged about it in the car. No one spoke. Elin's conclusion: she didn't know. But Toril is cool, so wd be okay, probably???

He's hoping she's right.

'Actually, that wasn't true. I'm sorry. I don't smoke or anything. I was . . . I went to Nilsbakken to meet someone.'

'Oh! Okay . . . Couldn't you just tell me that?'

'It was a guest. Someone I met at Easter. And he came back for the weekend – to do some hiking.'

He can see her thinking back to the Easter guests, sifting through the candidates. Frowning.

'I didn't know how to tell you because . . . well, I don't know. It's not like we're . . . boyfriends.'

'No? So, what are you?'

Now, she looks horrified. He has a cold sensation. He can't hold her gaze.

'It was just a thing, you know. It was nice, but not, like, you know, long term.'

'Okay. That's okay. But, sweetheart, he must be quite a lot older than you?'

'Well, I mean – he's, like, thirty.'

David could be thirty. From a distance. He'd said he was thirty-four, but it occurs to him now that perhaps they'd both lied about their ages.

'Jesus, Benny! I'm . . . No, it's fine. It's fine! Sorry. It's just that, you're my son. I know you're growing up. But sometimes, you know, on one of those dating apps, *I* match with men in their thirties.'

Benny has a distinctly vertiginous sensation. 'Probably not the same ones, though.'

She gives a strangled little laugh. 'You didn't meet him on an app?'

He shakes his head vigorously. 'No. I've never . . . He was part of that group from Oslo, and we got talking, and he was really nice.'

Toril looks like she's trying quite hard not to throw something.

'Well, I'm glad he was nice. Thank you for telling me. I hope you don't ever feel you have to hide things from me. I mean, I'm not saying you have to tell me everything, obviously. God . . .'

Benny sees, to his horror, that she is crying.

'I'm just . . . I love you, and . . .' Her voice disintegrates.

Benny finally bursts into tears and throws his arms around her. 'I'm sorry, Mum.'

She hugs him. 'You don't need to be sorry. Oh . . .' She stifles a sob and tries to turn it into something else. 'You're so great. I can't bear to think of anyone using you, or hurting you.'

'He didn't use me. Honestly. Or hurt me. I mean . . . I used him, if anything.' He wants it to be true, but tears threaten to betray him. 'I love you, too.'

'I know, baby.'

She shushes him, stroking his hair.

Fifteen

Nilsbakken: just a huddle of wooden houses built on the mountain to accommodate the miners, way back when. For such a backwater, it's surprising how often we keep coming back there. When I knew it first, in the late sixties, Nilsbakken was a very different place from the fancy resort it is now. It was a rough place: a cluster of temporary housing for single men who worked in the higher, more remote mines. Not a place where a decent woman had any reason to go.

As soon as I left school and could shake the village dust off my feet, I moved to Trondheim and trained as a secretary and bookkeeper. To my surprise, my parents, who made no secret of how happy they were to see the back of me, actually produced some money to pay for the training. It was a loan, they said. A loan that, on principle, I never repaid. I became a whizz at shorthand and typing: all the sorts of things young women were encouraged to learn, because that was all anyone would pay you to do. Well, there was also teaching and nursing, but I didn't have the qualifications, or the inclination, for those. And the most popular female occupation – marrying a man like my stepfather and turning into my mother – well, that was never going to happen in my life. I liked the work. I wrote in code. I controlled machines and made order out of chaos. It felt modern and clean and wonderfully unlike everything I had come from.

I started work at the mining company, Sulitjelma Gruber, in 1967. I'd already begun calling myself Svea Hustoft, because, while I didn't get on with Ingvild, I preferred that name to being reminded of any association with Erling Øvergaard – and what other choice did I have? Although it was in the same county as Gammelsøy, moving to Sulis was not like going home – it took several hours by train, bus and boat to travel from there to the village where my parents lived. Or would have, if I'd ever done it.

By then, I liked to think that I was unrecognisable from the Svea Øvergaard who had left the village dressed in her mother's cast-offs. New name, new look, new face – or, at least, new make-up. I was fashion-conscious. I read magazines and copied trends: black eye-liner, pale lipstick, fake Chanel suits with shortened skirts. I always had my hair cut in a thick fringe, but that was in style then. My appearance got me a lot of attention at Sulitjelma Gruber, where I was the modish, and slightly mysterious, Miss Hustoft. My immediate boss, Mr Tollefsen, used to brush past me accidentally-on-purpose, and liked to stand behind me kneading my shoulder when I had taken down a dictation. In those days, that was just what happened to secretaries, and I had to learn how to deflect it without causing offence – a vital part of the job. I invented jealous boyfriends or nameless maladies, and affected a religious faith I did not feel. I lived and worked in Sulis, at the company head office, and didn't have anything to do with the actual mines. I had only been up the valley to Nilsbakken on a couple of occasions, the summer I started there, for picnics and walks with female colleagues. I never set foot inside a mine. Why would I? They were dirty, dangerous, and full of miners.

I had been there less than a year when the bosses dropped their bombshell: the Nilsbakken mines were to be closed down. I hadn't realised the company was in such a bad way, but those mines were the most remote, so the ore was that much more expensive to transport. It was decided to henceforth concentrate operations in the mines nearer Sulis, which meant that scores of workers had to be laid off. This was not a popular decision, as you can imagine. Sulis and the surrounding area *was* the mines – if you weren't working for them, you had no job at all.

The company threw a party to commemorate the closure. A wake, dressed up as a thank you to the two hundred men who would be losing their livelihood and the homes that went with it. That night, there was copious free alcohol and a hall full of resentful men without a future they could see – what could possibly go wrong? As a secretary in the main office, I never saw the miners; the closing-down party was the first time that I'd experienced the workforce en masse. To begin with, they were on their best behaviour, scrubbed and buttoned into unfamiliar suits, and the wives were there too. But married men were in the minority and, after the food was eaten and the speeches had been made and received with varying degrees of enthusiasm, the evening, not to put too fine a point on it, degenerated.

I have always been careful not to drink too much in public, and that night I was keen to avoid drawing attention to myself, knowing – as all girls know – that one slip-up could lead to disastrous consequences, but I couldn't avoid going to the bathroom. By then, men were milling around, gathering in knots, laughing, shouting, smoking – a thick haze hung overhead. I passed a group of men on the way to the bathroom, and, as I turned down the corridor, someone barrelled past me and blocked my route to the ladies: a big man, blond, moustached; his arms stretched from wall to wall.

'Excuse me,' I said firmly, not looking him in the eye. 'I need to pass.'

'So, you're the famous Miss Hustoft,' he said. 'I can see why all the lads are talking about you.'

I turned around to go back to the main room, but he caught my arm.

'Hey, I just wanted to say hello. You're very pretty.'

At this point, he was grinning, still relatively amiable, trying, I suppose, to flirt – in a clumsy, boorish way.

'Thank you. Now, if you will let me pass . . .'

He didn't move. I waited. Surely another woman would soon come to the bathroom, or leave it, and give me a means of escape.

'Are you too good to talk to a mere miner, like me? You're just for the bosses, I guess, aren't you? Looking for a rich husband, when you could have a real man . . .'

'Please let go of my arm.'

That was the first time I looked properly at his face. As I have said, I had nothing to do with the miners or even the payroll. I couldn't have told you any of their names and I had absolutely no idea that *he* was there.

I went cold with shock. Literally cold – I froze into place. Because, although I hadn't seen him for some years, I knew him. His name was Jens Gulbrandsen, and we came from the same village. He was several years older than me, a teenager when I was a child, which was probably why he didn't recognise me – that and the fact that I had changed my name and appearance. I had gone out of my way to obliterate that child, erase her completely, and one of the reasons for that erasure was him.

He pulled me into a room – some office or other – with frightening ease. Of course he was strong: he was a young man with miner's arms that had hammered at rock walls and shovelled ore. The funny thing was, after that first moment of paralysing shock, I don't think I was afraid, because he clearly had no idea who I was. A moment later, he had closed the office door and I was pressed up against it. Blasts of beery breath hit me in the face.

'Have you ever had a real man?' he said, his teeth bared, his lips wet with spittle.

With one arm, he pinned me easily against the door, fumbling at my skirt with the other.

He was smiling. He was pleased with himself for finding this little piece of entertainment.

I tried to fight him off, but he was too strong for me. I turned my face to the side to avoid the slimy, questing mouth.

I said, 'You don't know who I am, do you?'

He just grunted. He was attacking my foundation garments, which were thankfully sturdy.

'We've met before, Jens Gulbrandsen.'

'Ha! I think I'd remember a little firecracker like you . . .'

But his grip slackened a little and he slowed down, confused, searching my face, drunkenly casting his mind back, presumably, to all the other girls he'd had like this, in his power. Not far enough.

'You'll remember me, Jens. Look!'

I stopped fighting off the arm that was tugging at my skirt and pushed up my fringe, uncovering my forehead – the skin that is always hidden. I willed him to look.

It had changed, of course, over the years, but it was still visible. He blinked at me, struggling to focus, irritated, but also, for the first time, unsure. With my other hand, I pressed the light switch, and the fluorescent strip light blinked once, twice, then flooded the office with the cold, undeniable truth.

Sixteen

As far back as he can remember, Odd Emil has been in awe of Svea. He was at school with her younger sister, Magny, and from her he used to hear how Svea stood up to the craziness of their parents. She shielded her sisters from their drunken rages, and, in return, they practically worshipped her. Karl, the baby of the family and only boy, was the parents' favourite and largely escaped their wrath – or their abuse, as we would have to call it now. Svea had it the worst for the simple reason that she was the illegitimate child of a German soldier who had been stationed in Nordland during the occupation. Her stepfather frequently referred to her as 'the Nazi bastard', even in public. Probably as a result, she had a steely aura that was like a warning to steer clear. She looked different from the rest of the family – tall, with poker-straight dark hair and brows, which she must have got from the German – she didn't in any way resemble her pale, mousy mother, and, obviously, looked nothing like the meaty, raw-boned Erling.

Svea doesn't talk about her childhood, and, on the whole, Odd Emil is careful not to refer to those years, which obviously weren't happy for her. He was thirteen when she left Gammelsøy for good – she moved to a city and became almost a creature of exotic fable. Magny would

129

tell him excitedly how fashionable she was, how accomplished. She had a good job in a smart office; she was independent. She even – and this was unusual for that time – lived on her own. It made her seem louche, bordering on scandalous, because why would a young single woman live on her own, unless she was up to no good? From time to time, Svea sent her sisters little parcels, and these would be addressed care of Odd Emil's family's store, as they contained magazines and other small, forbidden pleasures, like lipstick, or nylons. Mrs Øvergaard found one of these lipsticks in Magny's drawer, hidden among her underwear, and she threw a fit. She called Svea a Jezebel who wanted to corrupt her sisters, and stamped on the lipstick tube, shattering it. She told Magny it was 'the devil's muck'. Odd Emil had been surprised when Magny told him about this, as Mrs Øvergaard wasn't especially religious, nor was her husband, but she would dredge up the wrath of God if she felt like using it as a weapon. Odd Emil was not surprised when Magny, too, left home as soon as she could and moved away to work – as far as he can remember, she became a nanny. He missed her; she had been a good friend. Later, in the seventies, she married a Dane and moved to Denmark, where she lives still – although now, Svea has informed him, with an unreadable expression, she is married to a woman.

It was while Odd Emil was working with his father at the store, learning the business, that he fell in love with the youngest Øvergaard sister, Nordis. Where Svea was aloof, and Magny was pragmatic and funny, Nordis was wild. Looking back, across the chasm of years, you would probably have to say that she was eccentric, even a bit odd. She was prone to inexplicable giggles, blank stares, odd swerves of thought. He couldn't keep up. But she was also lovely, with soft, curling, light-brown hair, and a rounded face that changed expression with remarkable suddenness – a wild rose that had sprung from an unpromising patch of dirt. He wonders now whether her oddness was related in some way to Elin's condition – was it a genetic thing from the mother's side? Perhaps Nordis would have been diagnosed with Asperger's or one of those syndromes, except back then no one used those words. In those days, people could just be a bit odd. But he had loved her, partly because of her feyness, and despite the fact (he feels sadness, and also shame, remembering this) that he always knew he wouldn't marry her. She was too strange, too wayward. He couldn't see her keeping house, couldn't imagine her calming down and looking after his children. He supposes that this is a terrible, and terribly old-fashioned, thing to say. But that was how it was.

In the last few days, he has wondered – his mind has been on some odd excursions recently – how his life would have been different if he had married Nordis instead of his dear Ann-Karin. Then, he supposes, his daughter wouldn't have been Maria, and his grandson wouldn't have been Daniel – maybe he wouldn't have had any grandchildren at all. And then, his favourite among them (I'm so sorry Sindre, and Vivi, and Ebba and Lasse) wouldn't have disappeared.

Maria is amazing. He doesn't know how she is holding it together. Of course, there are the younger two to look after. Odd Emil has spent a lot of time at her house over the past week, but, on the phone this morning, she said, 'Dad, it's okay. You don't have to come over today. You look so tired, and I don't want to be worrying about you too. Please.'

Now, he feels rejected: a useless old man.

'Oh, all right. Sure. I just want you to know that I will do whatever you need. I'm sorry I'm not able to be more useful.'

She sighed. 'Dad, you've been wonderful. And you will be. I just feel like I have to keep checking in with you, and it's too hard. And, actually, I want to go back to work. I can't stand sitting around the house for another day. I'd rather be doing something.'

'All right. If you're sure. If you think that's a g—'

'I don't know if it's a good idea, Dad. But I'm going crazy, here. What else can I do?'

His daughter clings to the idea that Daniel has run away. A couple of days ago, she told Odd Emil that Daniel has been on medication for anxiety and depression for the last eighteen months. He was shocked, and tried not to show that he was hurt she hadn't told him before.

'He didn't want anyone to know, Dad. It upset him. That's why I didn't tell you. He asked me not to.'

She thinks that he may have set up something online (not that they've found anything in his history, but you can hide these things, can't you, if you know how). Maybe he arranged with someone to give him a lift – maybe he walked over the border to Sweden, and then . . .? He might call any day. He might email. Swedish and Finnish police have been alerted.

On Thursday night, there was a wonderful, terrible spasm of hope. Someone had reported a sighting of Daniel, down in Trondheim. It was quickly proved to be a false alarm – the usual nonsense. Wishful thinking. But this is the sort of thing that happens when someone goes missing. People want so much to help. To be the one to help. This is what Hanne Duli tells them. She is the officer who keeps them updated and talks them through the procedures of the case. She's also a friend of Maria's from way back. Odd Emil is glad it's her. She's good at it – steady, kind but not emotional. She doesn't exaggerate the odds. But it keeps hope alive.

The police have widened their search. They began at Nilsbakken, where Daniel's car was found, and the circle ripples outwards. They're not saying much, but Odd Emil has heard that divers have been seen up at Langvatnet and Kjelvatnet. Police divers! Sweet Jesus. When Maria told him about the medication, he thought – of course his mind leapt to the awful prospect – has Daniel taken his own life? Maria says no way. He might have problems, but he isn't suicidal. No way. No. He's always been a lovely kid: kind and happy and confident. At least, he seemed happy. Odd Emil has even (God forgive him) secretly congratulated himself on having such well-adjusted grandchildren. Sporty and nice-looking and popular. Not like Svea's weirdo grandkid, Elin. Daniel has always seemed so normal, so *fine* . . . even over the last year, when he was apparently taking those pills. The pills that are still there, up in his room . . .

Is this his punishment? (Don't be stupid, he tells himself. It's not about you.)

What signs did he miss? Was he wilfully, unforgivably blind? Was he that smug?

How did he fail his beloved boy?

Svea is sitting at their usual table. Asta is lying under her chair, but, when she sees it's him, she jumps up and wags her tail, tugging at her leash in her eagerness to greet him. He is ridiculously grateful for this. When he looks up from petting the dog, he finds Svea regarding him doubtfully.

She says, 'I won't ask you how you are.'

'Hm. Well. You know.'

'Or whether you've heard anything.'

'No. Thanks.'

They order tea.

'Hanne Duli – you know Hanne Duli Bodøgaard? – she's the main officer on the case. She mentioned something that Elin said to them.'

'Elin? You mean my Elin?'

'Yes. I didn't know she and Daniel knew each other. But she told them that, just a week before he . . . disappeared, she was with him at a party, and he told her that he couldn't wait to get out of this place.'

'This place? You mean, Fauske?'

'I suppose so. But she came forward with this – she thought he might have really meant it. Have you spoken to her this week?'

'Yes, but only briefly. I didn't think they knew each other well. That's the impression she gave. But maybe she wouldn't tell me.'

'Maria thinks he's run away. She's holding on to that, you know – that perhaps he was terribly unhappy, and she didn't know. She's hoping that he was unhappy! He was taking antidepressants, apparently— God! I keep saying "was" and I don't mean to – except that he's left them behind, anyway, so it *is* "was" . . .'

Svea puts her hand on his, surprising him. He feels as though he has forgotten how to talk like a normal person. How do they do it?

'Sorry.'

She shakes her head. 'Don't be silly.'

They sip their tea in silence for a minute.

'You know what I've been thinking about, recently? I mean, you think all sorts of things, that's what's so awful, but . . . I've been thinking about your sister.'

Svea doesn't need to ask which sister; she knows he means Nordis. When someone has disappeared, who else would you think about?

'And how it must have been, for you. You've never talked about it. I should have asked, shouldn't I? I'm sorry.'

Svea sighs and looks down at the table. She has withdrawn her hand. She makes a tutting noise with her teeth. 'No. I wouldn't have known what to say.'

'How long was it? Before they—?'

'Six weeks and one day.'

He means, how long before they found something that belonged to her, floating in the cold sea, not far from the house at Gammelsøy. It was a woolly hat, he thinks: that was all they ever found. They had to reconstruct the ending of her life from a sodden clod of wool. And so the story became that Nordis Øvergaard drowned in the sea off Gammelsøy. She liked to walk along the beach and scramble over the rocks. She had always liked that, from the time she was a girl, but by then she was old (although not nearly as old as he is now) and she must have slipped and fallen, maybe hit her head, and then . . . It was December. Dark. You could imagine the rest. The sea does not forgive.

'That must have been awful.'

'I honestly can't remember what it was like. I suppose it was awful.' She frowns. 'We'd grown apart, by then. And I think I knew quite quickly . . . no, I think I knew right away that there would only be one outcome. So, it felt like I was just waiting for the inevitable. But it wasn't the same.'

She means, not the same as Daniel. Odd Emil appreciates it, but he also knows that no one's assurances mean anything.

*

The woolly hat was found not far from the house where the Øvergaard children had been brought up. The house that Nordis had moved back to when their mother was diagnosed with early-onset dementia. Which meant alcoholic dementia, everyone knew. The postman found no one at home for a few mornings in a row and, because this was unusual, he eventually raised the alarm. Not right away, because this was Norway, and he didn't want to presume, or interfere. Someone came (who comes in such circumstances? The police, Odd Emil supposes) and had to force an entry, whereupon they found the house empty and neglected. There were no signs that Nordis had taken a trip – all her personal belongings were still there. No passport, but Nordis had never owned a passport. This was in 2012. The previous year, the mother had been moved to a nursing home as she had become too difficult to take care of at home, but Nordis had looked after her for more than twenty years. The wild, quicksilver girl had become her mother's steadfast carer. Odd Emil would never have foreseen that. By the time she moved back to Gammelsøy, he and Ann-Karin had had their children. By the time Nordis died – it seemed only the blink of an eye later – his children had children. The waters of life had run on, as they do.

When Nordis died, Odd Emil hadn't seen her for many years. She was sixty-two – not young, but not old either. Some people speculated: they muttered in low voices that it was suicide; she had always been strange, that one, and the stress of caring for Ingvild – a thankless task, for sure! – or maybe it was the grief over her mother's worsening condition, had tipped her over the edge. But this was unproven – just a rumour. Sometimes it was meant unkindly, more often not. Either way, impossible to know the truth.

All that happened a few years before his wife died and he and Svea became friends. Odd Emil heard about her death, of course, because everyone hears everything around here, and he had felt sad, because Nordis was a tender, if distant, part of his past.

He has never asked Svea what she thinks happened to her sister. There are some things you don't ask.

Seventeen

Over the past week, Toril Iversen has found herself frequently bursting into tears. It's not like her, but that poor boy, Daniel. His poor mother. And the rest of his family, obviously. Presumably it's the same for every parent in the area – they're thinking, What if that were my child? God forbid. Keep them close. Pray to never be so unlucky. Pray, even if you don't pray. Bargain frantically with whatever you have. (The unvoiced suspicion: was it, in some never-defined way, the mother's fault? Is everybody thinking that?)

When she looks at her son now, it is almost with hunger, because it is inconceivable that anything bad should ever happen to him. And she is quietly raging at that bloody man, David Mæland. Benny had said no, he didn't hurt him; no, there was absolutely no coercion involved. He had been a very willing participant. It had been 'nice': his word. But she knows him – talking about it, he is uncertain, a little evasive – and there is a sadness in his eyes. Of course he was willing – he's a teenage boy – but being willing doesn't mean you are prepared for everything that might happen. He has been through something that did not turn out the way he hoped, and it has bruised him. He is quick to absolve David of blame, but it's not as easy as that. So what if Benny

138

lied about his age? That doesn't excuse a grown man – an adult *in his thirties*, for fuck's sake – from taking advantage of her child.

Toril probes as delicately as she knows how, and Benny tells her that David has ended things (as if they needed officially ending!) and that he is understandably angry that Benny lied to him. Understandable to Benny, that is. Benny could have cost David his job! Now Benny feels guilty as well as everything else; he feels that he is the one to blame for putting David at risk. Well, no, sorry. Toril is not having that.

She searches online for David Mæland. She finds a picture of him on the website of his employers: a good-looking man, with a rather fierce face. He does look about thirty, although it could be an old picture. She vaguely remembers him from the group of investment-fund managers. They were the sort of people that she tries not to reflexively dislike: overpaid, entitled, full of themselves and their opinions about every little thing. There had been one woman who seemed to think she was more of an expert on yoga than Toril. She'd been (of course she had) on a luxury wellness and yoga retreat in fucking *Bali* . . .

David Mæland hadn't come to Toril's yoga classes – because he was with Benny? God, no, don't! Her mind keeps ambushing her with things she doesn't want to see. She can't access his social media – he seems careful about that sort of thing. While Benny is at school, she guiltlessly invades his computer and finds a contact number for David. She doesn't yet know what she's going to do. She has toyed with the idea of posting some shit online – shaming him, somehow. But she knows she won't do that. Apart from anything else, he would just assume it was Benny.

While she's in her son's room, her anger is refreshed. His room is full of things that proclaim his proximity to childhood. A sleepy

Pokémon plushie that seems to be some mad mixture of cat and cactus, misshapen from much cuddling, is on the shelf next to his bed. She can't remember its name, but Benny was always crazy about all that Japanese kawaii stuff. Now, he's teaching himself Japanese online. There is nothing he can't do. Stuck to the wall is a set of drawings of made-up creatures that he must have done . . . God – it must be six years ago! He was so proud of them. On his desk there is a framed photo of him and Elin, mugging for the camera. Just kids. Another of a group of his friends from school. And, in pride of place above his bed, there's a poster of a beautiful youth, someone young and sweet – that's who he should be mooning over, not some hawk-faced uber-capitalist who has fucked him and chucked him, and has now made her son feel bad about it.

She dials the number before she can change her mind. It's answered on the third ring.

'David Mæland.'

The voice is smooth and confident. His work voice.

'Hello, Mr Mæland. My name is Toril Iversen.'

A pause. At least he recognises the name. Some background noise is quieted; possibly a door closes.

'Oh. You're Benny's mother?'

'Yes. Benny doesn't know I'm calling you. I know he told you he was eighteen, but for God's sake! He's a kid! He's only sixteen. And you need to know that you've hurt him. You shouldn't play with people's feelings like that. I mean, maybe it's okay when you're an adult, but he's only sixteen and he doesn't have the . . . the emotional maturity to deal with it!'

David Mæland is trying to speak. But she barely notices.

'And now, as well as feeling hurt, he feels like he's the bad person in all this! You've made *him* feel like he's the one to blame! Can you see how cruel that is? For God's sake!'

'I'm sorry. I . . . I'm sorry. That's all I can say, Mrs Iversen. I was scared. I've had the police on the phone to me more than once, and I can assure you that they've said much worse than this. I could have – I could still lose my job. I realise that I . . . but I believed him, for what it's worth, since he was working there, and . . . I'm sorry.'

'It's him you should be apologising to, except that I sincerely hope he never has to see or hear from you again.'

'No . . . I understand. Can I send him a message – just to say sorry?'

Toril lets out an expulsion of air. A hiss. 'That's up to you. I don't police him. But I won't stand by and see him made to feel like shit when it's not his fault.'

'Well . . . I'm sorry, again. And I am really sorry to have put Benny through this. He's . . . he's lovely. He's a great—'

'Don't you *dare* tell me about my son!'

Her voice has gone much higher and louder than she meant it to. She ends the call before she says anything else. That was enough. She's glad. Her heart is pounding. Her hands are shaking. She needs a cup of mugwort tea.

Actually, she thinks, as the kettle is coming to the boil and she looks out of the window to where the first flowers are struggling out of the damp earth, he didn't sound all bad. He sounded genuinely ashamed – perhaps it was all for himself, but it's better than nothing. Now, she has to think how she will explain it all to Benny. She'll have to tell him, and she knows he won't be happy about it.

*

141

She drives down to the Co-op in Sulis, where she bumps into her friend Marylen Sundfær. Toril would never say so, but she feels a bit sorry for Marylen, what with her clinically depressed husband and her profoundly disabled daughter. She's prone to heaviness and tends to struggle when – infrequently, these days – she comes to one of Toril's yoga classes. And now, as a teacher at the high school, she's in the middle of this terrible Daniel business.

But, today, Marylen looks surprisingly well; she's even maybe lost a bit of weight. Her face can look puffy and heavy, but now she seems brighter. Normally brisk and matter-of-fact, she greets Toril with enthusiasm, before checking her grocery basket and lowering her voice: 'Listen, Toril, are you in a rush to get back? Do you have time for a quick coffee?'

'I feel sort of bad that I'm happy. You know – at the moment.'

They are sitting by a window in the restaurant of the Sulis hotel, well away from prying ears. It's not busy, anyway. It's too early for the short summer season to have begun.

Toril is reeling from what she's just heard, but trying not to show it. A part of her is – to put it bluntly – a bit jealous. She's very fond of Marylen – and, God knows, she deserves a bit of happiness (doesn't Toril, also?) – but to hear that she's having an affair! And with Eskil Torstensen! The vicar is admittedly handsome in a grey-blond, wintry way, but she has always found him austere and rather condescending. The sort of Christian who thinks yoga is a hair's breadth away from witchcraft. Although she is not and never has been a churchgoer, he has the sort of manner that makes Toril feel vaguely guilty. In the past, she has tried flirting with him, mostly out of sheer devilment, but he gave the impression that, if he noticed at all, he rather looked down on her for it. Well . . . damn.

'Does Elin know about you two?'

Marylen looks down, shaking her head. 'Eskil doesn't want to tell anyone, so I don't think so.'

'But why on earth not – I mean, if Petter knows and he doesn't mind?'

Marylen makes a face. 'I think "doesn't care" would be the more accurate way of putting it. He seemed almost surprised that I was telling him, as though he didn't consider it any of his business. Maybe he assumes I've been up to all sorts, for ages. I don't know. But it was a huge relief, I must say.'

'So, then, what's the problem? I mean, Eskil's divorced, isn't he? And you're effectively separated.'

'I know. Eskil just has this terror of being seen to be – I don't know – less than perfect. He worries that people won't respect him. He torments himself.'

'But he just couldn't resist you!'

Marylen grins wickedly, raises her plump arms heavenwards in a massive shrug, and they both burst out laughing. Eventually, she manages to wipe the smile off her face.

'It's just bizarre. Everyone is so worried about Daniel – and I'm worried too, of course; it's a terrible strain. But I keep forgetting for a few minutes, or half an hour, then I suddenly remember. The atmosphere at school is horrible. I think the kids feel awful, but they also don't know how they should be feeling – you know? Am I appropriately sad? Am I doing it right? They're all over the place.' She shakes her head. 'What about Benny? Is he holding up okay?'

'Oh. Well, I think so . . .'

143

'What is it?'

Toril shakes her head. 'Sorry. Not my secret. Kids deserve some privacy, I always think. But he seems okay – as okay as anyone could be when something like this happens. He spends a lot of time with Elin. It's nice that they're so close.'

Marylen smiles at her. 'Toril, you're such a model parent. So, what about you? We haven't had a proper catch-up for too long. I've told you my secret . . . and you won't tell Benny, will you – what with school, and Elin?'

'No, of course not. God!' Toril puffs out her cheeks and looks at the ceiling. 'I honestly don't think I have anything to tell. I haven't even been on a date for ages, you know, ever since that wanker . . .'

She rolls her eyes and Marylen nods, remembering. A few months ago, Toril had a depressing dating experience with a quantity surveyor from an app and hasn't felt like risking her bruised self-esteem since.

She looks at her friend and pulls a face. 'In fact, I have no secrets at all. God, isn't that sad?'

Marylen smiles, but then the word brings them both up short.

Eighteen

Benny has never less wanted to be alone. For the past few days, it has seemed as though everyone is angry and disappointed with him, including himself. The police were clearly disapproving because he didn't come forward immediately about seeing the Hellraisers' cars. Then he got a message from a furious David: *Do you realise what you have done? You should not have lied to me! I could lose my job because of you!*

So, that was that. He had suspected, the last time he saw him – on that ominous Saturday night and Sunday morning – that it was over, and he had felt sad and small. He was obviously too inexperienced and boring and femme for David. Now, he feels hot with guilt and shame as well. His mum isn't angry with him, not exactly, but she certainly isn't happy about it. He feels as though he's let her down; in telling her about the affair, which had been his exciting, sexy secret, the whole thing just came across as embarrassing and a bit weird.

When he comes home from school the next day, Toril comes into his bedroom and says she has something to tell him. She sits on his bed and says that she has spoken to David. Benny feels sick. The whole thing is a total nightmare.

'God, why did you do that? It's nothing to do with you!'

145

'I know you probably wish I hadn't done it, but he needed to hear it from someone like me – that he shouldn't have been so careless. I can see that he's hurt you. And then he makes you feel guilty! I can't forgive that.'

Benny shakes his head. 'But I lied to him, Mum! It's my fault. He asked me how old I was, and I said I was eighteen. I knew what I was doing.'

'Nevertheless . . .'

'What was he supposed to do – ask to see my ID?'

'I don't know, love. But he needs to take responsibility. He's the grown-up here, and he should have . . . done whatever it took. I know you feel grown-up, but you're sixteen, and I'm still responsible for you. I can't bear to see you unhappy, and you are not to blame in any of this.'

Benny plucks at his duvet cover. 'I'm to blame for lying.'

'Okay, you shouldn't have lied. You won't do it again.'

Benny says in a small voice, 'He's not going to lose his job, is he?'

Toril shrugs. 'I don't see why he would. It's not actually against the law. But, to be honest, I don't care what happens to him. I'm not going to speak to his employers. I just had to talk to him and tell him I don't think what he did with you was okay. I told him it was nothing to do with you and you didn't know I was ringing. But I want to be open with you about it, so – well, now you know.'

Benny is crying. What if he's ruined David's life?

Toril looks upset. 'Oh, sweetie . . . I really don't think he's going to lose his job. I'm sorry about all of this.' She puts her hand on his arm. 'Can I give you a hug?'

Benny holds out for about five seconds, then leans against her and she hugs him.

'I think you're amazing,' she says.

'No, I'm not. What about Daniel? I should have told the police sooner, then maybe they'd have found him, but I didn't because . . .'

'Shh. You didn't know what the boys had said. And it wouldn't have made any difference.'

'You don't know that.'

Toril sighs and strokes his back, the way she used to when he was little and couldn't sleep. 'I'm sorry this has all been so hard. It's bad luck, all of it.'

Benny sits up, wiping his eyes on his sleeve and his nose on the back of his hand.

'He didn't have parents like you, you know. His father used to call him "Gayboy". He was terribly bullied. He couldn't come out until after he'd left school.'

Toril makes a sympathetic face. 'Well, I'm sorry, but it's not an excuse.' She reaches for the Pokémon plushie and tries to squash it back into shape. 'What is this meant to be – some sort of cat?'

'What, Bulbasaur?'

'Bulbasaur, that's it.'

'It's a grass/poison-type Pokémon. First evolution.'

'Right.'

'It evolves into Ivysaur, then Venusaur.'

'So . . . it's meant to be a dinosaur, then?'

'I think it's a mix of a frog and a garlic bulb. You used to know them all.'

'Well, I've forgotten. So, it's not a cat?' She looks at its face. It has pointy, triangular, cat-like ears.

'No, obviously not.'

147

'Why has it got cat ears, then?'

'They're not cat ears! They're, um . . .'

They look at each other.

'There's nothing childish about having old toys in your bedroom,' Benny says.

'Sure.'

'These are worth a lot, actually, on eBay. Especially this one, cos it's asleep.'

'Oh. Going to sell it, then? Put that in your travel fund?'

Benny takes the toy from her and puts it carefully back on the shelf. 'Maybe.'

Elin is not cross with him, but he can tell she doesn't approve. When he finally admits David's age, her face reminds him of her father's in one of his more judgemental, churchy moments.

'Thirty-four! Benny! He could be your dad!'

'No, he couldn't – he'd have been eighteen! That's ridiculous.'

'That's more than twice your age! The rule is: half the older person's age plus seven, to not be really creepy. So, your upper limit should be . . .'

A pause – she's trying to work it out.

Benny smirks at her. 'Yeah, come on, Rain Man.'

'Fuck off. Anyway, what would you think if I slept with a man in his thirties?'

The thought of Elin being with a man like David, even with the necessary adjustments, is inconceivable. He shakes his head impatiently. 'It's totally different from straight relationships.'

'Is it? Why?'

'Because there's an inbuilt, you know, power imbalance, between men and women. Because, you know: the patriarchy.'

'And if I went out with a woman in her mid-thirties? You'd be absolutely fine with that?'

'You can't compare. Gay male relationships are different.'

Elin looks at him. 'You literally said, you felt that he had all the power.'

Benny can't meet her gaze. He can't deny it. And then there was the money. Whenever he thinks of that, his face goes hot. He hasn't told Elin, hasn't told anyone, about the two thousand kroner, because he is too ashamed. He has wondered about sending the money back, in a grand, noble gesture, but he doesn't know where he would send it. Also, it's two thousand kroner and he kind of doesn't want to.

'It's twenty.'

'What is?'

'Your upper limit. The other person – they should be twenty, at most. Actually . . . nineteen and a half – but I'll give you the six months.'

'Really?'

Benny frowns and takes out his phone to check.

'Huh. That's not a lot, is it? Where does this rule come from?'

'It's in the Bible.'

He giggles. 'Oh, yeah. Of course. That'll be in the Book of Elin.'

'Yeah. It's the best one.'

It almost works, for a minute – she's cheering him up. But mentioning the Bible just makes him think: the Book of Daniel. Daniel. And there it is again – his guilt.

Nineteen

Elin has also given a statement to the police. She didn't know whether she should, not wanting to get Daniel into trouble, but, after telling Benny that facts are always important, she supposed she couldn't withhold it. Also, that sort of trouble could hardly matter to Daniel now, could it? So, she rang the information line and spoke to the young officer, Merete Nordheim. She told her how, at the russ party, he had talked about inner voyaging. And he had offered her a pill. Half a pill. No, she didn't know what it was. She'd said no – and that was clearly disappointing to him and was kind of the end of it. But it couldn't have anything to do with his disappearance, could it? Because afterwards he was fine. He'd been at school the following week, just like normal. Merete tapped it into her computer, and thanked Elin. That seemed to be all.

Until . . . The day after, she's walking down the corridor on the way to science, blotting out the noise of the outside world with her headphones, when someone grabs her by the arm. It's her cousin, Lorentz.

'Hey, Elin.'

'Oh, hey.'

She thinks he looks cross. Or perhaps he's just upset. Sometimes it's hard to tell the difference.

'Listen.' He pulls her to the side of the corridor and lowers his voice. 'Did you tell the police Daniel offered you ecstasy at the party?'

'Is that what it was? Yes. Well, he did.'

'Why would you tell them that, Elin? Everyone does it. It's got nothing to do with him . . . with this!'

'You don't know that.'

'Now, they've been on my case – do I know where he got it? Did I give it to him? That sort of thing. And they've been on to his family, and his mum – I mean, think about how she must feel, knowing that.'

Elin says, 'I thought maybe it was relevant.'

Lorentz grimaces. 'How could it be?'

'I don't know. That's up to the police to decide, isn't it?'

Lorentz glares at her, then he sighs and drops her arm. A few metres away, Solgunn Ingebrigtsen is fiddling with her bag, pretending she's not watching. You never see one of the Hellraisers on their own, these days. Elin supposes she would be the same, if her best friend had disappeared without trace. Except that she only really has Benny, so, if he disappeared, she would have no one.

'What else did you tell them?'

'What else would I tell them? That party was literally the only time I ever spoke to him. I told them he said he couldn't wait to get out of this place, because he did – but that's just the sort of thing people say, isn't it?'

'Yeah. It is. Sorry I snapped at you. I'm going crazy worrying about him. We all are. It's just . . .' He shakes his head.

'Yeah. It must be. I'm sorry.'

151

He looks at her, widening his eyes in a look that is almost pleading in its helplessness. He looks as if he might cry. Elin has never seen Lorentz cry – not since that time he broke his leg skiing, when he was nine.

'Yeah. Okay. Well – I'll see you around, Elin.'

He heads back towards Solgunn, who puts her hand on his arm, and they go off down the corridor together, her arm securely around his waist.

The new, revised story from the Hellraisers is that Daniel had set off on his solo hike from further down the valley, towards Sulis, and the others were afraid to admit to driving the cars up to Nilsbakken because they'd been drinking. So, what Benny and David saw from the cabin doesn't seem to have changed anything, except that the police gave the boys a hard time for not telling the truth and therefore wasting valuable search time.

It is eight or nine days since Daniel disappeared. The police have combed a wide area around Nilsbakken: dog teams have criss-crossed hills and trails, divers have searched lakes. Volunteers have walked and driven all over the area, looking for anything. Most of them are locals, but people have also come from further afield to help. Daniel's disappearance has made national news. At school, people are saying that they're following leads in Sweden. Possible sightings. That maybe he arranged to be met by someone with a car and has been spirited away to . . . somewhere. The more time elapses, the more elaborate and far-fetched the theories become.

In the afternoon, Ulrikke Haubakk and Elle Maja Somby, both second-years and the sort of cool girls who don't normally speak to

152

her, come up to Elin in the library. They start by chatting, being unusually friendly, and then Ulrikke says, 'We're writing an article for the school magazine, and we wondered if we could interview you.'

Elin says, 'Why?'

They glance at each other. 'It's about dealing with trauma, like what's going on at the moment. We think it's important that people are aware of, you know, what resources there are to help when you're going through something as difficult as this. I mean, we can't just ignore what's going on.'

'But why me? I didn't really know Daniel. I mean, I don't really—'

'Yeah, no, sure. But, in your family, there was something like this, wasn't there? Your great-aunt disappeared? I mean, like, years ago? And was presumed drowned? We wondered if you would be prepared to talk about it – it could be really helpful for other people, to hear your story.'

Elin is astonished. 'I was four. I don't remember anything about it. I didn't even know about it, at the time.'

As she says it, she wonders: or did she? In her head, the mystery around the vanishing great-aunt – whom she doesn't remember ever meeting – is somehow linked with her mother and Oda leaving. She does remember Klara being shouty and tense – and Elin knew that was her fault. It was all around the same time, wasn't it?

Ulrikke says, 'Maybe you could ask your parents?'

Elin doesn't answer. Don't they know that her mother lives in Oslo? As the silence lengthens, the girls exchange glances.

'Well, would you maybe think about it?'

Elle Maja, sensing that Elin's confusion might tip over into something darker, smiles apologetically and begins to steer Ulrikke away.

'I'm sorry if it's upsetting to bring it up. We thought, since it was such a long time ago . . . Okay, well . . . no worries. Anyway – sorry.'

They walk away and Elin just stands there. She can't think of a single thing to say.

154

Twenty

Years ago, when Hanne Duli Bodøgaard was pregnant with her son, she became good friends with Marylen Sundfær. For both of them, it was their first child and they were full of excitement and nervous hopes. They met at antenatal classes, and their children were born within a week of each other, although not in the order expected. Marylen's daughter, Nora, arrived early, then Hanne Duli's son, Lars, was late. During those first exhausting months, they met up regularly, and their friendship deepened. They had more in common than just the coincidence of life events. Hanne Duli admired Marylen – her senior by a few years – for her awesome experience teaching in war zones, and her generous good sense. Hanne Duli herself had not seen much of the world – had never left Scandinavia, in fact – but they shared the same sense of humour and made each other cry with laughter. They had taken leave from their jobs, as police officer and teacher respectively, and both enjoyed the novelty of being at home – for a while, at least.

Over time, it became apparent that Marylen's daughter was not doing well. Lars was sitting up, laughing, reaching for things, being a generally delightful baby, while Nora lay flat on her back, either oddly quiet or screaming without stopping. There were visits to specialists, and scans, and tests and more tests. When the news came that Nora was, as they put it, 'severely impaired' and that her outlook was 'poor', Hanne Duli was broken-hearted for her friend. But she also felt fierce gratitude at her own luck. Little Lars was fine; he was perfect. She had the sense that terrible misfortune had struck so close it could have been meant for her, had it not been for the accident of Nora arriving early, shielding her son from the curse – which was nonsense, of course.

For a while, Marylen found it hard to see Hanne Duli with her normally developing child. Nora was so demanding and helpless that Marylen's maternity leave stretched from one year to four. Hanne Duli had her daughter, Elizabeth, and urged Marylen to try for another baby – it would put things into perspective, she thought – but Marylen said she couldn't cope with another child. Her husband, Petter, slid into a severe depression. It has taken years for the friendship to properly rekindle, but rekindle it has. Hanne Duli has even more admiration for Marylen, who has somehow come through the last twenty years with her sense of humour intact. For a while now, Nora has been in residential care, and things are, if not fine, then certainly easier than they were. And the heady enchantment of baby Lars settled into the humdrum business of children growing and developing personalities which are mysteriously theirs. Her son, currently, seems to have become a rather dull, uncommunicative young man, but perhaps (she hopes) she doesn't see all sides to him now that he is at university. Her daughter periodically struggles with an eating disorder, but is on track to graduate from school next year. So . . . a normal, average, lucky life. Or so it had felt, until she was put in charge of the search for Daniel Fjordholm.

In more than twenty-five years of policing, her work has not included the need to make public statements, to stand up in front of TV cameras and journalists from all over the country: immaculately made-up strangers who shout her name and clamour for her attention, which makes her feel as though she herself has committed a crime. But she's in charge of the case and it's her job. That sort of exposure is difficult enough; what's worse is the knowledge that so many people she knows are devastated and bewildered by Daniel's disappearance, and they are looking to her for answers. Eyes follow her wherever she goes: when she's walking down the street, when she's picking up groceries, when she's filling her car. They're too polite, too Norwegian, to say anything, but she knows what they're not asking. How can she possibly do enough? Then, when she goes home, she finds herself wasting her precious time off worrying whether she will have to appear in front of the cameras tomorrow, and if so, will the new, ominous pimple on her chin show?

And now this. The call came in just over an hour ago, and she has been feeling physically sick ever since. She and Merete Nordheim headed for a car and drove up the valley, barely saying a word, trying not to even think.

They leave the car on the road beyond Nilsbakken, although it's barely a road up here – more a narrow dirt track that peters out at the furthest of the old mine workings. They get out and head up the slope to meet the dots wearing bright yellow vests. There's a small cluster of them, standing around a golden stain on the hillside – an outflow of spoil from the old workings. It's a mild day, with fitful sunshine and a breeze that pesters the leaves of the birch trees. A stream gurgles in its bed, hurrying to join the small lake at Nilsbakken, now below them, flat and grey as a sheet of zinc; while above, stark against the sky, stands the four-legged, two-wheeled dinosaur that broods over the valley – the old winding mechanism.

The mine entrance they are heading for, like the others scattered along the mountainside, is just a tiny door in the hill. The ground leading up to it is still scarred with spoil, but grass and scrub have veiled it, and birch trees provide meagre shelter. Until this morning, the entrance would have been almost invisible. After the mine was closed down, the doorways were blocked and sealed with concrete, but, over the intervening decades, the weather has gnawed away at it. Freezing winters, spring melts and summer heat have honeycombed the concrete with fissures and cracks, and now it has become so fragile that a couple of blows with a sledgehammer are enough to reduce it to dust. The hole beyond is blacker than the darkest thing.

Hanne Duli turns to the dog handler who called it in. 'What made you open it up?'

'The dogs were indicating strongly enough that we couldn't ignore it.' The cadaver dogs, he means. 'The concrete was completely rotten. There were cracks everywhere – see here . . .' He shows her the photos on his phone. In places, the concrete is almost like lace. 'But it hadn't been recently broken or disturbed, from the look of it.'

She shakes her head – he's right.

'So, no one came in this way. Is this the only entrance? Does this join up with the other tunnels somewhere?'

Shrugs greet her question.

'We'll have to access company records.' She glances at Merete. 'Geological maps.'

Merete nods, taking notes.

The forensics officers are on their way, but they have further to come, so Hanne Duli and her team will just have to wait for them to record the scene before they can go in and take a look. The dog handlers who broke into the tunnel only had torches, so their opinions cannot be conclusive, but they both said it looked old. 'Old', as in, it had been there a long time. 'It', as in, the body. The body of a man.

'Boss . . .' Merete says, in a warning tone.

Hanne Duli follows Merete's gesture and sees a movement down the valley – three or four cars are heading towards them.

'It's not us – I mean, not the forensic team. They're only just past Finneid.'

Hanne Duli narrows her eyes. 'I hope that's not what I think it is.'

She means, they could be freelance news hounds who have picked up the police communication. Which would be infuriating, but not altogether surprising. Daniel's disappearance has not only made national news, it's on the Swedish news – and Finnish.

Merete, with her sharp young eyes, identifies one of the vehicles as an outside-broadcast van.

'Fucking bastards. We'll need more bodies up here to get this cordoned off.'

Hanne Duli radios a request for more cars and some uniforms to close off the road at Nilsbakken. Her initial anxiety has lessened. She thinks, It can't be Daniel, not here, not sealed behind old, unbroken concrete in a long-disused mine. It can't be – can it? She was dreading breaking the worst possible news to Maria Fjordholm today. But, in that case, suddenly there is another missing person in their little valley . . . What are the odds of that?

*

At long last, the evidence team is finished and the lead forensics officer, Anders, a new guy from Bodø whom she knows only slightly, allows them into the hole in the mountain. To call it a tunnel is to pay it a compliment it barely deserves. It's a roughly hewn crevice: close, dark, airless, cold. The air is damp, but also lifeless and without any smell – shocking, after the juicy, springlike abundance of outside. And, after the first few steps, it's as silent as a vacuum: no wind, no birdsong – just their own shuffling footsteps and the heavy breathing of humans who are trying not to think about the tons of rock and earth pressing much too closely over their heads.

They don't have far to go. After a couple of minutes, Anders stops and flattens himself against the wall to let Hanne Duli and Merete squeeze past. He points, but she doesn't even see it at first, despite the powerful flashlights and yellow evidence markers. She would have taken it for a pile of earth, a brown mass lying at the side of the tunnel. It only gradually reveals itself to be a human body, huddled in a foetal position, its face to the wall. It looks dry, shrunken. It wears remnants of clothing, but the fabrics are so discoloured and rotten that it will be a while before they can say what they are. She thinks the body is male. There are the remains of trousers, a jacket, work boots, but definitely not the brightly coloured, technical garments Daniel was wearing. It's not even modern outdoor gear, but something duller and more natural – denim, wool, leather . . . a hint of pale shirt collar – patterned? Possibly. Hanne Duli plays her torch over the corpse and finds rusty hair and, beneath that, a flash of something yellowish. The bone of a skull. She allows herself, at last, to feel the rush of relief.

*

The forensics team have packed up and gone, with their samples and scrapings and measurements and photos. And the body has been carefully stretchered to a mortuary van on the nearest piece of driveable ground. Basically, it is bones. Years spent in this damp tomb have winnowed it to almost nothing: it only weighs a few kilos. Hanne Duli spends some time on the phone with her boss, Gunnar, discussing the statement they will put out – everyone will assume the worst, so it will be chaos. Gunnar is worried in case they are wrong. What if they say it isn't Daniel, and then it turns out to be him? That's unthinkable.

'It won't,' says Hanne Duli, for the fourth time, although now she is starting to doubt herself and her own eyes.

'You're not a forensic specialist,' he replies. 'I'll need confirmation from them.'

'Hello . . . ? Can you hear me? Gunnar?'

Hanne Duli is so cross, she pretends she has lost the faint phone signal. He'll have to take the consequences. And she will have to take the consequences for ringing Maria Fjordholm and telling her, confidentially, what she knows, because God knows what that woman is going through.

Hours have passed since they arrived this morning. Hanne Duli and Merete trudge back to their car. The police have set up a cordon to prevent anyone coming up the track, but she can see several parked vehicles scattered around Nilsbakken that weren't there earlier. Some idiot has already chanced his luck, scrambling up the slope with mobile phone held high, before being chased off by the uniforms.

Hanne Duli has been mentally checking through records of those reported missing – outstanding cases, the long-term lost – but she has come up with nothing. No one local, nothing at all. A notorious case springs to mind – but that was old, and somewhere in England, wasn't it? – where the police had dredged a lake for a missing French-woman, but the body they turned up wasn't that of the lost tourist; it was the body of a woman who had been murdered years before. Not knowing who she was, they called her the Lady in the Lake. Perhaps this one is a tourist, a foreigner – not that the valley was any kind of draw for tourists until relatively recently. Will he be given a name? She supposes it will depend on how long they take to identify him. And, at the moment, they have no clue as to whether he met his end naturally – that is, dully – or otherwise. Can there be an innocent expla-nation for someone going into a disused mine and dying there, alone?

How long had the tunnels stayed open? Records will have to be combed. The mining company, Sulitjelma Gruber, was wound up dec-ades ago – in the nineties, she thinks. Pre-internet. Somewhere in a document warehouse there will be crates and crates of cardboard files that have been gathering dust for more than thirty years. That will be fun for someone, but this, surely to God, is a separate case, so that person won't be her.

The one thing she hopes is that he was dead before the mine was sealed. Being buried alive – that's everyone's deepest, darkest night-mare, isn't it? She thinks he was already dead, because he was not next to the entrance, had not been clawing at the concrete, had been lying with his head pointing away from the entrance, face to the rocky wall. His bones had settled where he had lain, down there with no animals to disturb them. It hadn't seemed a posture that suggested violence, but only the forensics team will be able to say for certain, and, after such a long time, perhaps certainty will not be possible.

'Can we stop off at Nilsbakken?' asks Merete. 'I really need the bog.'

'Yeah. Me too. And I'm starving. We need to have a word with the Fagerheims, anyway. And then I want to drop by Maria's house.'

'You rang her earlier, didn't you?'

'Yeah, but . . .'

When Hanne Duli spoke to Daniel's mother, the first thing she'd said was, 'It's not Daniel, Maria.' There had been rumours of something going on, and it was hard to make Maria understand what she was saying. Once she had calmed down, she asked the obvious question: was she absolutely, absolutely sure? Hanne Duli told her, yes, this man had been lying inside the mine for a very long time.

'But how can it . . . ? I don't understand why . . . The poor man . . .' Maria burst into fresh tears. 'God, sorry, I don't know why I'm crying now.'

'It's fine,' said Hanne Duli, who knew.

Twenty-one

The house where I grew up has long stood empty, rotting away on the hillside at Gammelsøy. It's a wooden house from the 1920s, but don't go thinking it's picturesque or quaint. Even when I was young, it was ugly, shabby and mean, the rooms too small, the ceilings too low. If that house were a face, its expression would have been a frown. It was draughty and uncomfortable, freezing in winter and, in summer, too hot. It had been built by Erling's father. Perhaps he was a drunk too; he certainly didn't do a good job, and Erling just let the house moulder away like he didn't give a damn. When my mother nagged him to fix something, he would moan and swear, and would end up doing it too late, and badly. After Nordis died, with our mother in the home she was clearly never going to leave upright, Magny and Karl and I tried putting the house on the market, but no one was interested. Eventually, someone bought the land, but, as to the house, I have no idea if it's still standing. I have better things to do than go and check.

Last night, I dreamt I was back in the house at Gammelsøy. It was one of those dreams that seems more real than the world around you, even after you wake up. Nordis was there. In the dream, my sister didn't look like her, but I knew it was her in the way you know things in dreams. She was in the kitchen, by the window that wasn't high enough to comfortably look out of, and she turned to me and said, 'It'll be all right, you know,' in that light, teasing tone of voice she had when she was young. Then she laughed and said, 'Why wouldn't it be, silly?' In the dream, I knew what she was talking about, but, on waking, I couldn't remember. I hardly ever dream about her, which saddens me.

It has left me in a peculiar mood. The air in the house feels charged, as though someone came in during the night, opened all the windows, and a sea wind has blown through. I can almost smell the kelp. I sit in the conservatory, under my grapevine, ignoring Asta's unsubtle hints about going out. The sky grows dull and it begins to spit with rain. In this light, the pinks in my marble tiles are flatter and more visceral. Less Roman atrium, more butcher's shop. Why am I thinking that?

After Nordis died, our brother Karl said that she always seemed to have one foot in another place. It was a most unlikely comment, coming from the hard-headed businessman he was. I thought, perhaps he really loved her too. He was right. She was always eccentric, increasingly so as she got older and became interested in all her occult nonsense. She clung to numerology as some people cling to God; numbers told her what to do, explained everything.

Magny, who came over from Denmark for the memorial, was uncharacteristically tearful. She said she felt that she'd abandoned Nordis. I said I did too, but that was what she seemed to want. No one could ever make our little sister do anything else. Unspoken: we thought she'd done it on purpose. I asked Magny where Dolly was. Dolly is her wife. Magny jerked her head in the direction of Karl and said, 'She wanted to come, but I knew it would be awkward, and I really don't need that right now.'

I nodded my understanding. We talked about my going to visit her in Denmark. We both knew it wouldn't happen. How could I have left Tommy?

As for Klara, she seemed devastated. She was at the memorial with Eskil, but we hardly spoke. We aren't close – have I mentioned that? I know it's my fault. Even when she got married and was living in Sulis, we saw each other only rarely. She brought the girls to see their grandmother every so often, but Klara would have a look on her face that said she was doing her duty by them, but she wasn't going to go any further than that. She used to talk to me through the girls, rather than addressing me directly. For example: 'Oh, look! Granny's made a cake for us – isn't that nice?' and, 'Sit down, Oda! Tommy's made a mess on the carpet. Granny's very fond of Tommy, isn't she?'

I could see that Klara was unhappy. I don't mean not happy in the normal way that people at funerals are sad, but she appeared, additionally, under tremendous strain. Of course, looking after young children is exhausting, and Elin, who was then about four, was particularly difficult. She could seem almost demonic in her ability to wind up those around her. On the other hand, her sister Oda was a charming child: good-natured and sweet, but with a tough core. She had a steely focus that reminded me of how Magny had been at the same age: you knew you wouldn't need to worry about them.

I don't think Klara and Nordis were close. I know that Klara never took the girls to visit her or Ingvild. I suppose that sounds harsh, since Ingvild was the only grandparent that Klara knew, but again: my doing. I'd made sure that Ingvild had nothing to do with her – I wouldn't allow Klara to be tainted by her craziness and her hopelessness. I put Klara's misery at the memorial down to something else, possibly her hatred of me. I'm not saying that because I think I'm so important, but because I know what an angry, unhappy parent does to a child.

Suddenly, the phone rings (is there any other way for a phone to ring?). Anyway, it makes me jump. I suppose I have come, like everyone else in town, to start at the sound of a phone. You immediately think, What if this is it – there is news? And then there isn't, but your heart is still pounding.

'Svea?'

Or – because one day there has to be – there is. Odd Emil's voice sounds hoarse, and he's panting, as though he's been running.

'Svea, I wanted to tell you, the police are saying they've found some-thing.'

I grip the phone so tightly my hand hurts.

'But they say it's not Daniel. It can't be Daniel.'

'What? Why?'

'They've found some human remains in a mine, up at Nilsbakken. But they're old. Years old. It definitely isn't Daniel. There'll be a lot of rumours going around, so I wanted to tell you before you hear some rubbish that isn't true.'

'My goodness. So –' my mind races – 'who do they think it is?'

'I have no idea. They haven't said anything.'

'But those mines haven't been open since . . .'

'Yeah. I don't know. We just know that, thank God, it's not Daniel.'

'Yes. Thank God,' I echo, sighing out the dread that gripped me when I heard his voice. But it doesn't leave me, not entirely.

'Can I come and see you?'

'Oh, goodness, now? Well, it's rather late . . .'

'Come and meet me, then.'

'Um, I suppose . . .'

'Please,' he says. 'I need you.'

I'm so surprised – no one has said that to me since . . . actually, I don't think anyone has ever said that to me – I just reply, 'All right,' or something like that.

As it's late and the café is closed, we meet instead at the bar by the station. It feels decidedly odd to be meeting somewhere different – as though it alters our relationship. Into what, I'm not sure. Odd Emil is there before me. He stands up to greet me, ever the gentleman, and insists on buying my astronomically expensive glass of wine.

'You look tired,' I say.

'Thanks, Svea. I am tired. I don't sleep much at the moment.'

'But this is positive – isn't it? They must have looked everywhere now, and they haven't found him, so . . . he's not here.'

'Well, that's the hope.'

'How is Maria?'

'I can't believe how strong she's being. She says she has no choice, what with the kids, but I'm really in awe of her.'

'Well, she has a good dad,' I say.

'Oh, hmm, well, she takes after Ann-Karin,' he says, looking down at his glass of beer. He's not used to hearing compliments from me.

I get the next round of drinks, and some peanuts. I should think about improving my diet. I've been eating a lot of rubbish recently. And, I have to admit, I've been drinking more than usual. When I took my bottles to the recycling, there were so many, I had to decant the bag into my wheeled shopper.

'I wanted to ask you about Nordis,' he says, eventually. 'I said I'd been thinking about her – and I suppose she's been on my conscience.'

'Good heavens, why? You broke up when you were still so young. And she broke up with you, didn't she?'

Odd Emil sighs. 'I know, but I always cared about her – yet I let us drift apart. It's so easy to do, when you have a family and so on, but that shouldn't be an excuse.'

'Everyone does it, Odd Emil.'

'Yes, but I could have made more of an effort to keep in touch when she moved back to Gammelsøy to look after your mother. Give her some support, I don't know. I used to go up there to visit my parents. I could easily have gone to see her, but I didn't. Not once.'

I shrug. He isn't saying anything that I haven't said to myself. I could have tried harder to maintain my relationship with Nordis when I moved back to Nordland, but I didn't want to see Ingvild, and they were in the same house. Also, I had little patience with my sister's numerology fixation, which by then had gained what seemed to me an unhealthy prominence in her life. The last time I saw her was in Bodø, when I had to do something for work, and I persuaded her to come and meet me. This was after Ingvild moved into the nursing home. I assumed that Nordis's life would open up again, now that the self-imposed duties of caring for our mother were over. She certainly didn't have to stay in that house. She was only sixty-one, and we – Magny, Karl and I – waived our interest in the house, so it was hers to do with as she pleased, do it up or sell it or whatever. Although, as previously stated, it wasn't worth much. But, in the hotel where we met that day, Nordis seemed distracted and grumpy – in some ways, odder than ever. After twenty years of little conversation with anyone but our demented mother, perhaps that wasn't surprising. At some point, she had started spelling her name with an extra *S*, which I thought was ridiculous. It made the letters in her name add up to nine, and the number nine was a talisman to her. I didn't probe, as I didn't want to encourage her, although I suppose living your life by the tenets of numerology is no more illogical than following horoscopes – or, for that matter, believing in God.

Although she didn't say so, I got the feeling she was angry with me. I assumed it was about our mother. I refused to visit her in the home, just as I had refused to visit her in Gammelsøy. I thought Nordis accepted my decision and understood it, but perhaps I was wrong. I would like to stress that she didn't say anything, and I didn't ask what was on her mind. I suppose I didn't want to have that sort of conversation. For whatever reason, it was not an enjoyable or successful meeting, and I was, I'm ashamed to say, relieved when it was over.

I remember, at one point, her asking, out of the blue, 'Do you regret nothing you've done?'

I said something like, 'I regret lots of things. But what's the point of dwelling on the past? This is a new beginning for you. You can do whatever you want.'

I expect I mouthed more platitudes along those lines, but Nordis just sighed and looked out of the window, as if I was irrelevant, and said something about being sixty-one. I said she was far from old (after all, I was sixty-six), but she ignored me and said that sixty-one was the number for moving away from the physical to a purely spiritual plane. What are you supposed to say to that? As far as I remember, I didn't say anything, but afterwards I thought about it a lot.

When, a few weeks later, I got the telephone call to say that Nordis was missing, I asked myself, Was that a sign? A cry for help? What more could I have said?

From her post under his chair, Asta whines and puts her head on Odd Emil's thigh. He strokes her head.

'When I got to know you, I was so bound up with my own grief over Ann-Karin that I didn't ever think to ask you about yours, and what you had been through. I want to apologise.'

'Good heavens! Nordis died long before we met. You don't need to apologise.'

He carries on: 'These last few days, it's made me realise what it's like to not know what's happened to someone you love, and you had so much of that – weeks and weeks – and, in the end, you never really knew what happened. And I'm sorry.'

He looks anguished on my behalf, which is absurd, so I tell him about my dream, and how peaceful it made me feel. I tell him, whatever went on in the past, I figure that Nordis has forgiven me.

'I never understood why she moved back in with your mother when she did. I mean, she was young! She wasn't yet forty. Nordis had her job, and her life, even though . . .'

He trails off. What he means, I think, is that, from the outside, Nordis appeared to lead a small life. To someone like him, it must have seemed empty and lonely, moving as she did between her flat and her menial job. Without partner or family. No social life that anyone could see. But of course that is only a judgement from a distance.

'I know you had it the worst in Gammelsøy, but Ingvild wasn't exactly mother of the year to Nordis either.'

'What do you mean, I had it the worst?'

'Well . . .' He looks uncomfortable. 'You know, being Erling's step-daughter, and, er . . .'

'Being the *naziyngel*.'

He looks down and shrugs in acknowledgement. Just for a moment there, I wondered what else he might know.

'Why did she do it?' he asks. 'Why did she go back?'

I shake my head, because I don't know for sure.

Twenty-two

Marylen heard the rumours in the afternoon. They all knew something was going on: police cars and TV vans had been seen heading up the valley, breaking the speed limit, and the atmosphere in the classrooms became impossible. Everyone was checking their phone for news, scrolling through messaging apps. People were crying. They feared the worst. Helene Shirani-Lund tried to calm things by ringing the police station to find out what was going on, but no one was saying anything definite and she was told they would have to wait for the official statement. Johnny Skarstein collapsed in the corridor and was taken to hospital with a suspected anxiety attack. After that, it was mayhem, and they decided to close the school early.

The police released a statement late that evening to the effect that they had found human remains, but they belonged to someone other than Daniel Fjordholm. This body had been lying in a disused mine for decades. No connection was being sought between the boy's disappearance and this new discovery. It was coincidence, nothing more. The police were, of course, continuing to prioritise the search for Daniel. A coincidence, they repeated.

The next day, school is still in a state of mild chaos. There is the hysteria of relief, but only at times, and only for some. The news has released some pressure, but conspiracy theories bubble up all over the place. The students look at each other in uncertainty and confusion – whatever emotional response they had subconsciously lined up for such an eventuality, it doesn't quite fit. Is this news good or bad? It's neither. Well, it's bad, clearly, for the unknown body and for some, possible, family, somewhere. But not for them personally. They cannot even conceive of 'fifty years ago'. It can be nothing to do with them. How could anything that old really matter? But Daniel is still missing.

After lunch, Marylen has her third-year class, the one with the Hellraisers, including Johnny, who was sent home from hospital without treatment after yesterday's panic attack. Tobias Mero has his head down, frowning at his textbook, next to Lorentz Jentoft. She feels – unfairly, probably – more sympathy with Tobias than with the others. His family moved here from Syria, and he is bright and conscientious. The school has high hopes for him, as long as he can keep it together through the exam period. It's very hard to know how he feels. When she asks him how he is doing, he always replies politely that he is okay, thank you, and then says he is trying to focus on his work. This response has not changed since Daniel went missing. His demeanour suggests he does not want to talk further about it, and of course she can't make him. She has said – she has repeated it to all of them – that she is there if they want to talk about anything, but so far none of them have expressed a desire to do so. There is the school counsellor too, of course, and he is sworn to uphold confidentiality, but Marylen knows that none of the boys have been to see Martin, because he has vented his frustration, slightly miffed that his training and talents are going to waste. Marylen responded that he should be glad. It means the students are doing all right – but, of course, it doesn't mean that at all. She doesn't think she would choose to confide in Martin, at eighteen or any other age.

The most marked change, even before his collapse yesterday, has been in Johnny. Marylen previously searched for hidden depths in Johnny, but they remained hidden. At that age, especially the boys, they can appear all cocky surface and bravado, clinging on to an abrasive social persona to hide their fear of not measuring up to whatever ideal of manhood they have imbibed, but Johnny's behaviour is more obnoxious than most, and his track record, especially with girls, has raised a few eyebrows. He is so beautiful, he can get away with things that others can't. Marylen tries to reserve judgement about all her students, but with some it is harder than with others. She even thought, at one point: Why couldn't it have been Johnny who went missing, rather than Daniel? God forgive her.

Now, Johnny rarely raises his voice in the classroom or corridor, he keeps his head down, and his pale, angular face looks haunted. His classwork has only ever been average, but now it's terrible; he struggles even to complete a piece of work. Sometimes, Marylen looks up to see Tobias quietly explaining something to him, but any help given seems to bounce off his chiselled cheekbones. Lorentz is also subdued and seems permanently glued to his girlfriend, Sol-gunn Ingebrigtsen. It's nice that she is being so supportive, Marylen supposes, although there is something a bit, well, creepy, frankly, about the way she is always with him – a mostly silent, watchful presence, like a heavily made-up ghost. Probably she's prejudiced, Marylen admits; she is revelling in her new relationship, which is lovely – cosy and free at the same time – that, and her age. What a relief it is to be safely through the choppy headwaters of youth, and having never had to live up to these warped, Instagram-era standards of beauty.

After school, she finds Elin and Benny waiting for their ride, as usual.

'Hi, guys,' says Marylen.

'Hi, Marylen,' they say.

'Been quite a day, huh?'

Benny says, 'Yeah. It's been weird.'

'How are you doing?'

'Okay,' says Benny.

Elin says, 'Fine.'

They said the same yesterday, when they didn't really know anything. She had tried to talk a bit about the dangers of listening to rumour, but didn't think it helped any.

'It's so weird to think that this is nothing to do with Daniel,' Benny goes on.

'Yeah. But it's not. It's some poor, unfortunate person, from years ago. Coincidences do happen. I hope you're not listening to those daft conspiracies about demons and . . . whatever else it is.'

'Dark-web crypto mines!' says Elin.

'Alt-right bot farms, run by ghosts!' Benny's smile fades. 'Those tunnels were closed more than half a century ago, weren't they? So, it must have been someone from before then.'

'They don't know anything for sure, Benny. Maybe there were other entrances, or . . . Anyway, all we can do is wait while they run their tests and so on.'

'Yeah . . .' He stares out of the window, thoughtful. 'God, to think

I've worked up there. Maybe it was a miner who lived in one of the rooms I've hoovered.'

'Do they think it's murder?' Elin voices the question on everyone's mind.

'I don't think they think anything yet, Elin. I know as much as you do – only what was in the police statement.'

'Yeah, but you're friends with top cop Hanne Duli Bodøgaard, aren't you?' Benny says, slyly. 'So, you could ask her.'

'I certainly could not! I would never ask her to break confidentiality. Anyway, it'll be an entirely separate case. And I hope you're not bothering Elizabeth Bodøgaard, because she definitely doesn't know anything. Hanne Duli never takes her work home.'

'No, of course not,' says Benny.

Elin says, 'She wouldn't talk to me, anyway.'

After that, the kids spend the rest of the journey staring at their phones, occasionally snickering at what they see. Marylen doesn't know why they don't just talk to each other, but she isn't about to ask. She suspects that it's not because they are shy of her overhearing their conversation; more that there is something intrinsic to this mode of communication that can't be reproduced in speech.

Question: If you get so used to expressing your emotions in emojis, does that mean the feelings themselves will alter, shape themselves more closely around a little yellow symbol? She has read somewhere that, in people who have had Botox, they report feeling less emotional, simply because their faces are less capable of expressing emotions. Although, you have to wonder about the methodology of such studies – at least, she does. How do you measure the intensity of your own emotions? It changes so much over time. For long periods when Nora was little, Marylen believed that she had no feelings at all – unless you counted exhaustion.

Texting with Eskil, she has used heart emojis and kissing faces, but that's it. Normal words, correctly spelt. Anything else would be a foreign language. Somehow, demeaning.

If you constantly express love as a red, shiny heart, bouncy and unbreakable, does that diminish the complexity and subtlety of your feelings?

Discuss.

Once the kids have been dropped off at their respective homes (she spots Eskil pruning roses in his garden and waves to him – casually, of course, so that no one will guess – and then tries to suppress her grin) and she arrives at her own house, she sits in her car for a few minutes, relishing the time alone. The sky is almost entirely clear, and the mountains above Sulis are washed with golden light. Tomorrow is Constitution Day; the weather has cleared up just in time for the parade. The town, like every city, town and village in Norway, will be bristling with flags. A holiday. The forecast is for warm, sunny weather, but the celebration will be muted, under the circumstances. She can't say she's looking forward to it.

Now, there is one more thing on her mind, which is coalescing into a dark shadow, like the threat of bad weather. Reluctantly, she turns her head to look towards Nilsbakken, up to where the old miners' houses and mine workings are folded secretively into the mountainside. The spoil heaps glow a warm ochre in the evening light, but, from this distance, they could be natural outcroppings of rock. The ugliest scars have been softened by grass and heather, and, apart from the old, rather quaint winding gear, you would never guess at the valley's industrial past. But it was up on that hillside, somewhere, that it was found: the body, in a sealed-up mine. She corrects herself: not 'it'; that 'it' was a man, a person whom someone once knew and loved. It makes her shiver – the thought that one day, back then, that person went into the mine and, for some reason that can only be terrible, never came out.

The Nilsbakken mines closed down before she was born, but her father had worked there as a young man. He never talked much about his job – didn't talk much about anything, really. That wasn't the way for a man from a modest background, back then. He worked hard and provided for his family, and, when he came home from work exhausted by manual labour, he read the paper and smoked, ate his dinner and watched television. Marylen loved her father, but she realised a long time ago that she didn't really know him. They never talked about things like feelings. Her mother did the talking in their house. Her father passed away some years ago, and her mother followed a year later, so there is no one left to ask about what's on her mind.

Twenty-three

Eskil had been lurking in the dining room, because from there he can keep an eye on the road. When he thought Marylen's car was due to appear, he went outside and fussed with the rose bush by the front door, looking for dead twigs to remove, a roll of twine in his pocket. That way, he could turn around, as if surprised by the car drawing up outside, and give Marylen a casual wave, and capture the answering smile on her face, as Elin stumbled, hang-headed, out of the car. It thrilled him.

Normally, Elin grabs her after-school snack, which is always the same – two glasses of oat milk, four biscuits and a banana – and disappears up to her room until supper. Eskil will ask, 'How was school today?' and she will answer, 'Fine.' If he presses for more detail – about a particular piece of homework, or a swimming lesson – she answers in monosyllables. Today, though, she hangs around the kitchen, munching her way through the biscuits.

She says, 'So . . .'

This is how Elin prefaces her announcements – irritatingly ungrammatical, to his mind. Probably her age. All the kids seem to do it.

'So . . . did you hear the news?'

Eskil never watches TV – rarely even listens to the radio. 'I've been writing most of the afternoon. What news?'

'They found a body at Nilsbakken – but it's not Daniel.'

'Oh, my goodness . . .'

Eskil's heart dropped in his body at her first words, and his instant thought was, Well, this was inevitable. It takes a second to recover himself.

'They think it's old – like, decades old. Not recent, anyway.'

Eskil remains speechless for a moment. 'When did you hear this?'

'People at school were talking. It's been on social media. There's TV crews up there and everything. The police made a statement.'

'Oh, how terrible – but I'm glad it's not your friend. Very glad.'

'He's not my friend. Not really.'

'Oh. Well . . .'

'But, yeah.'

'My goodness.'

Elin says, 'I know. They haven't said anything else, I don't think.'

'How do you feel? Do you want to talk about it?'

'About them finding a body?' She shrugs. 'Dunno. What's there to say?'

'Well, you've had a lot to deal with recently. It must be a strain.'

This is what Marylen has told him – that the kids at school are 'under psychological strain'. He feels quite pleased with himself; he's working on his emotional intelligence, he thinks.

Elin looks as if she's thinking about it, then shrugs again. There is a pause, but she still doesn't make a move to leave.

'Dad, people at school have been asking me about Great-Aunt Nordis.'

'Really? Good God. I'm sorry, sweetie. Why are they asking you about her?'

'Because of all the stuff that's going on with Daniel being missing, and they said she was missing, and how did the family cope with that and stuff . . .'

Eskil experiences a surge of fury that anyone would inflict that on Elin. He wants them expelled with immediate effect.

'I hope you told them it was none of their business. How dare they! Who was it?'

Elin shrugs again. 'Just some girls. It's no big deal. I didn't say anything. I don't know anything. But it made me realise that, you know – that I don't know what happened.'

'I don't think anyone knows what really happened, Elin.'

'But I don't want other people knowing more than I do. And they must have heard about it or read it somewhere.'

'Right. Okay. What do you want to know?'

'I know that they found her hat in the sea, and she's supposed to have drowned.'

'Yes. That's right. That's all anyone knows. Nothing else was ever found.'

'And – well –' Elin squeezes her eyes shut, as if the effort of marshalling her thoughts is painful – 'I know that it was because of me that Mum left—'

'Oh, goodness, of course it wasn't, Elin. It wasn't because of you!'

'No, but sort of – anyway, that was around the same time as Great-Aunt Nordis, wasn't it?'

Eskil sighs. Thinking about that time can pull him back into the depths of sadness. Klara's hysterical anxiety before any trace of her aunt was found; her morbid conviction that her family was cursed; the awful memorial service, where Svea had stared at her daughter like some malevolent ghoul . . . How had the family coped? By falling apart.

'Nordis died in December 2012. Klara was struggling with her mental health – she always had – but the uncertainty of Nordis disappearing, and then realising what might have happened – it did make her worse. She wasn't well, darling. She was ill. That's why she left.'

'Yeah. I know.'

The matter-of-fact way she says this makes his heart hurt.

'But did it contribute to Mum leaving, do you think?'

'I think so. She felt that . . . well, her family wasn't the most stable. Your grandmother had been pretty hard on her when she was growing up.'

'But she was a war baby – *Bestemor*, I mean. Her father was some German soldier.'

'Yes, and that must have been difficult, but it doesn't excuse Svea's behaviour.'

'You never say what that was. Did she beat her or something?'

'I . . . You should ask your mother, but she may not want to talk about it.'

Elin stares at the floor, and Eskil hopes that she will drop the subject.

'So, did Nordis commit suicide?'

Eskil takes a breath. He has never discussed Nordis's death with Elin, because . . . when is the right time to discuss such things with your child?

'There was no reason to think it was anything other than an accident. She left no note. But I suppose there's no way of knowing for certain.'

'But Mum thought she did.' Less a question than a statement.

183

Eskil shrugs. 'Perhaps – I don't know.'

'That's what Oda says.'

'Oh . . . Well, it was a difficult time for her, clearly. But our marriage was also . . . in trouble, by then, I'm afraid.' He gives a little, mirthless laugh.

Elin says, 'Well, her loss.'

Eskil realises she means it as a compliment to him and is profoundly touched. 'Certainly, as far as you're concerned, love.'

Elin snorts, but he thinks she's glad.

'I'm sorry I'm such a pain,' she says.

'Sweetie – you're never . . . Well, you're worth it, anyway.'

To his surprise, she shuffles towards him and puts her arms around him, leaning awkwardly so that only her arms and shoulders touch him. He knows better than to hug her back.

She steps away again. 'Dad . . . ?'

'I don't think there's anything else I can tell you about it. You could ask your grandmother, of course. Or Great-Uncle Karl.'

'Mm. No, it's not that. It's . . . are you going out with Marylen Sundfær?'

Eskil opens his mouth and nothing comes out.

'It's fine, if you are.'

'Well, I . . . we've . . . yes, I suppose, we have started, er . . .'

Why is it so hard to talk about?

'Dating?' Elin offers.

'Dating. Yes. But her husband knows about it – they're separated, really. They haven't been together for years.'

'Yeah, I know. It's cool, Dad.'

'Right. Okay. Good. How did you know?'

Elin shrugs. 'I think everyone knows.'

'Oh.'

He has a cold feeling – the dread of judgement that is never far away. Had they been careless? Or has Marylen taken matters into her own hands? Perhaps it doesn't matter.

'Elin, love, I don't want you to worry that things are going to change around here. We're . . . we're just friends, really, so . . . things will carry on exactly as before. I want you to know that. I didn't tell you before because it is still very, uh, early days, and, um, we don't know – well, you know, whether . . . Nothing is going to change.'

He knows that Elin hates change above all things.

'It's fine, Dad. She's nice.' Elin's face gives in to a smirk. 'I see her every day. I probably know her better than you do.'

That brings him up short. His daughter spends two hours with her every day in the car. God knows what they talk about on those journeys . . . Him? He goes cold at the thought. But, no, Elin isn't like that, nor is Marylen.

'I mean, it's been going on for a while, hasn't it?'

'Er, no, not really . . .'

Although, if you count that first kiss in the church, all those months ago, perhaps it has.

Twenty-four

Benny is dreading the Constitution Day parade. It is meant to be a celebration, but everything has been so weird lately, he can't imagine it being anything other than awful. Some of the seniors, including Daniel's closest friends and all his past, current or alleged girlfriends, have abandoned their red overalls in a show of respect. This has led to outbursts of anger from both sides – from those who think it is crassly insensitive, not to say hurtful, to carry on as though nothing has happened, and those who say that this is their only chance to take part in such an important tradition, and who is to say that Daniel hasn't just run off somewhere? And, in any case, would he – a kind and positive person – want everyone else to be miserable? Friendships have been sundered over this.

This afternoon, in geography, Benny's phone buzzed: it was a message from David. In it, David apologised for making Benny feel bad and acknowledged that he should have been more responsible. Benny would have been more moved if it hadn't come after Toril's phone call, but at least it's an apology. He said Benny had no reason to feel bad, as it was absolutely not his fault. He also asked him not to reply, *and it's probably best if you delete me.* Benny imagines that he has

186

already been deleted from David's phone, and his life, which makes him feel sad. David was his first real boyfriend – only they weren't boyfriends, were they? They weren't anything. But, still, his first . . . partner. That should be something joyful and fun, and it had been, to begin with, only now it has changed into something else, something that changes its colour and taste every day, but always for the worse. It's like the dreams he has in which everything he does turns to shit. He no longer understands what he'd been thinking when they first hooked up – who even was that person?

Maybe he should give Jonas-from-Bodø a go, but at the moment he feels soiled and much too tired. What he wants is for all these *things* to stop happening, so he can calm down and work out where he is with everything. But every day there is a new shock. Today, at school, in the canteen, he saw two senior girls staring at him and whispering, and he had the awful suspicion that they knew about him and David being at Nilsbakken. That's impossible – the police said they had a duty to protect him and would not reveal his name to anyone. But Lorentz and the others know there were witnesses to them parking Daniel's car at the cabin, and what if someone has worked out it was him?

And still sitting in his savings account is the two thousand kroner that David left him. The weirdly generous 'tip' that he hasn't sent back. Only because he doesn't know how. But keeping it makes him a . . . what? He refuses to think about it, pretends it's not there; he tells himself that money is like water and, when you add it to other water, it loses its identity and becomes anonymous. Only, what seems to have happened instead is that all the money in his travel fund has become spoiled, tainted with something shameful.

It's after ten o'clock and he's in his room, failing to do his English homework. Benny catches a glimpse of his face in the mirror that sits on his desk – it's pale and his eyelids are swollen and tinged with red. He sticks his tongue out at his reflection. What a miserable, whiny monster he is. The upsetting things are not happening to him. He is fine. He has the best mum in the world. So, they found a dead body in the mine at Nilsbakken . . . It's someone from a long time ago, and nothing to do with him. Elin has just found out that her dad is sleeping with one of their teachers (they'd been speculating about it for a while, but tonight she confirmed it), and she has been hassled by people at school about a tragedy that happened in her family. Her great-aunt (whom she never knew, but still) disappeared when Elin was four, presumed drowned, although no one knows for sure because her body was never found. Benny was furious when she told him about Ulrikke and Elle Maja – how dare they pick on Elin about something so traumatic? He's disappointed in Elle Maja; he always thought she was cool – although, now that he thinks about it, that's mostly because she's a lesbian, and liking someone based on their sexuality is just as stupid as disliking them for it. Elin had seemed quite relaxed about it all – unemotional, in fact – but can she be, really?

And, hanging over everything, the ghost – no, *not* ghost . . . the questions; the missingness of Daniel. This not-knowing creates a void that aches – a kind of hunger that can never be satisfied. His absence has become bigger by far than his presence ever was. Benny and Daniel weren't close. Daniel was someone he knew vaguely, and kind of liked, and kind of fancied, and they had made out that one time, though only for a dare, as a joke. But Benny didn't – doesn't – really know him at all; maybe he wasn't that nice. At the party, he'd tried to get Elin high, knowing she's only sixteen and neurodiverse: that's not a nice thing to do. It's lucky Elin has such firm boundaries. She says it was fear, but it just seems like good sense to him. It means she doesn't get manipulated into risky behaviour, like taking unknown drugs, or having sex with age-inappropriate people.

Benny has begun to believe that Daniel has run away somewhere, for some unknown reason. Maybe he's not worth all the tears and prayers and emotions. Benny's not to blame for Daniel's absence . . . but he is to blame for David. He keeps coming back to that. No wonder he's exhausted. He cannot face the thought of doing anything as energetic as communicating with someone new, with all the being-your-best-self that that involves. His best self seems to be in a critical condition at the moment, and he doesn't know if it will ever make a full recovery. He feels – and yes, it's ironic, under the circumstances – about a hundred years old.

He picks up his phone.

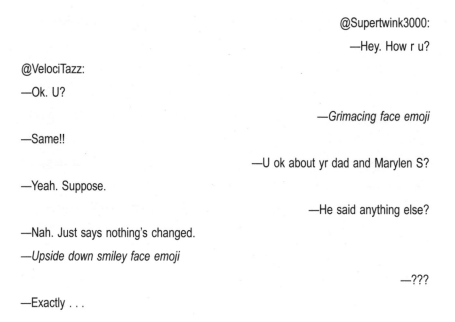

@Supertwink3000:
—Hey. How r u?

@VelociTazz:
—Ok. U?

—Grimacing face emoji

—Same!!

—U ok about yr dad and Marylen S?

—Yeah. Suppose.

—He said anything else?

—Nah. Just says nothing's changed.
—Upside down smiley face emoji

—???

—Exactly . . .

—Straight mouth face emoji

                                    —Yeah. I get it.

—Face hidden by smoke emoji

                         —Face with spiral eyes emoji

—Face without a mouth emoji

                 —Face with slanted straight mouth emoji

—Dotted line face emoji

                                    —Ghost emoji

A bit weak, that one. He could do better. . .

—Grey silhouette emoji

Damn. All he can come up with is. . .

                            —Two grey silhouettes emoji

No, wait:

                       —Two grey silhouettes embracing emoji

—Heart emoji x 3

                                    —Heart emoji x 6

As he dabs repeatedly at the screen, he finds that he is crying.

Twenty-five

Norwegian flags are strung between the lamp posts in the main street, so this morning Asta and I take a walk in the opposite direction, as far away from the town centre as possible. The parade is still happening, despite the shocks that have hit the town in the last few days. I suppose people want to cling to the normal, because it's better than the alternative.

I don't expect to find Elin hanging around my house when we get back. Usually, all the schoolkids take part in the parade dressed in the *bunad* – the traditional Norwegian costume – but she's wearing regular clothes: sloppy, hooded sweatshirt, too-big jacket, baggy jeans. With her short shock of hair, she could be a boy just as easily as a girl, until you get really close. I suppose that's the point.

'Hello, Elin. Aren't you meant to be in the parade?'

'Hey, *Bestemor*. No, I'm not doing it. Not this year.'

I find myself raising my eyebrows, but I just nod and let us in. She squats to make a fuss of Asta, who is overcome with joy at having a visitor.

'So, why don't you want to take part? Is it the costumes?'

'The costumes?'

'Well, the *bunad* is quite, er . . . gendered, isn't it?'

I'm rather pleased with myself for using this word, for the first time in my life.

'Oh. No, not really. You don't have to wear the *bunad* if you don't want to. I just . . . I wanted to talk to you.' She looks a bit shifty.

We go into the kitchen and I begin to make coffee, which Elin won't drink, but I don't know what else to do when someone comes into my house.

'Are you sure you don't want something else? Tea? Er . . . water?'

She shakes her head.

'Is everything all right? I suppose that's a stupid question.'

'No, it's okay. I'm fine.' She leans against the kitchen table and looks out of the window. Her fingers drum annoyingly on the tabletop. 'Dad's got a girlfriend.'

'Oh. Right. Is that a good thing?'

'Yeah, I think so. She's one of the teachers. I've been getting a ride to school with her every day. She's nice. I think it's good for him.'

'Mm. Well . . .' I don't know how to react to this news. 'I'm glad, if he's happy. And as long as you're okay with it.'

'I mean, he hasn't been out with anyone since Mum left – at least, I don't think so.'

'No. Well, I wouldn't know.'

'*Bestemor* . . .'

'Yes?'

'People have been asking me about Great-Aunt Nordis.'

'Oh.'

I don't need to ask why, but I'm shocked that they would bother

Elin about that. She was a small child at the time, and I don't know what her parents told her about Nordis's death then – or, for that matter, since.

'Who are these people?'

'Just people at school.'

'Well. I wouldn't have thought that it's any of their business. I hope you told them that.'

'Yeah. But it made me think. I don't know anything about what happened. And Dad says he doesn't know much either.'

'Mm. What do you want to know?'

Elin looks at the floor for a long time. 'You know, I just want to understand.'

'I don't know if I can help you. I don't think I understand.'

'But you were her sister!' She sounds affronted.

'Yes, I . . . Yes, I am.'

I tell her what I can, about what Nordis was like when she was young: my quicksilver sister who would not be pinned down. Then, how she pinned herself down to look after our mother, by which time she had changed into a person I didn't recognise. But I had been away from Nordland for nearly twenty years, and I only saw the result of the change, not the reason for it.

'But Great-Uncle Karl was here all the time, wasn't he? He must have known what was going on.'

'Possibly, but he was very taken up with his business. They were never close. Nordis became very . . . alternative, I suppose you would call it. She was obsessed with all sorts of strange stuff – numerology, rune casting, you name it – and Karl had no patience with that sort of thing. But, yes, you should talk to him, of course.'

193

'Numerology? I don't know what that is.'

'As far as I know, it's the belief that numbers can affect your life. The letters in your name add up to a certain number, and that . . . well, influences things.'

'Huh. So, what's my number?'

'I have no idea.'

'Isn't that totally random? What if you change your name?'

'Then your number changes, I think. I don't know, Elin. It always seemed like nonsense to me, but Nordis was very serious about it.'

'So, was she a bit crazy?'

'Not crazy, no. Eccentric, perhaps. Nowadays, I think she might be described as, what do you call it . . . ?'

'You mean, she was like me?'

Elin's face has sparked with wary interest. I look at her and wonder what she wants to hear.

'Perhaps. But she wasn't anything like you.'

'What about Great-Aunt Magny? When did she go to Denmark?'

'Oh, the mid-seventies, it must have been. Just after my stepfather died, which was in seventy-five. That's when she met – what's his name? Søren. So, she wasn't around either.'

'Great-Uncle Karl's not that easy to talk to. I hardly ever see him, anyway.'

'But you must know Lorentz, from school? Perhaps he knows more.'

Elin shrugs, and I think that she doesn't like Lorentz much. Since I am persona non grata with Karl, I barely know the boy. Perhaps he takes after his grandfather, who has always looked out for number one.

'*Bestemor*, do you think Nordis killed herself?'

I start shaking my head before I think what my answer should be.

'I don't know, Elin. I've thought about it a lot, but . . .'

'Mum does, doesn't she? Wasn't that why she left? She was afraid she would end up like her?'

'Oh . . . I don't . . . I think she was more afraid she would end up like me. I wasn't the best of mothers to her, I'm afraid.'

'What does that mean? That's what Dad says, but he doesn't say why.'

'Oh, well. Goodness, Elin . . . One tries one's best, but—'

'It's okay, *Bestemor*. I don't believe you were that bad. Mum did her best with me, too. She just couldn't. Dad said I had to make allowances for her.'

'He said that?'

'Yeah. A few times. But, you know, I was too difficult.'

I can't bear that she is making excuses for Klara, who I know for a fact used to hit and scream at her. I suppose that was only to be expected. I hit and screamed at Klara when she was a child, the same way that Ingvild had hit and screamed at me, so what chance did she have?

Perhaps I'm not being entirely honest about what I was like. You might be thinking, All parents get angry, that's inevitable. No one's perfect. True, but I would get so angry with Klara, I could hardly see. I lashed out at her when she whined and grizzled. The fear in her eyes only enraged me more. I called her names I don't like to think about. I'm not proud of myself. My mantra was: I'm not as bad as Ingvild was. As long as I could convince myself of that, I could live with myself. But it came to the same pass. Perhaps, in taking herself away, Klara did the best thing she could.

Elin says, 'I don't know why anyone has children. I'm not going to.'

'Well, you don't have to.'

'And, I mean, anyway, it's selfish. There are far too many people in the world already. The planet is burning, the oceans are rising, people are starving, refugees are dying, there are wars over resources. And it'll only get worse.'

'Well . . . er, maybe it won't be quite that bad. Things tend to go in cycles. You may change your mind, one day.'

Elin makes an impatient noise. 'I hate it when people assume you want to have babies just because you're a girl. Why do people think they know your mind better than you do?'

'Older people, like me, you mean?'

'Not just older people. People at school too, sometimes. They're so stupid.'

'I suppose older people think they know better because we remember what it's like to be your age. We know that you can change your mind.'

'That's why I'm genderfluid. It makes more sense to me than anything I've ever felt. It's like . . . when everything's in the right place. I feel safe.' She waves her hands around her to emphasise her words. She seems to really mean it.

Again, I feel that sting of sadness – or is it envy? – that I felt when she and Benny were getting ready for the party. To have so many possibilities, and so much righteous anger to power them. Anger was the one thing I was absolutely not allowed to have, and the one thing I've lived with every day of my life.

Elin says, 'Did you always want to have children?'

'No. Well – I suppose I didn't think about it. But you don't know how things are going to turn out. And it's not all bad – here *you* are.'

196

'*Bestemor*, so ... I don't know anything about my grandfather –
Mum's dad.'

'Oh. She never met him, of course. What has she told you?'

'Not much. Just that he was, like, Australian?'

'Tasmanian, yes. He was a Tasmanian hippy called Thomas Anstruther. He was sweet.'

Well. Or Rolf. It could possibly have been Rolf. But I'm going to stick
with Thomas. I always believed it was him.

'Do you have a picture of him?'

'Oh, goodness. I might have one somewhere. I can have a look, later.
But it wasn't a ... very long relationship.'

'Why didn't you get married? Do you mind my asking?'

'Oh, no. It was so long ago. It was the seventies, and we lived in a
commune in Thailand. Children were supposed to be brought up by
everyone and no one – who the actual parents were wasn't supposed
to matter. Which was naive. Especially as what it meant in practice
was that the men would sleep around and the mothers were left to
change the nappies.'

'That's crap.'

'Yes, it was crap. We thought we were liberated, living such a different life from our mothers. But, in so many cases, we ended up just
like them: angry and frustrated. I ended up behaving like my mother,
and I hated her. And Klara hates me ... so you're probably wise not
to have children.'

Elin goes silent. Perhaps I've shocked her.

'But, of course, Elin, you are you. You're not your mother, or your
father, nor are you anyone else.'

Elin says in a small voice, 'I don't think Mum hates you.'

197

'Well ...'

It's all I can think to say.

'She just feels like she failed.'

'We all feel we've failed. That's living.'

Asta whines at me. Perhaps I'm not being fair.

Elin stares out of the window. She looks as though she is contemplating a bottomless abyss. I realise that this is probably not what she wanted to hear when she came here today, but the realisation comes to us all sooner or later.

'Did you really hate your mum?'

All of a sudden, I am very tired. 'Oh, I don't ... It was difficult. We didn't get on.'

'You didn't know your father either, did you?'

'No.'

'But you had a stepfather? Didn't you like him?'

'Oh, my goodness, Elin, I don't think I can talk about this now. This is all ...'

I shake my head, and, once started, I find I can't stop.

'My stepfather was a horrible man, and I was glad he wasn't my father, even if my real father had been a Nazi. I'm sorry, Elin, but I can't talk about this anymore. I'm tired.'

Elin is crouched down, her back to me, scratching Asta's head. I desperately want her to leave.

In my youth, I became caught up in some things that ... Well, I should have known better. I'm talking about when I was in West Berlin, caught in the incandescent glow of Astrid's attention. As I think I've said, it was 1969. Does that give you a clue? Astrid introduced me to her friends, who were all fervently political. We demonstrated against the Vietnam War and discussed how women would change the world. We stayed up all night, chain-smoking and talking. Some of the people in her circle were quite a bit older than us. I was astonished to encounter men and women who seemed quite middle-aged – as in, they were married and had children. Yet they still burned with revolutionary ideals. They hadn't 'settled down', with the connotation that has of sediment sinking to the bottom of a lake. Not like my parents, who just greyly existed from day to day and had long ago stopped thinking for themselves, if they ever had. To meet people like Ulrike, the journalist, was thrilling. I was afraid of having my general ignorance exposed, so I rarely said anything at the late-night gatherings where everyone talked so fast and used such a lot of political jargon that I could barely follow.

At one party, I was introduced to a woman called Gudrun. She was tall and blonde, and seemed, going by the way the other guests treated her, to be some sort of celebrity. She was stunning and confident – all the men fancied her like crazy – and she totally ignored me. That was Gudrun Ensslin. So, now you know, if you hadn't already realised, that I was on the outer fringes of the group that became the Red Army Faction. Or the Baader–Meinhof Gang, as they never called themselves. The journalist who so impressed me was Ulrike Meinhof. I got involved in a very minor way with some anti-government protests – marching, throwing smoke bombs, painting slogans on the side of the parliament building. But I think I was deemed too uneducated and silly to be fully trusted or accepted. Once, someone asked me to drive a car for some unspecified action. I knew it was a compliment as well as a test, and I had to say, with a mixture of shame and relief, that I couldn't drive. Clearly, I was not a soldier. That was when Astrid began to grow away from me. I suppose my naivety saved me, but at the time I believed I had, yet again, been found wanting.

I expect you think I was a very foolish young woman, but I knew what was going on and I believed in it. No one here knows about that time in my life, although my brother has always acted as though my twenty-year absence was in itself evidence of criminal behaviour. And ... look, I know, I know, but I'm going to say it again – things were different then. Moral absolutism is all very well, but if you can be sympathetic to a different culture, then you should be sympathetic to a different time. The Holocaust was fresh in everyone's minds, and, for the German generation who had grown up in the shadow of that shame and guilt, there was nothing more vital than to reject the people who had perpetrated those crimes. Yet, in 1969, there were members of the West German government who had been Nazi politicians. Men who had pledged allegiance to Hitler were still in power: allowed to forget their pasts to keep the anti-Communist dollars flooding in. Astrid's father had held a low-level position in the Reich government and was now a successful lawyer. He had never been held to account and Astrid could not bear it. It was a mortal wound, because, as much as she hated him, he was her father and she couldn't not love him. For me, as much as for my German friends, such horror justified – well – almost anything.

And so, Astrid went missing, too, although in a different way from my father. She disappeared into the underworld of those who went on the run from the police. I never saw her again. I suppose what happened later hit the headlines while I was in Thailand and

living in the commune, which was off-grid, as you would say now –
although then there wasn't even a 'grid'. I didn't find out what had
happened until I was back in Oslo in the late seventies, working as
a bookkeeper once again, my free-love experiments long abandoned.
I was getting dinner for Klara when something penetrated my con-
sciousness like a flash of bright light. The newsreader had said the
name 'Astrid Junger', and the hairs on the back of my neck stood
up. When I turned around, there, on my little black and white TV
screen, was a photo of Astrid. Scintillating Astrid, smiling, looking
as she had done when I first met her. The image changed to another
picture of her, standing in a dock. She looked older and she wasn't
smiling. Then it switched to a picture of a boring concrete building,
which, the newsreader's voice informed me, was the prison where
she had taken her own life.

When Elin finally took the hint and left, I crawled into bed. My limbs
felt as though they were made of cast iron, and the pain that lives in
my hip had spread through my entire body. When it comes on like
that, the only thing to do is take a pill, lie down and wait it out. Stare
down the pain, and the memories, and see who blinks first.

While I'm lying here, giving the occasional theatrical groan, which
seems to help, Asta lies beside me and looks at me, furrowing her
brow, as if she's trying to work out how to fix me. In case you're
wondering, yes, I named Asta for Astrid, just as my dear Tommy was
named for Thomas Anstruther. I suppose they were the two great
loves of my life, if you believe in such a thing. Of course, I love my
daughter too, in spite of everything, but you can't call a dog after
your child, can you?

It has been so many years since I was with them, but I miss them both. I was wondering when you would notice about the names. I hold on to them in this unimportant, almost invisible way. People always let you down, dogs never do.

Twenty-six

Sometimes, Elin wonders if everyone is unhappy, or if it's just the people in her family. Even the ones who appear fine on the surface, if you dig down a bit, you always seem to turn up some terrible pain. She tells herself that it isn't so. Benny is happy, usually (just not at the moment). Toril seems pretty happy, too, although Benny says she is dying to have a boyfriend and never meets anyone she likes. Even Marylen Sundfær seems happy enough, although she has a severely disabled daughter and a clinically depressed husband, which is clearly a bummer.

She wanders back towards the school, but no one is there and the doors are locked. So, she walks on, avoiding the main streets and the crowds. The parade music is a constant muffled beating. She doesn't think she will do anything, because the police must all be out at the parade, and she doesn't expect to find anyone at the station, but she does. The younger officer who was at the school, Merete Nordheim, is coming out of an office just as Elin walks into reception. She gives her a nod of recognition before disappearing through another door. Elin goes up to the receptionist and speaks to her. Then she has to sit and wait for ages, kicking her heels. Of course, the police must be super busy, with everything that's going on – the Daniel thing, of course, and now this mysterious body in the mine. At length, Merete comes back out and beckons to her.

'Hello, Elin. How are you doing?'

'Um, okay.'

Merete closes the door to the reception. There are phones ringing in another room.

As she sits down next to Merete's desk, Elin has a mad thought – what if the body from the mine is here? Next door? No, it can't be. It must be in a special cold place for bodies. She wonders where that is.

'Sonja said you have something to tell us,' Merete says, sitting at her computer.

'Maybe. I mean, yes, but I don't know if it's important.'

'Don't worry about that, just go ahead.' She smiles encouragingly. Her blond ponytail swings; her eyes are bright and clear. She looks like an advert for being in the police.

'It's not a fact, or anything; it's just something I can't stop thinking about.'

'Okay. What is that?'

Elin tries to order her thoughts. Show your workings, as they say in maths.

'So . . . Lorentz and the others, they lied about Daniel's car, didn't they?'

'I can't comment on that.'

'Right, okay. Well, first they said that Daniel drove his car to Nilsbakken on Saturday night and went hiking on his own. But that wasn't true – they drove his car up there and left it. Daniel wasn't there.'

Merete is watching her closely.

'And you – I mean, the police – have been looking for him around Nilsbakken. Because that's where he's supposed to have gone. That's how come you found this other body, isn't it?'

Merete is tapping busily at her computer, but doesn't say anything.

'But what if he was never there?'

'What makes you say that?'

'Because it doesn't make sense to lie about the car for no reason. You tell lies for a reason, don't you?'

'And what reason would that be?'

'To make sure no one looks in the place where Daniel really was.'

'And where might that be?'

'I don't know.'

'You don't know anything about where they went that Saturday?'

She shakes her head.

Merete reads something on the screen. 'But, the weekend before, you had been with Daniel, you said. You and he had been quite intimate. And he offered you drugs.'

'Yeah, but, I mean, that was at a party. I had never done that before. It was just . . .' She has a horrible feeling that she's blushing.

'Just a hook-up? Is that what you mean?'

'Yeah. I didn't speak to him after that.'

Elin isn't sure, but it looks like a flicker of a smile crosses Merete's face. It's disconcerting.

'And did he say anything about what he was going to do the following Saturday? Any plans?'

She shakes her head again, and then says, 'No,' in a firm voice, in case it's like on the TV and the police have to hear you. Although, come to think of it, there is no tape. 'Nothing like that. He just said

205

he couldn't wait to get out of here. Said that everyone here was so conventional. And I would understand. But I didn't.'

Merete taps away, her eyes on the screen. 'Okay, well, going back to your theory, Elin. Is there anything in particular that makes you think Daniel was somewhere else and the others were trying to lay a false trail?'

'I don't know, but Lorentz is being really . . . odd. It's like he's afraid. I mean, everyone else is beginning to think that Daniel ran away somewhere, and they've sort of calmed down a bit, but Lorentz is still in a state.'

'How well do you know Lorentz?'

'He's my cousin. Well – second cousin. Actually, he's my half second-cousin. It's not that I want to get him into trouble, but . . . I don't know. It doesn't seem right. That's not very helpful, is it?'

'Well, you never know. Every little helps.'

'I mean, no one knows that he has run away. You haven't stopped looking for him, have you?'

'You have to understand that I can't comment on the specifics of an ongoing case, but, no, we haven't stopped looking for him. You're sure there isn't anything else?'

Elin shakes her head. She feels deflated. She doesn't really have anything to contribute, just a feeling. She really has no desire to get Lorentz into trouble. She has nothing against him, other than that he's a bit of a wanker and has always teased her. She felt an unwonted sympathy for him the other day, when he had looked at her as though he wished she could absolve him, if only she knew how.

But it's not right. And the not-rightness of it has been bothering her, causing her a nagging discomfort, like a piece of grit in her shoe. She feels it at every step.

Twenty-seven

There is nothing on the Nilsbakken body that leads to an easy identification. The clothing is like that worn by working men for decades
in the middle of the last century. The body has no watch, no wallet,
no letters. The only thing in the pockets is a crushed pack of King's
cigarettes. The deceased had bad teeth, but that was not unusual. The
tentative conclusion is that he most likely died between the time the
mines closed, in March 1968, and when the workings were finally
sealed up, which was later that summer. The remains have been dis-
patched to the police laboratory in Bodø, where forensic scientists
will examine them for signs of violence. A tooth is sent away for DNA
testing. There is no great urgency about this – it's not as though any
putative killer will still be prowling around, six decades on. From the
state of the bones, it's not clear there ever was a killer in the first place.

That doesn't stop people speculating. Those from the older generation cast their minds back, combing memories for stories of missing
people, but that's a lot of ground to cover. Memory grows woolly after
such a long time, and dates are hard to pin down. Still, anyone with an
internet connection goes online and googles whatever terms they can
think of: *missing people, Nilsbakken mines, Sulitjelma Gruber, bodies*

in mines, Nordland 1968 and so on ... A rumour goes around that a journalist is working on a podcast, although no one knows who it is, if it is someone local or not, but that's how people solve old mysteries these days, isn't it? Citizen detection, sharing information, getting the public involved. There was that famous one: back in 1970, a burnt body was found in an isolated valley near Bergen. Recently, someone did a podcast on the case which ... well, it hadn't actually solved anything, since the woman's identity and the reasons for her death are still a mystery, but it was all very interesting. In a clear bid to ride the wave of Isdal Woman's notoriety, someone at the local paper has dubbed the body *Jerngruvemannen* – Iron-Mine Man.

But, since the dramatic events of Wednesday, discovering Iron-Mine Man's identity is not Hanne Duli's priority. Her priority is finding any trace of Daniel – something that, thus far, she has significantly failed to do. At her desk in the station, she once again goes through the search reports. There are mountains of them now: the sniffer-dog teams, the police divers, the ground-search teams, the volunteers, the helicopters with heat-detection cameras – which, with little leaf growth on the mountain at this time of year, should have been more helpful. These cameras can spot a hare huddled on a mountainside at night; they should certainly spot a being as big as a human, as long as it is alive. All of these searches have come up with nothing. The searchers have spread out in ever-widening circles, covering roads, disused mining tracks, hiking trails. They have plumbed dozens of lakes and searched cabins far beyond the range of a person on foot, all with the same result: they have found not the slightest trace of Daniel, not anywhere.

She keeps coming back to the fact that there is nothing at all, which is weird. If he was on foot, the dogs should have been able to pick up some trace from where he left his car, but the results from Nilsbakken were so inconclusive as to be useless. After the boys revised their story, the handlers took the dogs further down the valley to try again, around the lay-by where the boys said they dropped him off and he set out on his solo hike. Nothing. A strong, healthy young man, competent in the wilderness, familiar with the terrain. Even if he was immediately picked up in a vehicle – whether by plan or in some more sinister event – there should have been some trace, but there was nothing. As if he were never there. Either that, or the worrying possibility: there are traces, and they have missed them.

For the second time that morning, she turns to the report of the girl's statement – Elin Torstensen. They'd not given it much attention initially because it contained no facts, just her opinion. But she had said – there are the words, in black and white – 'What if he was never there?' She had said, 'You tell lies for a reason.'

When confronted, the boys said they lied because they were scared of admitting they had driven to Nilsbakken when they'd been drinking – they all had, apart from Tobias, who doesn't drink, but also doesn't drive. They were trying to protect Lorentz and Johnny from potential drink-driving convictions? Does that make sense? Then there is the statement from the other kid, Bendik Iversen, who saw them parking Daniel's car by the hut at Nilsbakken ... With a few taps, she brings up his statement on her screen. Lorentz was driving one car, Johnny the other. Did they appear drunk? Bendik Iversen – and the man he was with, David Mæland (and that was a dodgy business, whichever way you looked at it) – didn't give an opinion as to that. But then, looking at the transcripts, they weren't specifically asked.

Hanne Duli has spoken to all three boys. First interviews were done by Merete Nordheim and Jesper Nystrom. She saw the boys a couple of days later, once they had changed their story. Fauske is a small town and Hanne Duli's daughter is a second-year at the high school, so the Hellraisers were familiar faces to her. Lorentz and Johnny, in particular, are well known in the town – everyone knows the Jentoft family is one of the wealthiest around, and Hanne Duli remembers Johnny's mother from her own distant schooldays – that's the sort of place this is. Linda Flakstad married Finn (was it?) Skarstein, who wasn't from round here and cleared off again before Johnny was two years old. Johnny is the only one of the boys who has crossed her radar in her police capacity. In the past, she has had to caution him for antisocial behaviour and for speeding. The car wasn't his own; Linda couldn't afford to buy him one. Hanne Duli had 'the chat' with Linda, not wanting to make too much of it, as Johnny was then only sixteen. Linda Skarstein was embarrassed and, Hanne Duli thought, slightly resentful. At school, Linda had been the pretty, popular girl, who should not, according to the laws of natural selection, have ended up in social housing, getting a dressing-down from the fat girl in the year below. Hanne Duli is no longer overweight, actually, thanks to unceasing vigilance, but it's hard to shake off words that, at sixteen, are burned into your soul.

'For God's sake, what is it now?' Linda glares at her. She has just opened her front door to find Hanne Duli on the landing of her apartment block.

Hanne Duli sketches a smile. 'This won't take long, Linda; I just want to go over a couple of things with Johnny.'

'You've spoken to him over and over again. He's on antidepressants because of all this. You know that he collapsed at school? He couldn't breathe! He had to go to hospital.'

'I didn't know that. I'm sorry. But it really is just routine.' Hanne Duli gives her a bland smile – the one that says, *I'm not leaving.*

'I know it must be awful, not knowing where your best friend is, or if he's okay.'

Johnny nods. He and Hanne Duli are in the living room, while Linda hovers in the open-plan kitchen, listening. Johnny sits in the corner of the sofa, as far away from Hanne Duli as possible. He hunches into himself and avoids eye contact – which, in a teenage boy, is not necessarily a sign of guilt. His angular features remind Hanne Duli of Linda's when she was young, but in him they are honed into something altogether more memorable. From her daughter, Elizabeth, Hanne Duli knows that girls cluster round Johnny like flies – normally, that is. Today, the school Don Juan looks pale and unhappy, his hair greasy, his skin broken out in spots. Linda doesn't seem to have exaggerated the effect of 'all this' on her son.

'I thought you'd come to tell me that . . .' His voice trails off into a whisper.

'No, I just want to go through the events of that Saturday again. I know it's tedious and you've done it before, but sometimes a person remembers something that slipped their mind. Something that didn't seem at all important, but it might help us to find him. That's what we all want.'

Johnny nods, then shrugs. He says, 'So, you don't have any idea where he went?'

'I can't comment on the investigation, Johnny.'

Johnny sniffs and rubs his nose with the back of his hand. 'I don't know what else to tell you. I wish there was something. I've been over

211

and over it in my mind, that night, trying to think of anything . . .' He shakes his head. 'I feel like we let him down.'

'Why do you say that?'

'We'd been drinking – not Tobias, but the rest of us. We were supposed to go up the mountain together, but Lorentz and I felt too tired and . . . out of it, and Tobias never wanted to go in the first place. So, we decided to go home – but Daniel insisted that he was still doing it.'

'Still doing what, exactly?'

'Hiking up the mountain behind Nilsbakken and watching the sunrise. Only the sun was already up, by then. We tried to talk him out of it, but, once he's made up his mind to do something, he won't budge.'

Hanne Duli takes him through the evening once again – where they started partying, what they had drunk. He says that alcohol was the only thing they took, but she's used to being lied to on that score, and she's sure he is lying. She gets him to recount when they changed their plans, what time they left Daniel. Why they moved his car up to Nilsbakken: 'Because he asked us to.' It's the same as before, chiming perfectly with the accounts of the other two. She's on the lookout for stories that sound too rehearsed, for syntax that is a repeat of the others'. Johnny keeps his eyes on the ground while he's speaking, his voice flat, hair falling in a curtain over his face. She feels there is something he's not saying, but nothing she can get a grip on, work her fingertips into and prise open. When he looks up again, Hanne Duli sees traces of tears.

Driving away, she thinks, Damn. She'd thought Johnny was the most vulnerable, but maybe she was wrong. What that girl said, when Merete asked why they would have lied about the cars . . . Was it to hide the fact that they were drink-driving? Or was it 'to make sure no one looks in the place where Daniel really was'? She'll have to get them in, lean on them a bit harder.

Her phone lights up in its cradle: Merete. She taps the button to answer.

'Hey, boss – are you driving?'

'Yes, but I'm not far from the station. About five minutes. Why?'

'You might want to turn around. I'm at the Sjønståfjell tunnel.'

There is something in her voice that Hanne Duli recognises – an urgency.

'I'm coming. What is it?'

There is a pause. 'I'd rather tell you when you get here.'

God knows how they spotted it, as it was deep inside the Sjønståfjell road tunnel, partially hidden in the moraine of silt deposited by recent rains. But someone saw something shining in the dirt as they drove through. The tunnels weren't searched by hand, but they have driven through here dozens of times since Daniel disappeared. The lights are bright enough; the walls are bare rock, there is nowhere to hide. Now, they've had to close the tunnel, which means closing the road which is the only way in and out of the valley – a logistical nightmare. A forensics team is here, sweeping the tunnel – and searching a tunnel three kilometres long is not a speedy operation. Traffic enforcement has come up to block the road and try to pacify the inhabitants of Sulis who are trapped in the valley like wasps in a bottle, and some angry tourists from Nilsbakken who had dinner reservations in Fauske. They can't set up a diversion, because there is no other road. Everyone will just have to wait.

The shining thing is a mobile phone. And it looks very much like Daniel's phone. There are stickers on the back: one, a warning to assume this phone is tapped; another, for a rock band he likes. A poster of the same band is stuck to his bedroom wall. The battery is dead and will have to be resuscitated before they can know for certain, but Hanne Duli is sure that it is his phone. The search, once completed, turns up nothing else. Daniel is not here – it would be impossible for a body to lie here unnoticed. There are no hiding places, no nooks and crannies that could conceal so much as a cat. There are no footprints in the dirt. The few items they scavenge from the tunnel floor are probably jetsam – cigarette butts, food wrappers, cans, that kind of thing – but every single one is put in an evidence bag, just in case. Samples of silt and gravel. Scrapings from the walls. No one walks through these narrow, bare tunnels; that would be suicide. No one even cycles. Anything here was most likely thrown from a car. Is that how the phone ended up here?

Twenty-eight

Magny hardly ever calls me. Admittedly, I don't call her either – somehow it never occurs to me to do so. With Karl, I don't speak to him because we have nothing to say, but, with Magny, it's not that I don't love her, I just take her for granted, which, as far as I'm concerned, is the biggest compliment you can pay a relative. Siblings remind you of what you come from – not their fault – and neither of us is big on nostalgia, for reasons you can fill in for yourselves. Also, she's lived in Denmark since the mid-seventies and rarely comes back to Nordland. Out of sight . . . you know.

I always believed, although she's never said as much, that she married the Dane so that she had a reason to get as far from our parents as possible. It clearly wasn't out of love, as subsequent events proved. By then, I was in Thailand, and she probably thought it was her turn to make a break for freedom. She left just before Erling died, which he did in that sudden yet unsurprising way that alcoholics have. I think she was thankful not to be on the spot to hold Ingvild's hand – and Karl and Nordis were nearby, although Karl, being a man of a certain sort, wasn't going to waste his valuable time 'caring' for anyone. In any case, Ingvild was a young widow – she wasn't yet fifty when Erling popped his clogs – so we assumed she would pick herself up and finally make her own life. I thought she would be relieved to be rid of him. I don't know, perhaps the years of alcohol abuse had rotted her brain beyond repair, or she was just – what's the word? – institutionalised by her hard life. They say women don't leave abusive men because they are too psychologically damaged. So, even though Erling was dead and couldn't hurt her anymore, nothing changed about her life, except that she was now knocking around the Gammelsøy house on her own. A big part of the problem, I think, was that she had never had a job outside the home, and it didn't seem to occur to her that she could start. She got some sort of state benefit, and I believe Karl helped her out with money. I heard from my sisters that she complained a lot. I stayed away, in case her hopelessness was catching.

That left Nordis in the frame, for which I still feel a certain amount of guilt. It is guilt without regret, because I was adamant that I would not see Ingvild again, and Nordis didn't seem to expect me to. But I do wish she hadn't felt impelled to take on that burden. I prayed atheist prayers for her to emigrate to the US, or somewhere equally far away from Ingvild – Australia maybe, or the Galapagos. But she never went anywhere, and when Ingvild was diagnosed with dementia after years of increasingly erratic behaviour, Nordis gave up her job and her little apartment in Bodø and moved back in with her. I was angry with Nordis, not because I felt pressured to do that – Klara was a child, so I had my cast-iron mummy excuse – but because it seemed a capitulation to the terrible Øvergaard legacy, a willing recycling of our same old shit.

This morning, Magny calls. It's quite early, and I have yet to take Asta out for her first walk. For a moment, I think something bad must have happened, then I feel a rush of gladness. There is no nonsense with Magny.

'Magny! It's so nice to hear from you. How are you?'

We chat for a few minutes. She is well; Dolly is well. Dolly has taken up paddleboarding, which she does from the beach near where they live, even in winter. Magny says she's too old to join in, but she drives to the beach with a flask of coffee and watches, phone in hand, in case Dolly gets swept away and she has to call the coastguard. It's true that Dolly is a lot younger than us – she's barely sixty, and she has always been very sporty. I was startled, when Magny first sent photos of them together, to see this youthful, attractive woman, with her dark, curly hair and dazzling smile – who was, apparently, head over heels in love with my homely sister, and bombarded her with romantic gestures until Magny gave in and married her. Why was I startled? Well, Dolly resembles an American actress I always found particularly beautiful. It's not that I think all lesbians look masculine, not at all – but, well, Magny does, rather. No doubt Elin would scold me about that.

Eventually, Magny says, 'I read about the body they found up at Nilsbakken. Awful. And with that poor boy missing as well.'

'God, has it made the Danish news?'

'No, but, you know, I keep an eye on things at home. So there's still no news on the boy?'

'No. They've looked all over the place – that's how they found this old . . . body. You said, "at home".'

I am touched by this. She has lived in Denmark far longer than she lived in Norway, but we are still home.

'Well, you know. So . . . have you heard anything about who the body might belong to?'

I switch the phone to my other hand. 'No. It's only been a few days.'

'Are people speculating? There must be plenty of people around who were living there then.'

'You mean, like me? I haven't heard anything. They haven't said how old it is, so . . . I mean, it's anyone's guess, at the moment.'

Magny says, 'Hmm,' and there is a rather odd pause.

'What? You're being a bit . . . I don't know. Like you think I should know something.'

'No, no,' she says. 'I was just wondering. I was there too, wasn't I, in Fauske? We all were. Aren't you thinking, Maybe I crossed paths with that person? You think, maybe *I* knew them? Maybe Nordis knew them?'

'Honestly, no. I mean, I was only there till the mine closed, and they couldn't have been in there before that. I left pretty much immediately afterwards, so . . .'

Another pause.

'You've obviously been thinking about it. Do you have any thoughts?'

Magny sighs down the phone. 'No. I don't know. I suppose they'll work out who it is eventually.'

'Maybe. Or maybe not. It's such a long time ago. I think they're more focused on finding this boy. I know his grandfather. It's devastating . . .'

After some more chat, she asks me the question that is always hovering in the background: 'Have you heard from Klara recently?'

'You know she doesn't speak to me. Why, have you?'

'Actually, yes . . .'

Have you ever stood in a forest in the depths of winter? When it's very cold – say, twenty below zero – tree sap freezes and expands. Under certain conditions, the tree will burst. You see them sometimes, with their poor, broken trunks, as though a giant axe has split them from top to bottom. When it happens, it sounds like gunfire. That's how I feel whenever someone mentions my daughter: like I'm frozen to my core, and the cold might cleave me in two.

When we were still in Oslo, I made an effort to change. I wasn't proud of the way I lost my temper with Klara and I hated it when I heard Ingvild's nagging, bitter tone coming out of my mouth. Sometimes, she would flinch in my presence, actual fear in her eyes. I admit that – quite often – I couldn't stop myself lashing out when she cried or whined, which seemed to be most of the time. I didn't want to be like my mother, but behaving differently seemed more than I could manage. When I couldn't stand it any longer, I plucked up the courage to mention it to my doctor. This was in the bad old days when people didn't talk about mental health, or their lack of it. Doing so was seen as the province of hopeless weaklings and people with too much money. I didn't think of myself as having a mental-health problem; I thought I was a horrible person who couldn't stop hitting my daughter. It turned out there was a waiting list for individual therapy, and I was strongly encouraged to join a group. I loathed the idea of sitting in a room with a bunch of crazy people. Meanwhile, Klara's father, who I was sure was Thomas, was on the other side of the world. I had written to him over the years, and sent pictures of Klara, but there had been a pure, unbroken silence, and I assumed he didn't care. Then, out of the blue, I got a short letter from his mother, who told me that Thomas was a long-term patient in a psychiatric institution. Kathy Anstruther wrote, *We hold on to the hope that he will get out one day*, which made it sound as though they had no hope at all. He had always medicated himself with marijuana, dimming his brightness, sometimes until he was practically comatose. I'd hated that about him. I didn't know whether that had contributed to his breakdown, or – possibly – postponed it. Poor Klara, doubly cursed by crappy genes. I gritted my teeth and went to group.

To my surprise, it became my favourite activity for the next year. On Tuesday afternoons, while Klara stayed at after-school club, I went to sit in the circle of plastic chairs in a hospital annexe. The building was too hot and the corridors smelt of disinfectant and artificial carpet. But our room was quite nice. The windows had a view of some gardens, and there was an ancient rubber plant in one corner – a scarred, ugly thing that seemed placed there as a metaphor for survival.

Of course, the others in the group were normal people with a smorgasbord of mundane psychological miseries: Per Erik was lonely and depressed, Annika struggled with her relationship and young children, Kari had suffered multiple miscarriages and Ragnar was a former addict who kept falling off the wagon. Ragnar sometimes came to meetings drunk, and I objected to this. I thought that, if I could make the effort to turn up sober, then so could he, which made him angry – although he was not an aggressive man; he was actually rather sweet. There were a couple of others in the group, but, after so many years, I've forgotten their names, and their faces. Apologies, whoever you were. There was no set pattern to the meetings. People talked about whatever they wanted, while our facilitator, a fat, kindly man called Bent, tried to stop Annika from talking all the time.

Did it work? It's hard to know, but I think it helped a little. I don't know that Klara would agree. In group, we swapped stories about variously abusive parents, or our feelings of helplessness and emptiness.

The funny thing was, without exception, everyone thought that the problems of the other group members were more serious and worthy of attention than their own. They were shocked and sympathetic when I told them about my stepfather calling me a *naziyngel*, or my mother's violence, while I, in turn, was horrified to hear that Kari had been locked in a cupboard during her childhood. She was very funny when she spoke about this. Ragnar's parents were, big surprise, alcoholics, but his family was wealthy. His father had been possessive and domineering. It was clear to us that he had been jealous of his wife's love for her son, although Ragnar was astounded when we said this. We made suggestions and gave advice, and the sincerity of our desire to help each other was . . . a distillation of goodness. I have the feeling that, in that group, I was a better person than I have been at any other time in my life.

Of course, there were things I didn't talk about. I'm sure that was true of everyone. There are wounds that you show people, things you can say because you've said them before and they're part of your repertoire. It was a relief to say them again, in this room, where people really paid attention and weren't (generally) stoned. I told them about my mother and stepfather. But I didn't tell them about Jens. They didn't know why I always wore my hair in a fringe. God knows what they didn't tell me. It was a shame it only lasted a year, but that was all you got for free. Maybe, if it had gone on longer, we would have eventually emptied out all the detritus in our heads, gone on pouring out the darkness until we were finally clean. But that might have taken more than our lifetimes.

Out of everyone, I liked Ragnar the most. I suppose I was attracted to him, although I was adamant that I was – definitely – never going to let another damaged fuck-up into my life. Despite Ragnar's background being so privileged, if I measured my current circumstances against his, I was pleased to find that I came out on top. Perhaps not a high bar to clear, but still. I had a child and a responsible job that paid my rent, whereas he stuck needles in his arm and claimed to be an artist, which I interpreted as meaning that, even though he was forty, his parents still paid for everything.

Anyway, nothing was ever going to happen because he was interested in Kari, and I thought they were either having an affair or hovering on the edge of it. I disapproved. It had been explained to us at the beginning of the process that we were supposed to maintain 'clear boundaries' – relationships between group members were meant to be therapeutic, not muddled with real, outside-world feelings. But, with people like us, there was always going to be some breaking of rules.

One day, I was late and, by the time I walked in, Annika was in full flow about something or other – something troubling and worthy of attention – but, while I sat there with my jaw dropping in amazement (as far I remember, her husband was demanding sado-masochistic sex, or he would leave her), Bent very gently interrupted.

'Annika, I'm sorry, if I could just stop you for a moment. I know you have a lot to talk about, but Per Erik has something he needs to say too. Is that okay? We will come back to this.'

Annika stopped for breath and nodded. Per Erik shifted in his seat. He looked a bit glazed, although he was not one to abuse drugs or alcohol, unlike Ragnar . . . Only then I realised Ragnar was not there. Probably fallen off the wagon again.

'Yeah, um, well, the other night, Ragnar came around to my flat and he was upset. He'd been seeing this girl, and they'd argued.'

Kari stared straight ahead. She didn't seem bothered by this news, so perhaps nothing had gone on there, after all – or she had sent him packing, having more sense than I'd credited her with.

'He seemed a bit out of it, so I said he could stay the night on my sofa. He went to sleep. And, when I went in there in the morning, he was brown bread.'

I remember his words exactly, that's how he put it. He couldn't say the word *dead*. It took us a moment to understand that it wasn't a joke, to translate the euphemism into cold fact. Then, the rest of us, like a perfectly trained chorus, gasped theatrically. I put my hand on my heart. Kari had both hands over her mouth. Annika moaned, 'No!' No one is original, at such a moment.

'I mean, he was cold, man. I called the ambulance and the police, and they took him away. It was too late to do anything. He'd died in the night. He'd taken something.'

'Heroin?'

Per Erik shrugged.

'Was it . . . on purpose?' This was Kari, the only one of us brave enough to say it out loud.

'Dunno. No. I mean, I don't think so.'

'Did the police say what was the cause of death?'

'They said it was heart failure. His heart just stopped.'

I said, 'That's not a cause of death – that *is* death.'

Per Erik looked at me and there was, for the first time, some raw emotion in his face.

'Well, that's what they said, Svea! They're the police! I don't know! Christ!'

The rest of the session has become a blur in my mind, but afterwards we went to a bar for a drink. It seemed the least we could do was raise a glass to Ragnar, who had been irritating and hopeless, but had a certain, moth-eaten charm. We toasted him, and exchanged our few desultory memories – we knew such intimate things about him, but we hadn't really known him, had we? As we sat round the small table, Kari kept touching Per Erik's arm, and afterwards, as we trailed off into the November evening towards our various bus stops, I spotted the pair of them in a darkened doorway, locked in a passionate embrace.

God, I thought, with a revulsion that bordered on violence. How pathetic. You think that's going to help? What's wrong with you?

Much later, when I thought about that night and Ragnar's sad, almost certainly accidental death, I wondered: What on earth was wrong with *me*?

Twenty-nine

Her mother's voice sounds aggrieved: 'Elin? What's the matter? Don't you want me to come?'

Elin says, 'No, of course I do. But why are you coming? Is something wrong?'

'No. Everything's fine.'

'Do you not want me to come to Oslo this summer?'

'Elin, no, of course I want you to come and see me. I'm just coming up north as well. It's not either/or. It can be both.'

'But you never come here.'

There is the sound of Klara breathing. Elin pictures her switching her phone to the other hand. No, she's put her on speaker; the sound has changed, become tinnier.

'I know I haven't been up there for quite a while, but that's not because I didn't want to. I just . . . I wasn't doing so well . . . but I'm in a much better place now.'

Something about the phrase grips Elin's insides with a cold fist.

'You're not ill, Mum?'

Klara laughs. 'No, sweetie, no! I'm fine, I'm really well. Really, really good, in fact.'

'Oh. Okay. Why are you so good?'

'Well, I've been seeing a wonderful therapist and she's helped me a lot. I feel like a different person – or rather, I feel like me again, after a long time. And . . . this is one of the things I want to talk to you about in person, but I've told your sister, so . . . well, ha ha, I've been seeing someone. A boyfriend, I suppose – well, a man friend! Or should I say "partner"? I don't know. Anyway, we've been together for a while now, and it's wonderful. I didn't want to say anything before because, well, I didn't know if it was going to work out. We're actually going to come up north together, so you'll be able to meet him. I'm sure you'll like him. I hope so.'

Elin stares at her phone as if it's about to bite her.

'Elin? Are you still there? I didn't want to spring it on you, but . . . Elin?'

'Dad's got a girlfriend.'

This time, there is a silence at the other end of the phone.

'Oh! Well, that's nice!' Klara gives that funny little laugh again.

'Yeah. She's my teacher. One of them.'

'Oh! So, do you like her?'

'Yeah. She's great.'

Elin has yet to sit in the same room as her dad and Marylen in their new incarnation as two people who are involved with each other, but it feels important to say this.

'Well, that's great. I hope you'll like Mikkel. He's been really good for me. He's wonderful – he's really supportive. You know, emotionally.'

'Right.'

'We're flying up to Bodø on Monday. We're staying in Fauske.'

'Why aren't you staying here?'

'Oh, I don't think your father—'

'I mean in Sulis. There's a hotel just down the road.'

'Well, Mikkel is going to be doing some work, so it makes sense to be based in Fauske.'

'What does he do?'

'He's a journalist. But I'll hire a car and can pop over to see you any time.'

'What's he doing here?'

'Well, he's working on a story for a Sunday paper. But I'll be completely free, so we can spend some proper time together.'

'How did you meet him?'

'Er, through friends. We've been seeing each other for six months, now.'

'Oh. Are you going to see *Bestemor*?'

'I don't know. Maybe.'

@VelociTazz:

—God. Mum's coming up tomorrow!

Here!!!

—*Weary-cat-face emoji*

@Supertwink3000:

—Wow.

—That's nice – right?

—Suppose. Also weird

—Why weird?

—She's got a boyfriend.

—Wow. Well that's good ?? – if she's happy?

—She's bringing him with her.

—Maybe he'll be nice??

—Maybe

—*Spiral-eyes emoji*

—Actually, sounds like he's bringing her –
he's working in Fauske & they're staying
in the hotel

—K

—He's a journalist

—Ohhhh. What's he working on?

—She didn't say. Can only be one thing,
right?

Benny says, 'You think he's coming up here because he's writing about Daniel and the Iron-Mine Man?'

They are now talking on the phone, the conversation having become too complex for texting.

'Well, what else is happening in Fauske?'

'It could be lots of things – maybe he's writing about ... fish farming ... or marble. I mean, it could be anything.'

'But coming now? When there are all those TV vans going up to Nilsbakken and it's on the news ...'

'Well, you'll find out. And does it matter why he's coming? I mean, it's just nice that your mum's coming up – that's the main thing.'

'Yeah. Suppose.'

'It'll be fine.'

'I'm just ... I don't know.'

'Yeah. It'll be okay, El.'

'Mmm. There's another thing . . .'

'What?'

She sighs. 'Dad's just told me not to tell Mum about him and Marylen. But I'd already told her, because she told me about her boyfriend.'

'And, so, is he cross?'

'I didn't tell him. He made such a big deal about it, I didn't know what to say. But now he's going to find out.'

'Well, that's not your fault. He can't be cross with you about it.'

'But I don't know how to tell him, now.'

Benny sighs. 'El? Are you crying?'

She shakes her head, which of course he can't see.

Klara suggested picking Elin up after school, but Elin refused. She thought it would be easier to meet on neutral territory, so she says goodbye to Benny in the car park and walks to the café where they have arranged to meet. Klara is sitting at a table in the window, but she jumps to her feet when Elin comes in. Her mum seems to have made an effort to look nice – smart, dark jeans and an expensive-looking sweater, and she's wearing make-up. Also, her hair is neater than usual. She smiles at Elin and holds out her arms. Elin leans in for a brief hug, and Klara kisses her on the cheek.

'It's so lovely to see you.'

'You, too. Is that new?' She indicates the small gold necklace at Klara's throat. It's not the style of jewellery her mum usually wears, which is, well, cheaper.

'Oh, this? Yes. Quite new. I like your hair like that.'

'So do I.'

'When did you cut it off?'

'A few months ago? Where's Mikkel?'

'He's back at the hotel. I wanted it to be just the two of us, for now. I know it must have been a bit of a shock, telling you over the phone like that.'

Elin shrugs. 'S'okay.'

They sit down, and Klara smiles at the server.

'What do you want to have?' she asks Elin.

'Can I just have oat milk and biscuits?'

'Do you have that?'

The server explains that they have organic cakes or oatmeal cookies, which they make in the kitchen here. But they don't serve brand biscuits.

Elin, trying to be on her best behaviour, agrees to the cookies, but they turn out to contain dried coconut and raisins, neither of which she likes.

'What about the lemon cake?' asks Klara. 'You used to like lemon cake.'

'No, I didn't. Oda likes lemon cake.'

'Well, sweetie, I think you should eat something.' By now, Klara is looking alarmed. 'If you want, we can always go back to the hotel. I'm sure they have biscuits.'

'No, it's okay. I'll have the sponge cake, please.'

Between Elin and her mum, there is always this awkwardness: Klara trying to accommodate her daughter (to show that she can); Elin trying not to need accommodating (to show that she's not a monster). But it's hard to keep the conversation going. They usually end up talking about her sister, Oda, as this is an uncontroversial subject of interest to both of them. Her mother seems keen to tell her that, these days, she sees Oda as little as she sees Elin.

'I mean, I think she's happy, don't you?' Klara says, talking about Oda's job working on a cruise ship. 'She says she likes it. I hope so.'

'She's doing what she wants, isn't she? Dancing. And going around the Caribbean. Sounds all right.'

'Yes, that must be lovely – although, I don't think she gets to see very much of wherever they go. And working on a cruise ship isn't the height of her ambition. I think she'd like to get a permanent position in a good contemporary company. But, for that, she'll have to come back and start auditioning again.'

'There must be loads more dancers than there are jobs like that.'

'Yes. It's very competitive.'

'What if she's, you know, not good enough?'

'Elin!' Klara gives an admonishing laugh. 'You know your sister's very talented.'

'Do I? I can't really tell. I mean, she seems good, but what do I know?'

Klara sighs. 'I'm sure, if she really wants to, she'll get there.'

Elin can't help herself. 'Mum, come on, that's just not true, is it?'

'Elin, please . . .'

'Everyone says, if you really, really want something, you'll achieve it, but obviously that's rubbish. I mean, millions of people want to be Beyoncé, but they aren't.'

'I don't think that's the case. I think people want to succeed in their own way.'

'Yeah, but they can't all succeed to the same degree, can they? And it totally ignores systemic inequality. Millions of people in the world today are the same age as me, and presumably they all have dreams, but how can we all succeed equally? Lots of them get blown up or don't have enough to eat, or can't get an education. Some of those dreams will be in direct competition – thousands of people want to play in the Norwegian football team, but most of them won't. There isn't the space. Even most normal jobs are going to disappear in the next few years, so what are we all going to do? We're surplus to requirements.'

'That's absolutely not true. You're certainly not surplus to requirements, sweetie.'

'Aren't I? I mean, the world would be far better off if lots of people like me didn't exist.'

'God, Elin, that's ... that's quite a bleak vision. Who on earth is saying that to you?'

'Not a person. The evidence. The news. I mean, just look around.'

Klara smiles apologetically at the rest of the café and pushes her hand, palm up, across the table for Elin to take, if she wants to. Elin is surprised at her own words. On the way to the café, she had determined that she was going to be pleasant and grown-up, but her mother always ends up saying something so monumentally stupid, she can't stop herself. Platitudes are the things she hates more than anything. *If you dream it, you can be it*, and all that nonsense. Well, clearly, no. I mean, look at Daniel ... what about his dream? Presumably it wasn't to disappear without trace (or was it?). What about Great-Aunt Nordis?

She looks at her mother's hand reaching towards her. Klara has rings on almost every finger and each ring has a cheap crystal – amethyst for healing, black tourmaline for protection, rose quartz for love. In the past, she has given Elin crystal bracelets as presents, but Elin doesn't wear them, because bracelets irritate her and, let's face it, they're just stupid bits of rock. She didn't tell Klara this. She wishes it were easy to put out her hand and touch her mother's, but it isn't. Her own hand seems to have turned to stone.

'Well, anyway . . .' Her mother turns the hand gesture into fiddling with the menu card. 'I thought I might take you clothes shopping while I'm here. We could go to Bodø. I'll buy you something nice. What do you think?'

Elin says, 'You mean, like, a dress?'

'Whatever you like. I was thinking, there must be parties you want to go to.'

'Dad told you, didn't he? That I'm . . . genderfluid.'

Elin really tries to hold eye contact when she says the word, but it's difficult. Klara drops her gaze first. Actually, she leans back in her chair as if avoiding something, averts her gaze and sort of laughs.

'He mentioned it, but—'

'Is that why you're here? Did he ask you to come?'

'No, he didn't ask me to come! And I think it's fine . . . however you want to be. I haven't come up here to make you wear a dress, Elin.'

Elin looks down, now. Nods.

Klara lowers her voice confidentially: 'I've been reading about it, you know, online. Those links you gave to Dad – he sent them on to me. I love you. I hope you know that. If you want to change your name, I'll still love you. If you want to be "they", I'll try really hard to call you that, and I'll still love you.'

'Okay.' Elin nods. Is she supposed to thank her?

'And, you know, if you wanted to transition, I'd—'

'God, Mum – I don't, okay! I'm just, you know, this is what I am. Jesus.'

Her mum smiles. 'Don't let your father hear you blaspheme.'

'He's fine with it, actually.' Elin feels defensive on her father's behalf.

'Do you want to talk about it? The, er, gender . . . thing?'

'I mean . . . as long as you know, then, not really. It just feels right for me. I feel less . . . trapped.'

'Did you feel trapped being a girl?'

'Well, yeah. It's shit, isn't it? I mean, if you got to choose, why would you choose all that?'

Klara smiles a bit. 'Well . . . I don't think it's always easy being a boy, either.'

'I'm not choosing to be a boy. I'm choosing something else. Something without all the crap.'

There is a silence. Elin looks round and catches the eye of a woman at the next table, who quickly looks away. She feels a thrum of wild energy coursing through her body.

'Well, it's good that you feel less trapped. How is it at school?'

Elin shifts in her chair. 'I haven't told that many people, at the moment. But it's not a big deal. I'm not the only one.'

'Oh? Okay. Is Benny . . . genderfluid, too? You're still friends, aren't you?'

Elin acknowledges that they are. 'No. He likes being a boy, but he's not constrained by old gender rules.'

'Oh. Good for him. Well, I'm just glad that you're happy.'

Klara smiles and Elin sketches a smile in return. Although, perhaps 'happy' is putting it a little too strongly.

'I'd love you to meet Mikkel at some point, but it's absolutely whenever you're ready. You know, we could walk over to the hotel now and . . . or we can leave it for another time.'

'I think I'd rather—'

'No, of course. Of course. Some other time. He's really looking forward to meeting you.'

'Is he? Why?'

'Well, because you're my daughter . . . you're important to me.'

'What if he doesn't like me? Most people don't.' She glares at Klara from under her fringe.

'Sweetie, that's not true! And Mikkel's very easy-going.'

Elin nods again, but the prospect of meeting Mikkel is terrifying. She is suddenly immensely tired. Not having her usual after-school snack makes her feel all wrong.

'Can I go home, now?'

'Of course. I'll get the bill.'

Thirty

Eskil is nervous about seeing Klara. It's been nearly a year since they last met, and that was last summer, when he took Elin to Oslo to stay with her. He always feels this apprehension, but in Oslo he has some semblance of control. She only sees what he permits her to see – an Eskil that is well dressed, busy, has things to do. And he has always previously felt – admit it – that he occupied the moral high ground, which is where he feels at home. Now, he's not so . . . comfortable. Technically, he's an adulterer, which will make Klara laugh when she finds out. He is dating their daughter's teacher – is that even ethical? He can't see that it isn't ethical, precisely, but it still makes him uneasy. At least – and he only knows this thanks to Elin – Klara is in Fauske with *her* new boyfriend, so she can't play the martyr on that front. He thought maybe she wouldn't even come to the house, the home they shared for more than ten years. So, she wouldn't be able to look around and judge him. It strikes him that, soon, he will have lived here longer without her than with her.

But Klara's rental car is drawing up in front of the house, and his ex-wife and Elin are getting out. Earlier, Eskil put on the new sweater that Marylen gave him, and, although he is now too hot, he doesn't want to take it off and reveal the old shirt beneath, so he'll have to suffer. To his critical eye, Klara looks sophisticated, for her. Subtly different. Perhaps this is the effect of the Oslo boyfriend – who, thank God, is not in the car with them.

The best form of defence being attack, he goes outside to meet them.

'Klara, hello.'

'Hello, Eskil. How are you?'

They embrace and kiss each other on the cheek, because they feel they should. Eskil notices that Klara is wearing perfume – something unfamiliar. He can't remember her ever wearing perfume when they were together, although this was partly – latterly, anyway – because strong smells made baby Elin scream her head off.

Elin walks past them into the house with barely a mumble of goodbye. Eskil raises his eyebrows in apology for her lack of manners.

'Fine. And you? You look well,' he says.

'Thanks. So do you.'

He indicates their vanished child. 'Was she okay?'

'Oh, yes. Yes. She was great.'

There is a pause. Eskil wonders if Klara is expecting to be invited in. He doesn't feel up to that just yet.

Klara says, 'I was wondering if, maybe, we could invite you for dinner while we're here? You could meet Mikkel, and, you know –' she gives him a coy glance – 'you could bring your girlfriend?'

Eskil opens his mouth and, for a second, nothing comes out. 'Yes, why not? That would be nice. Maybe at the hotel? Although that might not be up to your Oslo standards! Or – in Fauske there are probably more options . . .'

'Yes, that would be . . . I need to talk to Mikkel and call you, find a good evening. He's got a very busy week, but he should have sorted his schedule by tomorrow, so, yeah . . .'

Eskil wonders if this is intended as a sting – the Oslo boyfriend's important schedule a heavier weapon than his mere pastoral duties. 'What's he doing up here?'

'He's a journalist. He's writing a story about the, er . . . about all the things that have been going on here recently.'

Eskil can't keep the disapproval out of his voice: 'Oh? That's a very sensitive subject. Everyone from Fauske to Nilsbakken has been affected by the boy's disappearance, and now with this – with the body in the mine, as well . . . It's very upsetting for people. Very upsetting. We're normally so quiet and peaceful.'

'I think that's the point – how tragic events can hit a remote place like this, and how people are coping. There's a lot of interest, nationally. It's going to be a proper, in-depth feature.'

'I hope he knows to tread carefully.'

'Oh, absolutely. He's a very experienced writer – very sensitive. Media attention can really help in a missing person's case, or where they're trying to identify, you know . . . They haven't got an identity yet, have they?'

'Not as far as I know.'

'When you meet him, you'll see. He's a really good person.'

'Well . . . good! I'd better let you get back. It's a long drive.'

'Yes. So, I'll ring you about a date? Are there any evenings you can't do, or do you need to check with, er . . . ?'

'Why don't you suggest a couple of options?'

She nods. 'Okay. It's good to see you, Eskil.'

She smiles and steps backwards, and the old Klara, who has been

238

hiding somewhere in the background, is suddenly visible – less confident than this smartly-dressed Oslo woman, unsure, desperate for approval. And he feels a twinge of the old protectiveness. He wants to shield her from everything harsh, even if that includes his own judgement.

'Hey. Can you talk?'

It's much later, Elin is in bed – or should be. Eskil has allowed himself to stretch out on the sofa, feet up, staring out of the window to where the midnight sunlight is caressing the mountain behind the house.

Marylen says, 'Yeah, it's fine. Petter's gone to bed. I'm in the living room. Finished all my marking.'

'I expect you've heard that Klara's arrived.'

'Yes. Elin went off to meet her after school. Is everything okay?'

'Yes. It's fine. I mean, I never know what to say when I see her, but, apart from that . . .'

Marylen laughs. 'I'm sure you were marvellous.'

'Turns out, ha ha, she already knew about you and me. Elin must have told her.'

'Well, that's okay, isn't it?'

'I . . . yes. Yeah, it's fine. But now she wants us all to have dinner – her and Mikkel and me and you.'

'Wow. Really? Bold move.'

'Will you come? Please? Not here – it'll be on neutral territory. In Fauske, probably. So we can, you know, leave early.'

Marylen laughs at this. 'Sure. Why not?'

Eskil feels a warm rush of relief. He wasn't sure she would agree to come. They haven't really been out in public together, so sitting in a

STEF PENNEY

restaurant with another couple is tantamount to placing an announcement in the paper. Although, as Marylen says, who in the world is going to care? Sometimes he can't believe his luck. For a long time, he lived with the leaden certainty that he was going to spend the rest of his life alone. Not because he wasn't interested in a relationship – he just thought it could never happen to him, because he would never get it right. Truth is, his marriage to Klara was the only long-term relationship of his life, and that had ended in spectacular failure. Of course, he can look back now and see how unsuited they were, but he has often been drawn to unsuitable women. There was that time, years ago, when he fell violently in love with Benny's mother, and even fantasised about them setting up home together. It would be wonderful: their children were already the best of friends, and she was so pretty and sexy – and free, somehow. Not like Klara; certainly not like him. Hard to believe, now, how much he had worshipped Toril Iversen from afar. It would never have worked, him being a vicar, and her a pagan who's into all sorts of New Age spiritual nonsense. He kept his feelings secreted, never gave her the slightest sign, because it was clear she didn't even like him. She found him dull and desperately conventional. He can smile about it now, because perhaps, at last, his luck has changed.

Marylen is still smiling when she hangs up. The dinner will probably be awful, but they've set up a safe word for when either of them can't bear it any longer. Their safe word is 'pineapple', as in: 'I wonder if they have pineapple for dessert.' They agree it is very unlikely there will be pineapple. And she is curious to meet Klara again. She hasn't laid eyes on her since Klara left Sulis, ten years ago. They hadn't known each other well; they weren't close neighbours and both had their hands full with their domestic challenges. Marylen was in the trenches of coping with Petter and Nora, as well as teaching. She hadn't been the best teacher in those years – something that makes her sad, but most of the time she was so tired she could hardly see to drive home (and, really, hadn't wanted to go home) – it's a miracle that she didn't write off the car and herself in one of the tunnels, or drive into a lake. No matter how hard she tried not to, she would look at other mothers – the mothers at the school – and feel a grinding resentment. They would complain about their sweet, annoying, normal children, the dimmest of whom had expectations of an independent life. And she would look at Klara, whose eldest, Oda, was a near contemporary of Nora's. Oda was bright and outgoing – everything you'd want a child to be, everything that Nora never would be. Still, she heard how people spoke about lucky Klara in low voices: how she struggled to cope with her younger daughter (you should try mine, Marylen used to think), but then Klara was known to have 'issues' and to be 'fragile' – but wasn't that husband of hers a saint . . . ?

Eskil might not be a saint (this makes her smile some more), but he is a good man. Yes.

Thirty-one

These days, people are always telling me that mobile phones are like Big Brother in *1984*, that it's terrifying how 'they' know everything about us – our habits, spending, predilections, politics . . . you name it. Elin has a lot to say about the invasion of our privacy by shadowy corporations and how a smartphone is basically like the electronic tags they fasten around the ankles of criminals, but that doesn't stop her from using one.

At the weekend, the police found Daniel Fjordholm's phone in a road tunnel up the valley – Sjønståfjell. Nothing else, apparently, just the phone itself, which was, they think, thrown from a car. They managed to resuscitate the phone, and checked its location and call records and dusted it for prints – or whatever they do to these things – but it doesn't seem to have helped in their search for the boy. There is patchy signal in the mountains, so they can't be sure where the phone was, nor for how long, before it ended up in the dirt on the tunnel floor. Perhaps phones are not so sinister, after all.

Odd Emil tells me all this while we sit on a bench on the waterfront, with cardboard beakers of takeaway coffee. Horrible – I detest the feel of cardboard on my mouth – but he wanted us to sit where we would not be overheard, and so here we are. It is warm enough, I must admit, and the light off the water and the play of the fountain is dazzling – so bright, in fact, that it has the effect of making me feel light-headed. Maybe I should look into getting those darkening glasses, vanity be hanged.

'Ach. What am I supposed to do with this?'

The seat we are sitting on has a slight camber, so there is nowhere for me to set down my coffee, and Asta is restless and her leash is tugging on my wrist.

'You're supposed to hold on to it.'

'Well, I need to put it down.'

'Oh, give it to me.' Odd Emil sounds cross, but he relieves me of the beaker.

I unwind Asta's leash, thinking I'm going to have a bruise round my wrist and I'll look like a battered wife, and then she finally chooses to flop to the ground and rests her nose on my shoe. I hold out my hand for the coffee.

'I thought you didn't like it.'

He doesn't look at me as he gives it back.

'I've paid for it. I'm damned if I'll let it go to waste.'

'Actually, I paid for it.'

'And I wouldn't dream of disrespecting your generosity.'

He sighs gustily.

'People do lose their phones,' I say, again. 'And, if you wanted to run away, you'd have to get rid of it, wouldn't you? Maybe he threw it out of the car himself. It doesn't mean . . .'

Odd Emil says, 'How soon did you know, with Nordis? You said you knew.'

He means, when did I know that she was dead.

'I suppose it was after a few days. But it's not the same. It was just a feeling, and I might have been wrong.'

'But you weren't wrong.'

'Oh, who knows? Maybe she's living it up in Panama.'

'Do you think?'

I sip my coffee and decide not to answer. I'm not sure why he continues to seek me out, these days, when he finds everything I say so annoying. I'm clearly not providing him with solace or comfort, or even distraction. We stare at the fountain out in the bay – at least, I do. It sprouts out of the quiet fjord like an incongruous white palm tree. Or like someone has dropped a bomb in the water. Local businesses pay for it. It is supposed to beautify the harbour and increase the town's tourist appeal – ironic, really, when all they needed to get people flocking here was a missing boy and a long-dead body in a mine. The hotel and holiday rentals are booked solid, the restaurants are booming. The streets are awash with news crews and journalists.

Odd Emil says, 'I find it hard to be around Maria. She wants me to go with her in her crazy ideas. She's always going on about some kid or other in America who vanished and then turned up three years later. Sometimes I find myself wanting to shout at her, "You have to stop!" It can't be good for Sindre and Vivi for her to obsess like this.'

Since the phone turned up, he seems to have given up all hope that Daniel is alive. I'm not sure why this has convinced him.

'It's only been a couple of weeks.'

'Seventeen days.'

'Still. It's not that long.'

He finishes his coffee and then deliberately crushes the cardboard

244

cup in one hand, mashing it to a crumpled mess. I can't look away, mesmerised by this small, pointless act of violence.

'God, I'm so ... angry, Svea. I'm so angry and I don't know what to do.' He stares at the destroyed cup, as if he's surprised how it got to be like that.

'Sometimes there is nothing to be done.'

He gives this remark the attention it deserves. 'I wish ...' He sighs and hurls the cup away.

Sacrilege – I'll have to pick it up before we leave.

'Do you know what I hate the most in all this?' he says.

'What?'

'I hate going to bed alone.'

This is not the answer I was expecting, so I don't say anything. I suppose, when you have lived with someone dear to you for decades, you never truly get used to their absence.

The silence between us stretches, elongates, solidifies. It develops its own peculiar character. Asta lifts her head, as if she's listening for something.

'Svea, will you come home with me?'

'What for?'

'Tonight. Will you come home with me tonight?'

'Christ!' I can't believe my ears. 'What good will that do?'

'Svea ... Svea ...' His voice is so quiet, it's barely an exhale. The last deflation of a punctured tyre.

'What's got into you?'

'What's got into me? How can you ask that?'

'Okay, I meant—'

'I don't want to be alone anymore with this – pain.'

'And I'm ... convenient? What am I – an aspirin? Did everyone younger turn you down?'

'Dammit, Svea! You know how I feel about you. I love you.'

It is extremely shocking to hear him say this. It's also not the tone of voice in which you want to hear those words spoken – irritated and resentful.

'I know no such thing! We meet for coffee. Since when is that the mark of undying devotion? Is that why you bought me a coffee? Am I supposed to owe you?'

Odd Emil sighs with the about-to-snap patience of a parent with a whining child – just like I used to do with Klara. 'And you love me.'

I let out a snort. 'Well, thank you for telling me my own mind. Obviously, I can't judge that for myself.'

'Svea, for God's sake, it's you and me. And it's been years. Years! Why can't we ... comfort each other, after all this time?'

Because . . . I want to say.

Because.

But I'm speechless. I can't think of a reason, except for the most obvious one. Because you want a wife, or at least someone kind and caring. Whereas, when I try to care for people, I damage them beyond repair.

I start to stand up – not a speedy operation, at my age – and Odd Emil puts a hand on my arm, which is enough to disrupt my precarious balance, so I just have to sit there.

'How long do you think we have left, Svea?'

'What?'

'How long? How much longer are you going to be alive?'

'Good God. I don't know, but I'm not going to sit on this bench any longer.'

'You want to be alone and cranky until you die? Just you and Asta, because she can't answer back and that's just how you like it? God forbid anyone should criticise you or challenge you! Well, when you die – *alone* – you'll decompose in that fancy conservatory that no one is ever allowed in and your precious dog will end up eating your face.'

By now, he has let go of my arm, so I stand up, feeling more light-headed than ever. I collect myself for a moment, not looking at him. I'm trembling with rage.

'I'll live longer than you. How I choose to live and die is entirely up to me. And if Asta wants to eat any part of me, she is more than welcome.'

I can hear his breathing – fast and raspy. Maybe he's ill. He's obviously losing his marbles. Sometimes grief can do that: tip an elderly person over the edge.

'Don't you care that your daughter is in town and hasn't even rung you?'

This stops me in my tracks. Not fair, I think. Not fair. He should know better.

I wind the leash slowly around my hand, although Asta is stock still, waiting for me. Good girl.

'Come on, Asta.'

Odd Emil doesn't say anything else as I walk away. I'd like to say that I stride off with a majestic gait, head held high, but my hip is hurting like hell, so a stately shuffle has to do, past the crushed coffee cup lying on the ground. I consider retrieving it, as a pointed reproach, but my hip hurts too much. He can pick up his own damn litter. I don't look back. I don't know if he turns to watch me. I suspect not.

By the time I make it home, my phone is ringing. I ignore it. I need

247

to take a pill and go to bed. With a drink. But it rings again, and again, and in the end I put on my glasses and peer at it, because maybe he's calling to apologise. But it's not him.

'Hello, Mum.'

Her voice is brittle and youthful. It hasn't changed at all since she was sixteen, and, for a moment, I can't breathe.

I should have realised there would be an ulterior motive. Klara asks if I would agree to be interviewed by her boyfriend, a journalist who is working on a 'serious, in-depth article' about our recent dramatic events. He is speaking to a cross-section of the town's inhabitants to find out how our small community has been impacted. I suppose I represent the 'old' section. I can't think I will have anything of interest to say, but I agree to it, because – well, as Klara implies – granting her this favour is the least I can do. It will be one small drop to counter-balance the ocean of crap I left her with.

So, here they are, my daughter and her new beau, sitting in my nice conservatory – see, Odd Emil? It's not true that no one comes in here – and I study them both. Klara looks older, but then, she is a middle-aged woman, and I haven't laid eyes on her for – well, it doesn't matter. I see her so rarely that her appearance is always a shock, but I don't say anything. I suppose my mind has preserved her as her just-leaving-home teenage self, although she was always very young-looking; even when she was in her thirties and the mother of two children, there was something of the waif about her, something not quite complete. She has lost that unfinished look at last, which is a good thing, and she has ... solidified somehow. This is not a catty way of saying she has aged and put on weight; she just seems more definite and at ease with herself. I am relieved. It has taken decades, but it is what I always wanted for her. I know whose fault it was that it didn't happen before.

The beau is called Mikkel something-or-other. Looking at him, I would guess that he's slightly younger than Klara, and he's well turned out, although he appears to have forgotten to shave and his jaw glints with brown and silver. Perhaps it's a deliberate choice that is supposed to send a message, along with the trendy T-shirt and suit jacket, and the trousers which have lots of unnecessary pockets. What it's all meant to convey, I'm not sure – probably that he is successful yet unconventional; he is casual and approachable. To me, he is trying a little too hard. He is good-looking, though.

I've made a cafetière of coffee and brought out some biscuits, which Asta stares at without blinking. It doesn't work with me, but she always tries it on with other people. I try to remember if Asta has met Klara before, but, frighteningly, I can't.

'This is a beautiful conservatory, Ms Hustoft,' says Mikkel. 'And are those grapes? Wow.'

'They don't really ripen, here,' I say. 'But I like the leaves. And I hate "Ms Hustoft". Sounds like a primary-school teacher. Everyone calls me Svea.'

'Okay, er, thank you. Is this the local marble? It's lovely.'

He talks on easily, and I find myself warming to him. Obviously, it's part of his job to put people at ease, but he's good at it. It feels natural.

Klara puts down her coffee, only half drunk.

'Well, I'm going to go for a walk. I'll leave you to it.'

A glance flashes between her and Mikkel, and he smiles. She picks up her shoulder bag and says a casual, 'See you later,' which I assume is meant for him. I don't ask if she's coming back.

'Do you mind if I record our conversation?' He takes a small device out of his pocket.

'I'm sure you've heard plenty of stories about me and Klara's miserable childhood.'

Mikkel smiles again, this time in acknowledgement. 'I know you're doing this as a favour to Klara, but I appreciate it. I'm not here to talk about that. I have a pretty complicated background of my own, and I know there's more than one side to every family story.'

'Aren't you diplomatic.'

He shrugs. 'I suppose I have to be, but I mean it.'

'Well . . . I don't mind – record away. Though, as I said to Klara, I don't know what I can tell you. I have no privileged information.'

'That's not what I'm after. It's a picture of the town and the mood, I suppose – the atmosphere.'

'Right.'

I'm not going to tell him I am friends with Daniel's grandfather. Klara doesn't know. And maybe we're not anymore, anyway.

It has been years since anyone other than Odd Emil asked me for my opinion about anything, and I find myself enjoying this. When you're retired, most younger people treat you like a borderline idiot: deaf, weak-minded, and probably racist to boot. But Mikkel seems genuinely interested, empathic, a careful listener. I have to keep reminding myself that there is no way he doesn't think I'm a terrible person, but it doesn't show. Quite the opposite, in fact. He gives the impression that he finds me insightful and intelligent. Of course, that's his job. I know I shouldn't say too much – nothing too personal, nothing about Odd Emil or Elin – but there is something about him that makes me want to unburden myself. I fight against it. Perhaps Klara has set this all up simply so that he can harvest more evidence of my monstrousness. But this is unlikely, because she already has far more than she could ever need.

'Have you spoken to anyone in the police?' I ask, during a rare lull in the conversation.

He says, 'I'm trying to get an interview with the head of the case, but they're very busy. Wary, as well, which is understandable. I know there have already been quite a few journalists around.'

'I've been told that someone is planning a podcast. There's been a lot of attention – and even more since they found this . . . other body.'

'I can imagine,' he says. 'It's an extraordinary thing. Do you have any thoughts about that? You were living here at the time, weren't you?'

'I don't think we know what "the time" was, do we?'

'Sorry, I just mean that . . . Klara told me you worked at Sulitjelma Gruber until 1968, is that right? And they think that whoever the body belongs to must have gone into the tunnel – in whatever way that was – after the mines closed in 1968.'

'Well, I left before the mine shut down for good. I moved away.'

I don't know why I said that – it's a stupid lie to tell, and something that could be easily checked, but why would he bother? I don't like to think about that time. I don't like to think about any part of my early life.

'I can barely remember, it's such a long time ago. Then I went to Germany. Perhaps you know about that, too.'

Mikkel nods. If he knows about Sulitjelma Gruber, then presumably he knows about my *naziyngel* status and the futile search for my father.

'Before you left, you don't remember hearing any stories of anyone going missing? That sort of gossip tends to stick in the mind.'

'Goodness. Well, you should know that, in the run-up to sixty-eight, the Nilsbakken mines were losing money hand over fist. Several hundred miners were made redundant, and most of them left the area around that time. It would be easier to say who didn't go missing.' I shake my head. 'I can't recall anything like that. I worked there less than a year.'

'What made you leave?'

I shouldn't have volunteered that, either, but there were many reasons for my leaving. All I have to do is pick one.

'A common problem – my boss kept trying it on with me. In those days, we didn't complain about that sort of thing. There was no point.'

'Ah! I see.' He nods and frowns sympathetically, as if this has also happened to him, and perhaps it has. 'And what about your friends – contemporaries? Are they speculating about who it could be?'

I would put money on Klara having told him that I don't have any friends, but his face looks innocent enough.

'If they are, they're not doing it in front of me. We don't know anything yet – not when he died, or . . .'

At last, Mikkel runs out of steam. I made a fresh cafetière of coffee, but that has grown cold and the sun has wheeled round until it is touching the marble tiles on the wall behind me. We sit in a box of rosy light.

'Well, I mustn't keep you any longer, Svea. You've been wonderfully generous with your time. I hope I haven't tried your patience too much.'

'Oh, no. No one asks me what I think, normally. It's refreshing.'

His phone buzzes as he turns off his little red-eyed machine, and I realise that he has orchestrated our talk down to the minute. That'll be Klara, texting to find out if he's finished with the old witch, or if my baneful influence has reduced him to an empty husk.

'So, what now – more interviews?' I ask, as I walk him to the front door.

He has left his card on the table in the conservatory, 'in case you think of anything else.' Like a policeman. The nerve.

'I'm going back to the hotel, and I need to transcribe this.' He waves his gizmo.

'Don't you have . . . typists to do that sort of thing?'

'God, no. We do everything ourselves. Well, actually, I've got a program that does it automatically. I just plug it in. Well . . .' He turns on the doorstep.

In the street outside, there's no sign of Klara. I suppose she doesn't want to run the risk of seeing me again.

'It's been a genuine pleasure to talk to you, Svea.'

'Huh,' I say, although I shake the hand he holds out.

'No, it really has. If you would like me to say anything to Klara to try and ameliorate things – well, you have my number.'

'I don't think that would be very wise.'

He smiles at me and I smile back, and that is that.

Thirty-two

They're in the car again. Marylen is driving faster than usual because she has to drop them off at home and then go back to Fauske. She's going out to dinner with Elin's dad and mum and Elin's mum's new boyfriend, which sounds like literally the worst date ever. Elin was invited to join them, but declined. She has chosen instead to stay at Benny's overnight – a good move. Elin has seen her mum a couple of times already this week, but hasn't said much about it, other than that they're going clothes shopping in Bodø on Saturday, and that, yeah, she seems okay with the whole genderfluid thing.

They're approaching the Sjønståfjell tunnel. They do this every morning and every afternoon, but, since the police found Daniel's phone, it feels like a different place. Benny never shared Elin's anxiety about diving into its dark mouth, but now he finds himself tensing as they approach, and Marylen seems to put her foot down, as if she too wants to get it over with. Everyone knows the police have searched the tunnel – all the tunnels, in fact – and didn't find anything else. Or, if they did, they're keeping quiet about it. But the questions raised by the abandoned phone hover everywhere, especially here.

Benny doesn't know exactly where in the tunnel the phone was found. The dim rocky tube looks the same as it ever did – bare and grey and inhospitable. It gives nothing away. But they are speeding past the place where 'something' happened. Was it here? Or here? You can't help staring at the walls and wondering. Why is that part of the wall patched with concrete? And that hollow – what has it been used for? It's the same as always, but it isn't, can't ever be again, because of what they know. Yet, the only visible sign that anything untoward happened here is a flutter of police tape, caught on a bush at the other end of the tunnel. At school, people are saying that Daniel ditched the phone so that he could start a new life without being traced, like they do in films. Finding the phone only confirms it. But it doesn't confirm anything. They are saying that because they want it to be true.

After they've eaten supper, he and Elin go to his room and play games, but Benny's heart isn't in it. He puts down his console, vanquished for the third time.

'What's up?'

Sometimes, even Elin can tell something is wrong.

'I'm . . . I've been meaning to say I'm sorry.'

'Who to? To me?'

'Yeah. I've been rubbish – for weeks.'

'I don't think you've been rubbish.'

'I have.'

'No. Why? Benny – you're my normal person.' She looks almost alarmed, and flashes him her shy smile.

'Well, for one thing, I used you. I got you to lie so that I could go and meet David. And I so wish I'd never gone . . . It all got spoilt. I don't even know what I was thinking.'

'You liked him. Even I could tell that. You'd have done the same for me. And I didn't actually have to lie to anyone. So . . . it's fine.' She shrugs.

'I don't know if I did like him. Just the thought of him, now, makes me feel kind of sick. I don't trust myself anymore.'

Elin is silent.

Benny swallows. 'And I never told you, but at Easter he gave me two thousand kroner.'

Elin doesn't say anything, her eyes just widen slightly.

'I meant to send it back, but then I didn't know how, so I've still got it, and I hate myself – because what does that make me?'

'Well . . . did you ask him for it?'

'No! God, of course not! No! He put it in my coat pocket, and I found it after he'd left. But, you know, it's . . . isn't it?'

Elin ponders. 'But you get tips sometimes, don't you? From the guests.'

'Yeah, but not two thousand kroner.'

'So . . . it was a present?'

He shrugs. 'Who gives you money as a present? Your parents. Not friends. Not a boyfriend.' Benny stares fixedly at the ceiling. Maybe, that way, he won't cry.

'What about last time? Did he give you money then, too?'

'No. That time it was more, I don't know . . . He made me dinner. But it wasn't great. I don't think he liked me anymore, if he ever had. He *hated* that I dragged up to go to the party.'

'Well, then, you're better off without him. And he must have liked you. He didn't have to come back. And you liked him, for a while. What's wrong with that? Everyone changes their minds about liking someone – that's normal.'

He wishes she wasn't being so nice, but he doesn't think she understands what he's saying.

'But it's not normal to be interviewed by the police, and have them ask questions like, "Were you coerced?" And they look at me like they think there's something wrong with it! It makes me feel like I let something happen I shouldn't have. Why didn't I see that at the time? What's wrong with me?'

'Nothing's wrong with you. It wasn't coercion, was it? You were happy! Even I could see that. You were so happy, I was jealous.'

Benny shakes his head and feels the tears threaten.

She says, 'I thought you were bored with me.'

That pushes him over the edge. 'Oh, God, Elin, no – I was just being a dick. I could never be bored with you. I'm sorry for being weird and everything. Can you forgive me?' The tears spill down his cheeks.

Very unusually, Elin steps forward and puts her arms around him. 'Of course.'

After a few seconds, he feels her tensing and he lets her go. It's getting late and he pulls the spare mattress out from where it lives under his bed, already made up with a sheet. He gets the spare duvet from the cupboard.

'You said the age thing was creepy.'

Elin shrugs. 'Well, I didn't meet him. I mean, it was bad luck, the way everything turned out, but it wasn't all bad, was it? You got to have sex. Wasn't it nice?'

'Yeah, but I wish . . . That'll always be my first time. It was so nice at first, so exciting, and now it's all spoilt. I just feel ashamed.'

'If it was nice, then it was nice. You have nothing to be ashamed of.'

Benny smooths the duvet over the mattress. 'Sometimes, I see people at school looking at me and whispering, and I think, God, they know about me and David. They know it was me at the cabin. And I want to curl up and disappear.'

'They don't know. The police haven't told anyone, have they?'

He shrugs. 'They said they wouldn't, but . . .'

'People think the witnesses were tourists. They don't know about you. And you know I'll never tell anyone.'

'I know.'

Elin takes the pillow he's been holding and puts it on the mattress.

'You could give the money to charity. If you can't give it back, you know, then do something good with it.'

'That's a good idea.'

'I'm not saying you ought to. Just, you know . . .'

'No, I want to. I think it would make me feel less . . . yeugh.'

'I'm sorry it all got fucked up. It's just bad luck.'

Benny sighs. 'I feel so bad about not saying anything to the police earlier. What if it would have made a difference for Daniel?'

'I don't see how it could.' She looks at him, sensing that there is something else he hasn't said. 'What?'

How to say it? He really doesn't want to.

'The police were here last night.'

A police officer drove all the way out to Sulis to talk to Benny. Not the young officer who does yoga with his mum, but her boss, the one in charge, Hanne Duli Bodøgaard. Benny was doing homework in his room when he heard voices from the hall, then Toril called to him. There was a note in her voice that caused him a twinge of alarm, although, when he came down the stairs, Hanne Duli was smiling at him.

'Hello, Bendik. Nothing to be alarmed about,' she began. 'There are a couple of things I wanted to check with you. Are you okay to talk?'

It was the same as before, only now he was answering questions at the kitchen table and his mum was there. The officer ('Call me Hanne Duli') had a notebook in front of her. Benny had to once again go through the events of that Saturday night, nearly three weeks ago. Talking about it, there was a nasty taste in his mouth – bile, vomit, self-disgust. Hanne Duli kept referring to 'Mr Mæland' – as in, 'where you had previously arranged to meet Mr Mæland' – which made him feel as though he was on trial. He wondered if, when they spoke to David, they referred to him as 'Mr Iversen', which sounds absurd, or as 'Bendik Iversen' . . . or 'Benny' – or that young boy, little tart, gold-digging slut, stupid victim . . . There is no word that makes him feel any better about it.

Hanne Duli checked her notes. 'When you looked out of the window and saw it was the boys from your school, what impression did you get?'

Benny shrugged, eyes on the table. 'I was scared. I thought they knew I was there.'

'Was there anything about them that worried you, in particular?'

'No. Just that they were there – you know. How could it be a coincidence?'

'What was their demeanour? How were they acting? Did you form the impression, for example, that they'd been drinking?'

Benny thought. Actually, it hadn't occurred to him. Wasn't that, in itself, odd? Three Hellraisers, out on a Saturday night in the middle of russ time, not yelling or playing music or generally making as much mayhem as possible?

'I don't know. They were quiet. That's why I thought they were going to prank me. They seemed kind of . . . secretive. But I don't know. It was all over so quickly. From hearing the first car noise until they left – it was two, three minutes at most.'

'Did you hear them say anything?'

He shook his head. 'I think they barely spoke at all. But the window was shut and I couldn't hear. Then they were all in Lorentz's car, driving away.'

Hanne Duli wrote this in her notebook. He tried to read her writing upside down, but couldn't.

'I mean, I don't know about the drinking. I couldn't tell.'

'I understand.'

'It happened so quickly, and at the time we didn't think much of it. I was just relieved. But people have been asking me about it ever since, and it starts to feel . . .'

Hann Duli looked at him keenly. 'Starts to feel what?'

Elin has been listening intently, sitting cross-legged on the mattress and rocking slightly, hugging the pillow to herself.

Benny says, 'You know, I wonder whether I'm remembering what happened on the night, or just remembering the last time I talked about that night. I don't want to get anyone into trouble because I've got it wrong. I feel like I'm going crazy.'

'Did you get it wrong?'

Benny sighs. 'I don't think so.'

'Does she think they had something to do with it – with Daniel?'

He shrugs. 'I don't know, but . . .'

He hadn't asked whether she thought the Hellraisers were 'involved', whatever that slippery word means. Because it's unthinkable, isn't it? They're his best friends. Lorentz and Johnny and Daniel grew up together. Best friends since they were eight. And they took Tobias into their midst in a way that, well, it makes you think that Johnny and Lorentz can't be that bad. They have *Ride or Die* painted on the side of their bus. Even if you don't like them, the one thing you know is that they are devoted to each other. The other thing that's unthinkable is this: if he'd been more alert that night, less worried about himself, would he have realised that something was wrong?

Elin says, 'We know they lied. So, they're hiding something.'

'Yeah, but not necessarily . . .'

They look at each other.

She says, 'Do you think they know where he is?'

The question has been squatting in his head since last night, perhaps longer, but he hasn't wanted to say it out loud, because then he would have made it real.

Thirty-three

The quality of being 'missing' is a strange one. It is not an absolute thing, but a state of relation. The French have it right when they say, *Elle me manque*, meaning, 'I miss her', but, really, 'she is missing to me'. Daniel is 'missing' to his family and friends, but, really, he is either alive and knows very much where he is, or he is dead. Odd Emil believes in his gut that the latter is the case. If you were to ask him how he knows, what makes him so sure that his grandson is no longer alive, he wouldn't be able to give you a reason. He just, somehow, knows.

He can't say this to Maria, who spends most of her time diving down internet rabbit-holes, chatting on forums for the families of vanished teenagers. She is addicted to her computer and phone, can't go for more than a few minutes without checking for messages and updates. She has been talking to people all over Scandinavia, all over the world. Excitedly, she relays stories from America or Britain: cases of children who disappeared for months, even years, and then came back. That case in Australia – seven months. A girl in Peru – three years. This morning, the phone rang before he was even dressed. 'Dad, there was this boy in Poland, just listen . . .' And she reminds him again that Daniel is, technically, an adult – eighteen. Eligible to vote, marry, work, join the armed forces: able, in short, to look after himself.

He has begun to dread her phone calls. Over the past days, she has made huge leaps in her mind. Now, she wants her son to have been desperately unhappy. The thought of his misery comforts her. She imagines for him a life far away, perhaps in another country, where he is happy. Even if he never contacts her again, she seems to find solace in thinking this. Odd Emil wants to believe in this possibility, he really does, but wanting to believe and believing are two different things, and, in the end, what any of them believe is of no consequence at all.

His anger and frustration spilled over with Svea, and now he is angry with himself. Also, with her. Granted, he might not have put it in the best possible way, but surely they have this understanding – they have always known, haven't they? He is only too aware that no one lives forever. For God's sake, he is seventy-five, and she is even older. He seems to hear Daniel reproaching him. *It happened to me – to me – in the blink of an eye, so what are you doing? Don't waste precious seconds. Whatever time you have left,* Bestefar, *you owe it to me . . .*

He isn't too worried about his clumsiness in asking her to spend the night. She'll get over that. Nor is he that worried about confronting her with her lonely death. Svea has always given at least as good as she got. But taunting her about Klara – he shouldn't have said that. That might have been a step too far.

There are many things they have never talked about, because some wounds are too tender, too old, or both. Svea neither questions, nor invites questioning. She doesn't talk about the past. Odd Emil respects that – who is he to start poking and prodding? So, he has never pushed her on her relationship with her daughter, just as he has never asked her about her childhood in the house in Gammelsøy. But recently he has been thinking about it. He has been spending long periods dwelling in his own past, perhaps because, in the present, he feels so helpless. And now, since Iron-Mine Man was pulled from his long sleep inside the mountain, Odd Emil has been trawling his memory for people who went missing years ago, because one of them has now come back.

It is probably no one known to him. Because what are the odds? More than likely Iron-Mine Man was a stranger – a miner from back in the day. Or a drifter who somehow got stuck in the tunnel and fell ill, and no one missed him. Or it could have been from later, after the mine closed, when the housing at Nilsbakken was bought by the church – hadn't it been a retreat of some sort? A boarding school? A pupil, then – an orphan? God, he hopes it's not that.

But.

There is another possibility that he keeps coming back to. He really doesn't want to think about this possibility, but it has a way of tugging at him, popping its head up when he least expects it, and the more he tries to ignore it, the stronger it gets.

Odd Emil has – had – a brother called Trygve, who passed away a few years ago. He was seven years older than Odd Emil. The age difference meant that, when Odd Emil was a small boy, Trygve already seemed grown-up, and he hung on his every word. Trygve was a bit of a tearaway and messed around with some local boys who had reputations as troublemakers. The leader of this gang was a boy called Jens Gulbrandsen. When Odd Emil was seven, Jens must have been about sixteen. In every small community, there is usually one single person behind every bit of trouble, and in Gammelsøy it was Jens.

Today, he would probably be diagnosed with some sort of syndrome – the letters ADHD comes to Odd Emil's mind, although he's not clear what they stand for – but, back then, he was just seen as a bad lot. As a boy, he had been a bully, and Odd Emil was afraid of him. Odd Emil's parents did not approve of the Gulbrandsens, who, in the village pecking order, were on a par with the Øvergaards, or possibly even worse. The father was a drinker and handy with his fists; the mother struggled, and the boys – Jens and his younger brother, Birk – were out of control. They were what people used to term, in the old days, 'the undeserving poor'. Maybe Jens never had a chance . . . but, no, everyone can choose their path, can't they? Birk Gulbrandsen, for example, cleaned up his act and got religion, and thereafter lived a pretty blameless life.

But something terrible happened with the group that involved Jens and Birk and Trygve. This was all so long ago. It must have been the mid-1950s, although Odd Emil did not find out about it until later, when he was himself a teenager, around the time Svea Øvergaard moved away from the village for good. One evening, after school, Odd Emil was helping his father in the store when he heard the noise of a fight in the street outside. He looked up to see Trygve and Jens Gul-brandsen yelling at each other, and then they began to wrestle and exchange blows. Odd Emil watched agog through the window. At first, he thought it must be some sort of roughhousing, but quickly realised it was serious. Then, his dad rushed outside and Odd Emil heard his brother say something like, 'I know what you did!' Jens had an arm around Trygve's neck in a choke hold, but his dad managed to pull them apart. Trygve was coughing and gasping. Jens backed away, blood running from his lip, stabbing his finger at Trygve and saying, 'You won't dare! You're the same as me. You were there.' Something along those lines. Odd Emil was frightened by the aggression on show; he had never witnessed a real fight before, and they were grown men. It was like seeing stags in rut.

Afterwards, his father was very angry. Trygve had to promise that he wouldn't see the Gulbrandsen brothers anymore. Odd Emil found this astonishing, as Trygve was twenty years old, a grown-up. What could be so bad about the Gulbrandsens? Later, he asked Trygve what was going on – in what way was he the same as Jens Gulbrandsen? Trygve shook his head repeatedly, saying it was nothing, none of his business, but Odd Emil badgered him until he gave in. Odd Emil had to swear on his own grave that he wouldn't blab, and then Trygve, clearly longing to unburden himself, told him.

'Jens is a bad man,' said Trygve, which wasn't news. 'But I've done some bad things too.'

'What do you mean? What things?' asked Odd Emil, equal parts fascinated and scared of what he might hear.

Trygve sighed and rubbed his face. 'You know the Øvergaards? You know the eldest – Svea, the one who's just left home?'

Odd Emil nodded and felt a thrill shudder deep inside him. Magny's big sister had recently moved to a city to work. Of course, he was aware of her, but she was a young woman and he was a child. That's how she made him feel.

'You have to understand that this was years ago. Well, Jens persuaded Svea, somehow, to meet him down at the harbour, at one of the net huts. I think he'd made up some story, because she was shocked when she saw the whole gang: there were five or six of us. I had no idea what was going on. It was weird and I was scared.

But I was the youngest one there, and I didn't dare say anything. You know what Jens is like.'

Trygve began to cry; he made strange noises – the harsh, hiccupping breaths of someone who doesn't know how. Odd Emil was aghast, more horrified by seeing his brother in tears than by whatever wicked deed they had enacted on Svea – which he, at thirteen, couldn't really imagine. It took a while for Trygve to tell him that Jens thought it would be funny to lure this little girl – she was ten or eleven at the time – to the net huts and carve a swastika into her forehead.

'Because her real father was, you know, a Nazi,' Trygve added, as if he needed to clarify. As if that could be any explanation.

Odd Emil was dumbstruck. His pubescent imagination had painted some vaguely sexual, titillating naughtiness – not this. Nothing like this. It took a few minutes for the words to sink in and for him to absorb their meaning. He said, hoping to make it go away, 'You mean he drew it on her forehead? With a pen?'

'No. He . . . with a knife. He cut it . . . into her skin.'

He broke down into fresh sobs.

In his mind's eye, Odd Emil saw Svea's face, with blood spilling from the fresh wound. She always wore her hair in a thick fringe that covered her forehead. So, underneath that . . . Jesus Christ.

Odd Emil didn't know what to say, so he didn't say anything. He promised his brother he wouldn't breathe a word to anyone, on pain of death. He could see that his brother was sorry, and he could see that he felt shame. He wasn't sure that was enough.

This is a thing he has known all his life. A sticky burr that clings to the back of his brain, where the shadowy, shameful things live. After that night, the brothers never spoke of it again, because what was the point? Trygve had been a bystander; he was only thirteen, it wasn't his idea, he hadn't touched the knife. But, he admitted, all the boys had held her down while she screamed and the blood ran into her eyes. He had pressed down on one of her skinny arms, surprised by how strong she was and how much she squirmed and struggled. The other boys knelt on her limbs or clamped her head still, pinning her down by her hair. Jens made them all lay hands on her. Odd Emil asked himself if he would have done the same because he was afraid of the consequences of refusing, as Trygve had been – had said he had been. He hoped he would not, but how do you know, really, if you are being honest with yourself?

Soon after that confession, Trygve moved away from the village and life flowed on. The brothers had never had much in common and didn't stay close. Trygve married a woman Odd Emil didn't like and moved down south, and, latterly, joined a right-wing party and complained about immigrants whenever they spoke on the phone. You move on and you try not to think about those memories from long ago, when things were, everyone agrees, different – and, anyway, you can't change the past, can you? You think about what's in front of your nose: your wife and your children, and their joys and sorrows; and time passes and you think about your grandchildren, and their talents and their school grades, and your children's divorces, their successes and mistakes. Then more time passes, and you think about your wife's illness and her slow decline, and then you think about her death.

That was the time when Odd Emil encountered Svea again, in the café in Fauske, when Ann-Karin was dying and he felt utterly lost. Svea's hair had turned white, like his own, but she still wore it in a fringe cut straight and severe across her forehead, just touching her eyebrows. He thought about what was beneath her hair when he approached her. The terrified little girl she must have been. And he knew that he would never force her to go back there.

That is one side of the story that nags at him. The other side of it is this: in the early 1960s, both Jens and Birk Gulbrandsen moved to Sulis, in the valley of the Long Water, and began working for Sulitjelma Gruber. Mining was dirty, dangerous work, but it provided a more reliable living than the sea, and you were slightly less likely to die earning it. By then, no one in Gammelsøy would touch Jens with a bargepole. He'd blotted his copybook too many times before he even left school, with fighting and stealing and vandalism. Jens should have been punished. He was seventeen. He should have gone to prison, or to some reformatory, a place for young offenders. Odd Emil knew in some part of his brain that he should have reported it, but how could he, without getting his own brother into trouble?

Then Odd Emil fell in love with Nordis, and the three sisters were once again present to him. This was in sixty-seven or sixty-eight – which, by the way, was not the Summer of Love in northern Norway. Please don't think that. The hippy revolution happened a long way away, in warmer, less Calvinist places. His relationship with Nordis was intense but chaste; she was seventeen to his nineteen. When she got a job at a hotel in Bodø, Odd Emil would make the tedious journey by boat and bus to see her. It took hours each way. The journey ended up being far longer than the time he had with his sweetheart, but he did this every weekend for months, until things between them suddenly cooled. Nordis made excuses, became unreachable. He didn't know what had happened, if she had met someone else. She just didn't love him anymore.

Through Nordis, he'd known that Svea worked for the mining company at Sulis. He knew she was an 'executive secretary', whatever that was. Nordis told him how glamorously she dressed, told him how she was relentlessly chased by her boss. Possibly even more than Magny, Nordis adored Svea, and her love was fuelled by a fierce protectiveness that was unusual, given their ages, but understandable when you knew what had happened. The only other people who knew what Jens Gulbrandsen had done to Svea were her mother and her sisters. As far as the rest of the village was concerned, one day she had worn her hair pulled back off her face in a ponytail, the next day she had cut a fringe. There were times when he longed to confess to Nordis that he knew about the horrible thing, but couldn't find the words. How could he admit to being aware of something so dreadful, and that his own brother had been involved? He felt guilty just knowing.

After the mass lay-offs in sixty-eight, hundreds of miners and their families moved away from the area. Jens Gulbrandsen was one of them. You might have thought he would turn up to visit his parents once in a while. But the story filtered back to the village that Jens had got a girl pregnant and done a runner rather than face up to his responsibilities. Jens always used to talk about going to America, so probably that's what he did. In those days, when people emigrated, you accepted that you would likely never see them again. To be honest, the general feeling was: good riddance.

You see it now, don't you? Since Iron-Mine Man emerged and became their local celebrity, Odd Emil has been doing a fair amount of burrowing down rabbit-holes himself. Amazing thing, the internet. You can type in a person's name, and gaze, rather blankly, at lists of Facebook profiles for people with that name. More lists on something called LinkedIn. On social media. All sorts of nonsense. Sometimes, there are photographs. Then there are the genealogical websites where you can trace your ancestors, but those Jens Gulbrandsens tend to be long dead. He can't find a Jens Gulbrandsen who seems to be the right age, but that doesn't mean he hasn't lived a long and productive life somewhere. Even if Jens is alive, he will be in his mid-eighties and might not have an internet presence at all. It's not easy to put a suspicious mind at rest, and Odd Emil doesn't have the resources to dig deeper. He could take his suspicions to the police, but, let's face it, that's not going to happen. Because, ever since Maria told him about the man's body in the mine, Odd Emil keeps going back to that time in the late sixties when two people he knew from Gammelsøy both worked for Sulitjelma Gruber, and he can't help wondering: what if Jens Gulbrandsen hadn't gone to America? What if he had never gone anywhere?

Thirty-four

Marylen said she would drive, even though she had to drop Benny and Elin at Toril's house, then go home, before turning round and going out again. She wants to shower and change out of school clothes, because, however silly it is at her age, she can't escape a feeling of competitiveness at the prospect of meeting her boyfriend's ex. Eskil had said that Klara looked 'smart', which sounds ominous. She doesn't want to be the frumpy yokel, so she dresses with care in her favourite green blouse and smart trousers. Applies mascara, puts on earrings and brushes her hair till it shines. She collects Eskil at his house, reassures him that he looks fine. He tells her she looks wonderful. He is nervous. She finds this endearing.

It is something of a relief to walk into the restaurant overlooking the harbour in Fauske and be met by a Klara who looks as uncomfortable as she feels. It has been a decade since they met, but Klara hasn't changed much. She looks older, of course, but not dramatically, and, despite her nervousness, she seems less brittle than in the past. But then, the last time they met, she must have been on the verge of her breakdown. The boyfriend, Mikkel, is a handsome man who dresses rather young for his age, which is more or less what Marylen expects from an Oslo journalist. But he is friendly and garrulous, and easily carries the bulk of the conversation. In fact, he and Marylen do most of the talking. Whenever Marylen catches Klara's eye, Klara smiles quickly before looking away. Eskil doesn't say much either, but then, he's never been a chatterer.

Mikkel asks Marylen about her job at the school – how long she has been teaching, whether she enjoys it . . . and then: 'I expect you know why I'm up here,' he says, with a self-deprecating smile, 'and I would love to ask you about that – not now, of course – but I'm trying to build a nuanced picture of how the community is feeling, and obviously a huge part of that is the school where Daniel is a pupil.'

Next to her, there is a sharp intake of breath from Eskil. Mikkel notices.

'But let's leave that for another time. We're just here to have a nice dinner, right? Although, it must be kind of hard to talk about your job without acknowledging what's happened.'

'Um . . .' says Marylen. 'I don't find it so. Teaching is endlessly fascinating. And, yes, obviously the school is devastated, but I don't think I want to talk about that now.'

'No, of course not, I understand,' says Mikkel. 'This salmon is very good, isn't it?'

Eskil says, 'Is this why you invited us here?'

The question is aimed at Klara. His voice is quiet, but Marylen hears the anger in it.

Klara looks alarmed. 'No, of course not, Eskil. I know Mikkel is here for work, but I just wanted us all to meet.'

'Please,' says Mikkel. 'It's not Klara's fault. It's mine. Sometimes

I get carried away when I'm working on a story. Please, accept my apologies. I'm sorry. Marylen, you said you used to work in Syria – that must have been quite an experience . . .'

Before she can answer, Eskil says, 'Have you spoken to Elin?'

Mikkel and Klara both look at him.

'Have you spoken to Elin about Daniel?'

'No,' says Klara, glancing at Mikkel. 'Of course he hasn't. He's only met her once, briefly, and there was nothing like that. I've told him about her and that he shouldn't ask her about that.'

'But you thought he needed telling?'

Klara gapes at him.

Mikkel says, 'I assure you, Eskil, I wouldn't dream of questioning Elin. I'm not trying to abuse my position here.'

'It seems to me that's exactly what you're doing.'

'Eskil, come on . . .' Marylen puts a hand on his arm, which is rigid with tension.

In a soothing voice, Mikkel says, 'I totally understand your feelings about Elin. I have two kids myself.' He smiles in a way that is presumably meant to look empathic. 'I wouldn't want a journalist asking them about something like this.'

'But Marylen is fair game?' Eskil's voice is edged with diamond dust. It could cut steel.

'Eskil, it's fine. He's apologised. I can look after myself.' Marylen smiles reassuringly at Klara. 'If you want to speak to someone at the school, Mikkel, Helene Shirani-Lund is the person to approach. The deputy head. She's very good.'

Helene, she is sure, will give Mr Fancy-Pants Oslo Journalist short shrift.

274

'Yes. Erm, thank you,' says Mikkel, and she suspects that he has already found that out for himself.

Marylen turns to Klara and smiles at her. 'So, you're training to be a therapist? What sort?'

The conversation is steered into less choppy waters, and they make it to the end of the main course without further drama. Klara opens up about her plans to specialise in autism spectrum disorder. She is relaxed and engaging when discussing a subject on which she is confident. She says she suspects that her own mother is on the spectrum, which might go some way to explaining why their relationship has always been so fraught. Marylen finds herself warming to her, and even, a little, to Mikkel. He listens to Klara talking about her pet subject with intelligent interest, even though he's clearly heard it before. Eskil is still quiet, but he has calmed down. However, when their server comes to ask if they want desserts, he glances at Marylen with a significant look.

'No, thank you, not for me,' he says. 'I really think we ought to be going. It's quite a long drive back.'

'No, of course . . .'

'But don't let me stop you . . .'

Just then, they become aware of a kind of upheaval at the other side of the restaurant, an upwelling of talk and tension that ripples outwards. Mikkel's phone has buzzed and he puts his hand to his pocket. It buzzes again and again. Suddenly, all around them, people are pulling out their phones.

'Sorry, occupational hazard! Please excuse me . . .' says Mikkel, and he takes out the phone and stares at the screen. He says nothing.

'Oh my God,' says a women behind Marylen, in a choked voice.

Someone else gasps: a small cry. Marylen looks round and meets the stricken eyes of the woman behind her. She looks at Eskil and finds that she is clutching his hand.

Thirty-five

Hanne Duli has never felt so tired in her life. Ever since the call came in (four cavers had 'found something' and they thought it might be . . .), she has been moving like an automaton. First, collecting the team, including Merete; even though the young officer has been shunted sideways to work on the Iron-Mine Man case, she needed Merete for this. Then, driving halfway up the valley of the Long Water, arranging for the area to be secured, and making the steep climb up the mountainside to the mouth of the Marble Cave.

When she and Merete drove to Nilsbakken – that was only ten days ago, but it seems an unfathomable length of time – she had held a balance of hope and dread in her mind. Today, there has been no room for hope or doubt. The picture of Daniel that is pinned to the wall in the station, the same one that was featured in the media, the one spread all over the internet, shows him grinning on the beach at Mjelle, wearing a navy-blue and lime-green jacket. It was the flash of fluorescent green that caught the attention of one of the cavers – not a colour that naturally exists in a cave, even a cave like this one, with pink marble walls and a pale blue glacier at its heart.

Hanne Duli and the forensics officers followed the leader of the cavers on a silent trip into the depths of the cave, where ice meets rock in soundless, endless collision. All around them – and some of the chambers in the Marble Cave are huge – there was a chaos of shattered marble, heaps of rock that glittered with mica and fool's gold, water dripping down the walls. Every surface and every angle was off-kilter; in the bowels of the mountain, nothing is straight or flat, there is no reliable guide to up or down. Hanne Duli's eyes, and her sense of balance, became confused, untrustworthy. A silent, stumbling, nightmare journey, and, at the end of it, they clustered around the caver to point their flashlights into a gully where, tucked in a fold between the rock and the ice, they could clearly see the blue and green jacket, and that it was draped over the shape of a boy.

Afterwards, while Hanne Duli and Merete are outside the cave in the narrow defile that blocks any hope of a mobile signal, she has the sense that they are drawing their last breaths before the onslaught. They – the police and other officers in the little valley – are, as yet, the only ones who know this terrible thing. Merete cadges a cigarette from someone. Hanne Duli has never seen her smoke, but her face is drawn and her eyes are wet, and what are you going to say? She would smoke, if she thought it would help. There are so many questions facing them, the work they hoped would never need to be done, but here it is. The when and how and why – all of those, piling up into a mountain of need that will avalanche over them in a matter of hours. But the one question that Hanne Duli so miserably asks herself – and she knows that Merete is thinking it too – is why didn't they find him sooner? Why didn't they look here?

*

It doesn't take long to get out. The news spreads like branch lightning, from what source no one can tell. It instantaneously reaches every corner of the valley and far beyond. By the time it reaches Maria Fjordholm in the form of Hanne Duli, in the evening, she has already heard the rumours of intense police activity up the valley. When she opens the door and sees Hanne Duli standing there, she seems to draw herself up with immense effort, and says, dry-eyed and robot-voiced, 'It's him, isn't it? As soon as I heard . . . I knew.'

Hanne Duli nods. It's a while before she can stumble through the giving of information, what little she has. In answer to Maria's questions, all she can say is, 'There are no outward signs of trauma, so we'll have to wait for the forensic report.'

Maria's father, Odd Emil, is there, and one of Maria's friends, trying to comfort Daniel's distraught brother and sister. It's the old man who says, 'But hadn't you searched the cave already?'

Hanne Duli says, in a neutral voice, 'No. There was no indication that he had gone up there. We can only follow the evidence.'

The friend starts up, 'But he couldn't have walked all the way there from Nilsbakken, surely?'

Maria stops her. 'Please, Ingrid. Don't. It doesn't matter now.'

Odd Emil doesn't say anything else.

Thirty-six

Every year, in their first term, the seniors go on a field trip to the Marble Cave. Many of them will already have been with family – or they will have been to one of the other caves in the area. As caves go, the Marble Cave is an easy day out, and more rewarding of the effort than most. From the side of the lake, you wouldn't know it's there; it's an hour's climb up the mountainside, following a narrow valley that leads up from the shore. When you reach it, you see a low, wide mouth that, in summer, is hidden by trees. Inside, for good stretches of its twisty interior, there is reasonable head height and the ground is not too treacherous for the averagely fit. With good footwear, helmet and head torch, you can make your way from the entrance to a vast underground hall that visitors liken to a cathedral, where your torch beams cannot penetrate the full height of the soaring, convoluted ceiling. You will take many photographs, but none of them will do justice to the full majesty of the space. Then, as long as you don't suffer from claustrophobia, you can continue on, down steeper passages and through tighter squeezes, until you reach the underground glacier – and that really is worth seeing. All year round, the temperature in the deep of the cave stays the same: cold enough that the ice neither melts, nor grows. The glacier has been here, coiled like a dragon in its lair, hidden from the sun, for at least the last eight thousand years.

Elin has never been inside the cave, but Benny and Toril went last year, on a trip arranged by the Fagerheims as a thank you to their employees. Nordleif Fagerheim is a caving fan and knows every inch of its passages. Toril didn't like it much, but Benny was awed by it. He was fascinated by the vast spaces and the glittering walls, and especially by the swirling blue and white striations of the glacier, in a place where it seems impossible for a glacier to be.

Despite Nordleif's warning that photographs wouldn't come out well, Benny took scores of pictures, and was duly frustrated by his inability to capture the cave's enormity, or the subtle, beautiful colours of rock and ice. But, when he told Elin about it, he showed her his rubbish photos, and said that he thought she would be okay, at least with the first bit, and some people find that, even though they suffer from claustrophobia or anxiety, the cave is so extraordinary that their wonder outweighs their fear. Elin agreed that it sounded fascinating, but there was no rush to make up her mind about it. The cave wasn't going anywhere, and even the sleeping glacier is protected from the depredations that are shrinking the ice caps in the mountains around Sulis.

Elin thinks: she will never go there now.

Today – Saturday – was supposed to be the shopping trip with her mum, and Elin had begun to look forward to it. She met Mikkel a few days ago, and he was all right. She thinks her mother could do worse. Klara seems happier and more energetic than the last summer she spent in Oslo, so Elin is, tentatively, glad about that whole thing. She has even asked Benny which shops they should go to in Bodø – this being the sort of thing that Benny always knows.

The idea was that Elin would stay over at Benny's and Toril would give her a lift down the valley in the morning, to meet Klara at her hotel. Toril gives yoga classes in Fauske on a Saturday, and she doesn't mind being early. But that plan was made before the news broke on Friday night. Elin and Benny discovered it after they'd gone to bed. Elin always turns her phone off at night because it's too unpredictable, but Benny keeps his on, and around midnight the messages came flooding in.

—OMG, have you heard about Daniel?

    —*Crying-face emoji*

        —So so sad. Just can't believe it.

        Grey-silhouettes-embracing emoji

                —What???

—They've found him. It's not good news

    —*Grey-silhouettes-embracing emoji*

        —I'm crying so hard I can't breathe *Crying-face emoji*

                —No no no!

—It's always the good ones who get taken young RIP *Angel emoji*

    —*Broken-heart emoji x 5*

        —RIP Daniel, love you bro *Heart emoji*

                —WTF u talking about?

                Have they found him???

—I can't believe it. Such a tragedy

    —Is he dead then?

    —This afternoon, in the Marble Cave

    Grieving-face emoji

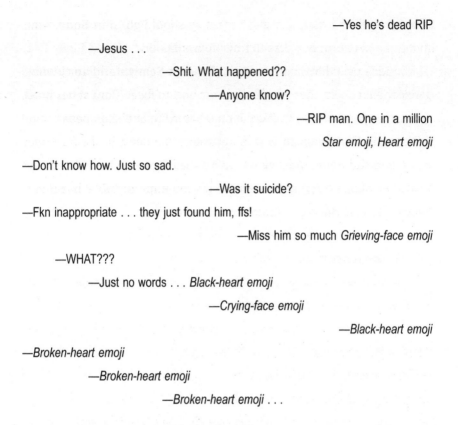

—Yes he's dead RIP

—Jesus . . .

—Shit. What happened??

—Anyone know?

—RIP man. One in a million

Star emoji, Heart emoji

—Don't know how. Just so sad.

—Was it suicide?

—Fkn inappropriate . . . they just found him, ffs!

—Miss him so much *Grieving-face emoji*

—WHAT???

—Just no words . . . *Black-heart emoji*

—*Crying-face emoji*

—*Black-heart emoji*

—*Broken-heart emoji*

—*Broken-heart emoji*

—*Broken-heart emoji* . . .

Elin woke up because Benny was crying.

'Benny? What is it?'

Benny didn't answer. His face was wet, tracks of tears gleamed in the light from his phone screen. She scrambled up off the mattress on the floor and sat on the bed beside him. Saw what was happening.

No one got much sleep, that night. Toril heard them talking and came in. She had seen the news too and sat on the bed, embracing them both. Toril and Benny cried. Elin couldn't cry. Didn't know if she wanted to. Wasn't this what they had all been expecting, really? She didn't say that out loud. Then they got up and wrapped themselves in bathrobes and blankets and sat on the sofa with glasses of wine and cups of tea. Benny fetched his computer and played Sigur Rós, which made even Elin cry. The three of them on the sofa, tears running down their cheeks. She suspected that was why he had done it. At three o'clock, Toril went to the kitchen and made them sandwiches, and then they all went to bed in her room.

'Do you think my dad's okay?' Elin asked Toril.

'He's with Marylen, isn't he? I'm sure he is. Marylen's very . . . strong. I hope she's all right. She knew him quite well.'

They all went quiet, thinking about who would be okay.

Who wouldn't be.

The only thing Benny hadn't liked about the cave was when Nord-leif made them all turn off their torches. 'This is true darkness,' he said. 'If this is your first time in a cave, you will never have experienced true darkness before.' They stayed quiet, waiting for their eyes to adjust. But your eyes can't adjust when there is no light, not a single atom. That is what Benny thinks of when he hears the news: Daniel, lying in that immense darkness, because that must be what death is like – nothing and nothing and nothing. Not an atom of light.

In the morning, Klara phones. Elin is supposed to meet her at the hotel at eleven.

'Hello, darling. How are you, this morning? I suppose you've heard the news.'

'About Daniel. Yeah.'

'I'm so sorry, sweetie. We heard about it last night. How are you doing?'

'Dunno. Okay.'

'Everyone seems to be in shock.'

'What, in the hotel?'

'Well, yes, and in the town, generally.'

'Do you want to cancel today, then?'

'Well, that's why I'm ringing, to see how you're feeling about it. Mikkel's working, of course, but we can still go. If you don't feel like it, that's okay. Or, if you do want to, that's fine too, of course. Or we could do something else. I'd love to see you.'

Elin is silenced by the responsibility of choosing.

'Sorry. I'm overloading you. Do you want to have a think about it and ring me back?'

'Okay.'

Her phone goes again – it's her dad ringing to ask her the same things. Have they heard? How is she doing? Does she want to come home? She doesn't have to go shopping if she doesn't want to.

She says: Yes. Okay. No. I know.

'Are you all right, Dad?'

Eskil sounds surprised at the question. 'Yes, sweetie, I'm all right. I'm just really sad for his family.'

'Mm. And is . . . Marylen all right?'

'Marylen? She's upset, of course. She was his teacher for three years.'

Thirty-seven

Marylen's first thought on hearing the news – after the initial shock – is for her friend Hanne Duli. She knows she will feel responsible. Everyone thought that every possible hiding place in the area had been searched – her included – but, when you think about it, that would be impossible. The valley and its surroundings make up such a vast and sparsely populated area, sprinkled with lakes, riddled with caves and mines – a wilderness of mountain and forest, water and ice. They'd brought in search teams from Bodø and even as far as Narvik, but still . . . She sends Hanne Duli a message, hoping she's okay.

She and Eskil drive home from the restaurant in silence. She is sad, but the silence is not awkward. She is glad she is sharing it with him. Eskil holds her hand for long periods of the drive. Of course, he is worried about Elin.

'Do you think she'll have heard, too? I don't know whether to call her or not. I don't want to break the news this late, if she hasn't.'

'I expect everyone who has a phone will have heard. She's at Toril's, isn't she, with Benny? She might be asleep by now, so I'd leave it. If she wants to call, she'll call, won't she?'

They drive in silence some more.

'I know you knew him quite well. How are you feeling?'

Marylen doesn't answer for a few moments. 'I think this is what I've been preparing myself for.'

Eskil knows how to listen. That's one of the things she loves about him.

'I suppose, until we know what happened – you know, whether it was an accident or . . . suicide – I don't know what I feel. I'm sad, of course. Daniel was so likeable. He made you smile. An ordinary, likeable young man.'

'Mikkel was thrilled, though, wasn't he?'

'Oh, well, I don't know if that's the word . . .'

'No, he was excited about it, you could tell. It's good for him, I suppose. For the story.'

'I don't think he's that ruthless.'

'Mm. I hope not.'

'It was nice to see Klara. I'm glad I met her again.'

'Thank you for coming. I don't think I could have coped with them on my own, what with everything.'

She squeezes his hand.

In the morning, she has to leave for her usual Saturday trip to see her daughter in Bodø. She goes home to collect her husband first. She had told him she was staying the night at Eskil's, and he had said, 'Fine.'

The thing about having a daughter like Nora is that it is impossible to think about anything else when you are with her. She lives so totally in the present, is so focused on herself, that time becomes suspended, all external worries are blotted out. About one in four of their visits is remarkably sunny – Nora will be in an affectionate and cheerful mood, finding everything funny, which is infectious. Today is one of those visits. Like a blessing. They are even granted a special Nora hug, which threatens to crack Marylen's ribs. When they emerge from the home after several hours, Marylen realises she hasn't thought about Daniel since morning. The sadness comes back, but it is smaller. She has seen many children pass through the school. Daniel isn't the first pupil they have lost, and probably won't be the last. She feels strangely calm.

As they are heading back along the coast towards Fauske, she says to her husband, 'There's something I need to do in Fauske. You can take the car, if you like. I can get the bus later.'

She pulls over in the forecourt of the Circle K, but, before she gets out, Petter says, 'Marylen, don't you think we should get a divorce? Now that you've got someone, and, well, I've been meaning to tell you for a while, I've got someone too.'

For a few moments, Marylen is too surprised to speak. He has kept that quiet, and, as far as she knows, her husband never goes out. Not that that is a bar to forming a relationship these days, she supposes.

'Oh. Right. Well, let's talk about it. Yeah. Do you want to tell me who it is?'

'She's someone I met online. She's Czech. And, no, it's not a scam. She's got more money than I have.'

She looks at him but can only see the side of his face. Petter is looking out of the window, to where the sun is spangling the fjord. Then he turns to her and smiles.

'I'm not an idiot.'

'No, I know. Well, that's good! So, are you . . . happy?'

'Let's not go mad. I don't know if I'll ever be exactly happy,' he says, with a glint of his old humour.

'Will you stay here . . . for Nora?'

'Of course.' He sounds shocked that she would even ask. 'Petra is going to come over for a visit.'

'Oh . . . Petra?'

'Uh-huh.'

'Petra and Petter. Well, if you think . . .'

He says, 'I'll be fine, you know.'

Marylen tries to agree, but tears are suddenly running down her face, and she can only nod.

When he has driven away, she walks up the side street, away from the water. What the fuck? Presumably, he'll tell her in time. Does she even have the right to ask anymore? She's pleased, of course she is, but also stunned. She has been so used to thinking that she is the one responsible for everything, that it is up to her to do, or not do. For the longest time, she has regarded her husband's depression as the ball and chain that has prevented her life from changing, moving forward. Now, that weight has turned into a balloon and it is floating away. Well.

In the police station, she goes up to reception and says that she thinks she has some information that might be relevant to the case of Iron-Mine Man. She doesn't see Hanne Duli, who is occupied with other things, but she is shown into a little room with a desk and computer, and is soon joined by a young officer with a bright blond ponytail. She remembers her from the visit to the school. Does that mean she's not working on the Daniel case anymore? Does that mean they know what happened to him?

'Hello, Marylen. Merete Nordheim,' the officer introduces herself.

289

'Yes, of course, we met at the school. I'm co-ordinating the Nilsbakken investigation. You have some information for us?'

Marylen takes a deep breath. Now, she feels embarrassed, as though she's trying to shoehorn herself into the case simply to get attention.

'Um, it depends. Have you identified the body yet? I've not heard . . .'

'No, not yet. Enquiries are ongoing, of course. Why, do you have an idea about that?'

'This is probably going to sound crazy,' says Marylen, 'but I think there's a faint possibility that it's a relative of mine. An uncle. I mean, I know it's a long shot, but I wondered, could we rule that out – with DNA, or something? Is that something you can do?'

Merete says, 'Okay. It'll be a while before we get any DNA results back from the lab, but, yes, sure. Why don't you tell me why you think it might be him? When did he go missing?'

Marylen sighs again. She feels like an idiot. 'I don't really know. It was before I was born – that was 1971. I never met him. My father's name was Birk Gulbrandsen. He was a miner for Sulitjelma Gruber from the sixties until the whole thing closed in ninety-one. He had an elder brother, Jens, who also worked in the mines until 1968. When they shut down the Nilsbakken workings, a lot of miners were made redundant and left the area, and he was one of them. My dad implied that Jens was angry because he was kept on, while Jens was given the boot. But Dad always said that his brother was a bad lot, so it wasn't surprising. Jens suddenly left; supposedly, he'd gone to America. But my father never heard from him again, and nor did my grandparents.'

'What makes you think that he didn't go to America?'

'Well, I don't know for sure that he didn't. But the fact that there was just no communication at all – no letters, cards, no news, nothing . . . Mum and Dad didn't really talk about it. I always assumed it was because Dad was ashamed of him in some way – whatever it was that made him call him a bad lot, but I don't know what that was. When you're a child, you just accept these things. You don't question it.'

'Mm. Yeah. And when you were older?'

Marylen smiles, but it's more like a wince. 'I don't know. We didn't really talk a lot in our family. Not about things like that. And my uncle had never really existed to me, so . . . When you're young, you don't care about family history – at least, I didn't. Then I left and worked abroad for twelve years, and, by the time I came back, my father was very ill. He could hardly speak.'

Merete nods. 'And your uncle was never reported missing, as far as you know?'

'I don't think so. I'm sorry, it sounds vague and silly now that I'm saying this out loud. I mean, it just could all be a coincidence. I'm probably wasting your time.'

'No, not at all. If you give me all the information you have on him – do I take it both of your parents are . . . ?'

'They've both passed away, yes. There isn't anyone else on that side of the family. Just me. And my daughter.'

'I'm sure we can get it cleared up, one way or another. It must be unsettling to have those doubts hanging over you. So, you would be happy to give a DNA sample?'

Marylen nods, relieved that this young woman isn't laughing at her.

'So –' Merete's fingers fly over her keyboard, her eyes tracking side to side – 'when you're ready, do you have a date of birth?'

291

'I'm pretty sure that he was two years older than my father, so he would have been born in 1939. But I don't know the exact date.'

'And the place?'

'They were from a village north of here. A tiny place. It's called Gammelsøy.'

Thirty-eight

It was inevitable, I suppose. Which doesn't make his death any easier to bear. I heard this morning, on the radio, when I was making breakfast for me and Asta. The news announcer said it in a voice of sad finality that made the back of my neck go cold: 'In Nordland . . . case of missing teenager . . . police confirm remains . . . family has been notified.'

Odd Emil has been notified. Poor Odd Emil. He was right, damn him. And I, who usually take the crown for assuming the worst at all times, kept mouthing platitudes and reassurances, because you do, don't you? Especially when you are a bystander, when it doesn't directly affect you. Now what am I supposed to do – ring him up? Pretend the ridiculous conversation the other day didn't happen? We haven't spoken since. All right, all right, I'm not a monster. Of course, I try ringing, but he doesn't answer. Odd Emil is of the generation, as I am, who have to answer a ringing phone if they can breathe and move a finger, so a sick fear grabs me in the gut. Maybe he just doesn't want to talk to me – that's what I'm going to cling to. Anyway, I can't just sit here. Asta needs her walk and there's no reason – none at all – why we shouldn't walk in the general direction of Odd Emil's apartment.

We set off, rather more slowly than I would like. My hip is hurting

a lot today, so I take the wheeled shopper, which is sturdy enough
to double as a stabilising device. I know I should get a walking stick,
because, let's face it, these things aren't going to get any better, are
they? Today, everything is shit. The heartless sun shines, and there is a
cruel glitter off the fjord – a sheet rippling with sequins: cheap, bright
things. I think back to the day when they found my sister's woollen
hat, wallowing in the strait between Gammelsøy and the heart-shaped
islet that has no name. That day, it was overcast and snowing, and it
went on snowing for weeks. The sun had the tact to stay away, but
that was in winter, when daylight is only ever a soft, blue haze, and
you don't have to face facts quite so harshly.

I wish I hadn't said to Odd Emil that thing about living longer than
him. People can die from a broken heart. There's even a scientific
name for it, although I don't know what it is. I realise how lucky I
have been in my life, to have got this old and to have experienced
relatively little grief. The loss of my sister was the only one that
truly hurt. The great griefs you expect – like when your parents
die – weren't such a problem for me. I suppose that is sad. Anyway.
I never married, have never lost a current partner in that way. Klara
is alive and well, despite everything. I know that, if something happened to her – well, it would be unthinkable. Elin, too. I could wish
that Elin and I were closer, but I learnt a long time ago not to ask
for the impossible.

I find that I'm nervous about seeing Odd Emil, so, on the way to his
place, I make a detour to the patisserie on Rådhusgata. Cakes are called
for at such times. Also, alcohol – so then I walk to the Vinmonopolet
and buy an eye-wateringly expensive bottle of malt whisky. By now,
I'm getting tired and I'm not far from the café, so I decide to stop in

for a coffee and *lefse*, to rest and get my strength up. It's not as though anyone is expecting me.

Odd Emil is sitting at our usual table, his back to the door. Even though I am on my way to try to see him, I pause in the doorway, wrong-footed. The first thing that comes into my head is: Could it be that he's meeting someone else? Has he replaced me this quickly? But anger stays me; the café is *my* place. I was here first. I walk up to him.

'Waiting for someone?'

He only half turns towards me, for a second, and doesn't raise his eyes to my face.

'Svea.' He shakes his head.

'You didn't answer your phone.'

'I don't want to talk on the phone.'

'Shall I sit down?'

'If you like.'

I sit opposite him. There is a half-drunk cup of coffee in front of him. It looks scummy, as though it has been there a while. Asta whines and rests her head on his thigh. Humans aren't allowed to do that, otherwise I would too.

'Hello, girl. Hello.' He doesn't look at me, but he communes with my dog via the medium of head-rubbing.

'I'm so sorry.'

'Yup.'

'I'm sorry about the other day, too. Perhaps I overreacted.'

Odd Emil shakes his head slowly. Whatever was said then doesn't matter a fig now, of course it doesn't.

'Do you want me to leave?'

'No.'

I can't think of anything else to say, so we sit there in silence.

Katrin comes over, sympathy smile pegged into place. She looks as though she's been crying. Clearly, she's already done the condolence speech bit with Odd Emil.

'Hello, Svea. Such a sad day. I'm just so, so sorry. It's terrible.'

I nod. I don't know why she's commiserating with me. Or why she feels the need to be 'so, so' sorry – i.e. twice as sorry as me. Like she wants to make me look bad.

'Can I get you the usual?'

'Yes. Um, no. Can you bring us two glasses and two plates for these?'

I take the box of cakes and the bottle of whisky out of my shopper.

'I know you don't have a licence, but you haven't sold it to us, so that's all right, isn't it?' I look her in the eye.

Katrin hesitates for a second, then says, 'Yes, of course it is.' Then she goes and turns the sign on the door to *CLOSED*, and locks us in.

'Katrin,' says Odd Emil, 'make it three glasses.'

He sloshes the whisky into three lemonade glasses, which is all they have in the café, and raises his glass.

'To Daniel,' he says, and Katrin and I clink glasses with him.

'To Daniel.'

Forty minutes later, we are counselling a weeping Katrin. She keeps apologising, and then bursting into fresh sobs. We've eaten the cakes – although, on reflection, I would have preferred *lefse* – and made a serious dent in the bottle. I'm not normally a whisky drinker, but an occasion like this seemed to call for something expensive and rare. The hot, smoky spirit attacks your throat like fire. It makes you choke and your eyes water – then, a minute after you swallow it, something wonderful happens. It's as though someone has switched on your own private sun.

Katrin blots her eyes. 'I should leave you two alone. I'm sorry to be so . . . This whisky is lovely, Svea, but I think I've drunk too much.'

'It's all right,' says Odd Emil, who hasn't shed a tear yet, probably out of politeness. 'This is a day for drinking too much.'

'You're amazing. I don't know how you can be so strong,' says Katrin, sniffing.

Odd Emil shakes his head. 'Oh, heavens, I'm not. Svea knows that.'

I see Katrin glance from him to me, and I wonder, not for the first time, what she thinks we are to each other. It could be that she's assumed, for the past eight years, that we are in an intimate relationship. People are sentimental like that, I find, wanting everyone paired off like the animals in the ark.

Katrin refuses more whisky, clears the table of cake rubble and goes into the kitchen. For the tenth time since the beginning of our little wake, a passer-by tries to come in through the locked door, clearly unable to read. This one rattles the handle for several seconds in disbelief, before swearing and going away.

Odd Emil says, 'We should probably go – let Katrin open up again.'

'What are you going to do now?'

'I don't know. I suppose I should go home.'

'What about Maria – should you be with her?'

He thinks and shakes his head. 'I was there last night. We don't seem to help each other much. She practically threw me out this morning. Some of her friends are with her now, taking turns.'

'You could come to my house. Or I could come to yours,' I say, carefully. 'I don't mean . . . you know – just as company.'

'Thanks. I think I'd like that. Go to your house, I mean. I don't want to go home.' He sits back and takes a deep breath. 'I should go home and pick up my medications first.'

I can't stop myself from saying, 'Rather presumptuous.'

Then I smile, to show him I don't mean it. Although, I'm not quite sure what I do mean.

Thirty-nine

Toril drives to Fauske, and Benny and Elin get out by the hotel on the waterfront. Elin asked Benny to go with her and Klara to Bodø, which is a relief to Toril. Benny is still visibly upset, though he assured her he's going to be all right. Elin seems to be doing better, but she is always hard to read, so who knows? Benny takes so much responsibility on to himself. Maybe it's the result of being brought up by a single mother (and therefore her fault). No matter what she says, he seems to believe that he bears some guilt for Daniel's death, and that's a terrible thing to think. Once they have worked out what happened to Daniel, it will prove to Benny once and for all that his delay in speaking to the police changed nothing. Because, surely? That said, she would still beat David Mæland to a pulp with a shovel, if no one was watching.

She has a couple of hours to kill before her first class, so she drives a little way out of town, to a place where she can walk along the shore of the fjord and be alone. There is no real path here, so she doesn't expect to meet anyone. There's nothing at all, really, except for the odd cabin and the campsite that won't be used before July.

As she walks, she thinks about Benny, about what an exceptional human being he is, and how she can't imagine herself going on living if something happened to him. But bereaved parents do that inconceivable thing – they continue. Maria has two other children, so maybe that would be different. No matter what she does, Toril can't ensure that Benny will always be safe. You can't guarantee anyone else's safety – you can't even guarantee your own. But they live in peaceful, comfortable, prosperous Norway, and really – she needs to get a grip – they are more than safe enough.

She picks her way along the shore, up to a place where great rounded rocks slope down to the water, and stunted trees and bushes provide handholds. Across the fjord, the further shore is likewise deserted and wild. She scrambles up to a good spot – the rock forms a smooth grey mound, like a breaching whale – where she can sit and feel the sun warming her face. She closes her eyes. It's good that Benny is spending the day with Elin and her mum – they'll be in Bodø, which will be a nice change of scene. Toril pressed some money into his hand before they left the house, which he protested about, but she insisted. She wants him to have some fun. Her thoughts slide back to Maria Fjordholm, whom she doesn't really know. She has seen her in passing, at the school: a pretty, blonde woman, with dark roots and slightly too much make-up. They've exchanged hellos, but Toril never got a friendly vibe from her. She has never been to one of Toril's yoga classes, not that you can judge a person from that. You never know, do you, what someone is really like?

She's startled from her reverie by the sound of footsteps on rock, and opens her eyes to see a slight, dark-clad figure bob into view. The face is half hidden under a black hoodie, but she can tell it's a boy around Benny's age or a bit older. He stops dead at the sight of her. He looks horrified. He has just scrambled up from the shore the same way she did, and there isn't anywhere else for him to go, other than come past her. But he stands there, caught, seemingly unable to either approach or turn back.

Toril says, 'Hi.'

'Hi,' mumbles the boy.

If he's local, he must go to the high school. She doesn't instantly recognise him, but that might be because of the hoodie and the way he's keeping his face down, as if trying to avoid scrutiny. If he goes to the school, he probably knew Daniel. Suddenly, Toril is worried.

'How's it going?' she asks brightly.

'Okay,' he says, in a low, toneless voice, and comes closer.

She realises two things: that he's hoping to pass as quickly as possible, and that she has seen that face before.

'It's Tobias, isn't it? Tobias Mero? You're at the high school? My son goes there, too – Benny Iversen.'

'Oh. Yes.' Tobias stops again.

'You win all the science prizes, don't you? I've seen your picture in the foyer.' She smiles at him. 'I'm Toril.'

He nods, but doesn't meet her eye. At least he has stopped walking, too polite to abandon her mid-conversation.

'This is a really sad day, isn't it?'

His eyes flick up to meet hers for a second and she thinks, You poor, poor thing. Of course, Tobias was a friend of Daniel's – was, in fact, one of the friends her son saw that night, parking Daniel's car.

'You were a friend of Daniel's, weren't you? I'm so sorry.'

The boy seems to grimace, and, without speaking another word, turns and begins to hurry back the way he came, trainers rasping and slithering on the smooth rock.

Toril, whose jaw has slackened with shock, stares after him, then she gets up and waits for a moment before following him. Surely it wasn't such a terrible thing to say?

She doesn't run, but walks fast enough to keep the slight figure in sight amid the rocks and trees. He doesn't appear to be aware of her presence – or, at least, he doesn't look back. Maybe he doesn't care. He crashes clumsily through the scrub, at times half-running, until he reaches the single-track road that travels down the spine of the peninsula, and there he pulls a bicycle from the bushes. He starts to pedal back towards town. That's a good thing, because . . . Toril finds her breath coming fast. She's thinking, He'll be all right for the time being, if he's going back to town. He'll be safe there, won't he?

She walks back to her car, parked a little way down the road. She needs to leave, too, or she'll be late for her class. Will anyone want to do yoga today? She should be there, in case. She starts the engine and then sits there, wondering. She knows Tobias's mother only by sight and knows that there are younger children. The Mero family are Syrian Kurds who moved here a few years ago. Tobias seems like a model pupil – or he did, until this business with Daniel. What *were* the boys doing with Daniel's car at Nilsbakken? When Hanne Duli came to talk to Benny the other night, Toril knew the officer was probing. She was very interested in how the boys had seemed that night – and why would she be, unless she suspected them of something? Dark thoughts erupt like black flowers in her mind. Tobias has just found out that his missing friend is dead: reason enough for him to be upset. Or is it more complicated than that?

Somehow, more time has passed than she thought. She drives off, heading for the gym and the first of her classes, but, when she's nearly there, she changes her mind, turns up a side road and parks by the police station. She'll just nip in and say something. It won't take more than a few minutes, and she's never late for class, so they'll forgive her. It's just that, if she didn't say something and . . . well, she'd never forgive herself. What if it was Benny? It's probably nothing and she'll be causing needless alarm. But the boy's expression had scared her: the eyes pleading, desperate, as though he was looking for the way out of hell.

Forty

Odd Emil falls asleep on my bed. There isn't really anywhere else for him to lie down, and he's clearly exhausted. I'm surprised it doesn't bother me more, having another person upstairs, in my room. Asta and I camp out in the conservatory and watch the sun being dimmed by clouds. Soon it will be midsummer, the pivot of another year, and then the long, slow slide into winter. A few weeks ago, Odd Emil and I were sitting in the café, joking about the russ and about Daniel, a boy I had never met, and now never will. I feel a great greyness settling on me. I'm trying not to think about myself, so I ring my granddaughter, but it goes to her voicemail. I have a feeling that she's spending the day with Klara, so I don't leave a message. In any case, I have nothing special to say.

I hope that, before Daniel died, he got to do some things that he really enjoyed – it sounds as though he did. He seems to have had a wonderful childhood, full of friends and nice holidays and fun. Odd Emil always thought he was happy, until Maria told him about the antidepressants. None of us knows anything, do we?

Sometimes, it seems to me that there is a finite amount of happiness in the world. Maybe Daniel burned through his allotted portion in the short time he was here. Whereas I have been eking out my share over many years, as if I'm planning to stick around forever. Obviously, this isn't true. I have been . . . what I've been, because of my parents, and doubtless they could pass the blame for their shortcomings to their forebears. How do you ever escape? I hope Elin escapes the worst of it.

There was one other thing that marked me out from a young age. Literally marked, like Cain, although he was punished for murdering his brother, and I was punished simply for being who I was. When it happened, I blamed myself, although I see now that blame can be handed to a number of other people: firstly, to Jens Gulbrandsen; then, presumably, on to his parents, to whatever made him the way he was.

When I was eleven, I spent as much time as I could out of reach of my mother's blows and my stepfather's jeers. I didn't have close friends – at school I was known as 'Nazi spawn' by some of my classmates, too – so, in summer, I hung around the harbour. I liked the huts – wooden sheds where the fishing nets were stored and mended, and the dim, strongly scented space under the sail stores. I could crawl under there and while away daylight hours reading and building structures out of wood, stones, bits of rope.

It was at the harbour that I first encountered Jens – a tall, blond teenager with an exciting reputation. As if recognising a fellow outcast, he talked to me, and I was bowled over by the attention of an older boy. The most shameful thing of all: I had a childish crush on him, and, in my naive way, I thought he liked me too. I was intrigued when he asked me to meet him at the huts one evening. He said, did I want to see something wonderful? And I said, feeling a wild thrill, yes.

I slipped out that evening and made my way down to the net huts, excited at the prospect of encountering something wonderful. When

I arrived, Jens was already there, smoking, with cigarette pinched between finger and thumb. I thought that was so exotic, like something a movie star would do. I felt important and grown-up, and this was what grown-ups did, take a leap into the unknown. He grinned and put his finger to his lips. Breathless with excitement, I followed him inside one of the sheds. After the brightness of the evening, I couldn't initially make out what was inside, but I heard odd sounds, some shuffling, a kind of snuffling. I remember what I thought: It's a dog! Maybe, I thought, it's a bitch and she has just had a litter of puppies? Then my eyes adjusted to the dimness and I saw the shadowy figures of the other boys.

I don't remember much of what happened. I thought he was going to kill me. I screamed, and someone put a clammy hand over my mouth. My limbs were locked in place by heavy, strong hands. Something immobilised my head. Jens took his time. I remember him staring at me with intense concentration. I remember the tongue poking out of the corner of his mouth. I know he said, 'If you tell anyone who did this, I'll cut your throat.'

I probably wasn't in there very long. Outside again, I was amazed and thankful he hadn't killed me and I hadn't suffered 'a fate worse than death' – which is how we talked about rape, in those days. I wasn't sure precisely what had happened, so how bad could it be? Everything hurt – my limbs, my head, my face – but I could walk. I seemed to be whole. As long as I said nothing, I would be safe.

Then, walking home, I saw the blood and realised my face was bleeding. More than anything, I was terrified of my parents. I had gone out, late, without permission, and I knew I would get into trouble. As for whatever had been done to me, I felt nothing but shame. I tried to sneak in unseen and creep upstairs, but Magny came out on to the landing and shrieked at the sight of me. My mother appeared, stared at me, and hissed at Magny to go back to bed and make no noise.

Mum hustled me into the kitchen and sponged my face. I really remember that – her unaccustomed gentleness. For once, she was kind, but her expression was tight-lipped. She pressed a cloth to my forehead until the bleeding stopped, then taped a pad of lint over it. After some thought, she fetched the kitchen scissors. She kept saying, 'You'll be fine, Svea. It'll go away. Leave the bandage be. Don't take it off or you'll make it hurt worse and then it won't heal. I'm going to change your hair so that no one will ask questions.'

She combed my bloodied hair and cut it into a fringe that hid the dressing. By now, my forehead hurt so much that I couldn't stop crying, and I hardly ever cried. Eventually, my mother got up and poured me a cup of akvavit, and I choked it down, and the pain slowly dulled to a throb. I began to feel numb and slack, and also that this horrible thing didn't matter so much. We sat at the kitchen table, drinking akvavit together, and I was dizzy with gratitude and an unfamiliar warmth towards my mother. She hadn't hit me, she hadn't shouted. There we were, me and my mum, drinking akvavit together, almost like friends. At that moment, I felt closer to her than at any other I can remember.

One more thing: she didn't ask me who had done it, and of course I didn't tell her. She told me not to say anything to anyone, which reinforced my sense that I was to blame. Perhaps – although I'm guessing, here, as we never talked about it – she thought it was an inevitable thing to happen to a *naziyngel*. An act of almost natural vengeance that we both deserved.

307

The morning after, I woke up with my first hangover. It wasn't my last. As far as I can remember, I stayed off school for a couple of days, then everything went back, more or less, to normal. My attendance at school improved. I didn't go to the harbour anymore. I tried never to be on my own outside. If I saw Jens in the distance, I kept my eyes down and turned in the other direction, shaking and trying to breathe. But, after that night, he ignored me. My memory of the whole thing was fragmented and bizarre, like a nightmare, and, as long as I didn't look under my fringe in the mirror, I could almost convince myself that it hadn't really happened.

For the best part of a week, I obeyed Mum's instruction not to touch the bandage, until my curiosity got the better of me. Magny, Nordis and I barricaded ourselves into our room with a hand mirror and peered under the crusty bandage – and then we saw what he had done. I was too shocked to scream. Even my sisters, at eight and six, knew what a swastika was. In my horror, I dropped the mirror, which broke – a million years of bad luck. And a serious hiding from Mum. But how could my luck get any worse? With trembling hands, I replaced the bandage. My sisters' little faces were frozen with shock and I couldn't bear to have made them look like that, to know of such a thing. I wanted to slam my face into the broken shards of mirror; I wanted to cut it, burn it, slash it until it was obliterated. I wanted not to exist.

I became more solitary than ever, because closeness increased the risk of someone else discovering my secret. I made plans to kill myself. I knew how to: when you live on the edge of the Arctic Ocean, it's not particularly difficult. I would go to the bay where rocky headlands hid deep, dark water and the current ran out to the sea beyond the islands.

However, I didn't want to do it in midsummer, under the endless sun. I was scared of being found and having people peer at my face and know. They would gossip; they would gasp and jeer. I would forever be the girl with a swastika carved on her forehead, and nothing more. I imagined my stepfather finding it funny. No. I would wait for mid-winter dark, the water so cold that everything sinks to the bottom of the sea, and then I could disappear without trace.

My mother never referred to it again, as though her silence and my thick fringe would be enough to conceal it for good. That was the way it was, in those days – people ploughed on, doing as best they could. There was a boy in our school whose right arm ended in a fascinating, puckered stump below the elbow. He had lost his hand playing with a half-buried German shell. How could I complain?

While I waited for winter, Nordis stuck to me like glue. She held my hand when we walked down the main village street. She told me she loved me more than anything in the world. She didn't talk about my scar; she didn't have to. By the time summer ended and we went back to school, I had recovered a little. Perhaps other things could happen in my life. I started paying attention in school and it was in a science class that autumn that I came up with my new plan.

It does not escape me that the fate I planned for myself, all those years ago, Nordis eventually made her own.

I must have fallen asleep, because the sun has wheeled round and is warming my right cheek when I become aware that Odd Emil is standing in front of me in his socks, looking exceedingly rumpled.

I quickly wipe my chin, in case – God forbid – I've been drooling. 'What?'

'God, you scared me, Svea. I've been saying your name for about five minutes. You wouldn't wake up.'

I pull myself together. 'You're exaggerating.'

'Aren't you hungry? We should probably eat something. It's nearly eight o'clock.'

'Oh! God. Asta . . . ?'

'I've fed her. She's fine. And she's been out in the garden to do her business.'

Asta is standing there too, wagging her tail.

'Okay. Thank you.'

I thought I was supposed to be looking after him, but whatever.

Then Odd Emil does something strange and unprecedented. He puts out his hand and gently combs my fringe with his fingers.

'What on earth are you doing?'

'Your hair was all skew-whiff,' he says.

My hand goes to my forehead, an automatic gesture to check all is in place.

'Let's see what's in the fridge,' I say, struggling to my feet. 'Don't get your hopes up. We might have to order a takeaway pizza, you know – behave like a pair of slobs.'

He says, 'Let's do that.'

310

Forty-one

It is midsummer, and it's evening. On a beach outside town, members of the school and the Fjordholm family hold a memorial for Daniel. There are speeches from staff and several students, and one from Daniel's grandfather, who cuts an impressive figure standing by the water, looking like a large, shaggy Viking. The beach is full. It feels as though everyone in town – perhaps everyone in the wider valley – has come to pay their respects. No one wears black. The senior girls have made little rafts out of paper and flowers (all biodegradable, Marylen was assured in class), and they light candles before wading into the water to set them afloat. It's a pretty sight, and a lot of people film the ritual on their phones. As a group of girls sing a sentimental song – rather beautifully, she has to admit – Marylen glances towards the Hellraisers, who are standing together with heads bowed. Their families are there too, but the three boys are standing next to Daniel's mother. Marylen feels a kind of awe watching Maria Fjordholm, who is there with her two younger children, but also, very publicly, stands with Tobias and Johnny and Lorentz. Marylen doesn't know how she has forgiven them, but it seems that she has.

The day after Daniel's body was found in the cave, one of the boys went to the police and admitted what had happened that night: it was a russ dare gone wrong. The recreational drugs they took that night as part of their self-imposed challenge – which was to get high while deep underground – reacted badly with Daniel's medication and he had a fatal seizure. It's called serotonin syndrome. Incredibly rare. Incredibly unlucky. Serotonin is the brain chemical that makes you feel happy, but, apparently, you can have too much of a good thing. The body overheats wildly, goes into spasm, and, if you can't get medical help in time, it results in massive organ failure.

Halfway up a mountain and deep inside the cave, the boys were freaking out. There seemed no point in leaving to get help; it would have taken hours. They tried. They attempted resuscitation for close to an hour, but it did no good. The autopsy concluded that Daniel had died almost immediately. It wasn't suicide and it wasn't murder. It was an accident. The boys panicked. Hanne Duli told Marylen that they had a confused idea that, if Tobias's involvement in the death came out, his family wouldn't get permanent residency – might even be deported. Daniel always insisted they look out for Tobias. So, with strung out, horrified logic, they did what they did: parked Daniel's car up at Nilsbakken, and, when Johnny found Daniel's phone on the floor of the car, he threw it out of the window without thinking.

Whatever happens to the boys in future, and charges of concealing a death and perverting the course of justice are yet to be considered, the general feeling is that they were more foolish and frightened than wicked, and they have already suffered greatly. If Daniel's mother finds it possible to forgive them, who is anyone else to argue?

Marylen makes her own short speech, then she goes back to stand with Eskil. They hold hands. It's not a religious service, but several people have come up to thank him for being there. Elin is here too, although Marylen can't see her at the moment – she's probably with Benny and their classmates. Later, once the adults and children have drifted away, the teenagers will start drinking and playing music, light a midsummer bonfire and let their hair down.

'Are you okay?' mutters Eskil, squeezing her hand.

Marylen nods. He has been extra solicitous for the last few days, since she found out – via an email – that her DNA sample shows she is a 'second-degree relation' to Iron-Mine Man. Twenty per cent of her genetic material matches that of the body in the mine. In other words, he is an uncle of hers, or a first cousin. They, meaning the lab and therefore the police, seem to think that is 'fairly conclusive'.

Marylen didn't – doesn't – know what she feels about this. When she managed to speak to a technician at the lab, she said twenty per cent didn't seem that much. Was the identification of Iron-Mine Man as Jens Gulbrandsen absolutely certain? A lot of technical jargon and hedging followed. The Gulbrandsens came from a small, isolated, rural population, and long-term inhabitants of Gammelsøy might be expected to share a certain amount of DNA. Another thing she has found out recently is that Eskil's ex-wife's mother, Elin's grandmother, came from the same small village. So, it is even possible that she and Elin are distantly related. But then, isn't everyone on earth related by only six degrees of separation?

She can't feel much sorrow for an uncle – if it is, indeed, Jens Gulbrandsen – who died before she was born, and had, according to her father, caused his family nothing but trouble when he was alive. A police artist is working on a facial reconstruction, and Marylen has said that she will look in the attic for any photographs that show her father and uncle when they were young. In those days, after the war, in a poor fishing village, photographs were a luxury. She thinks there are one or two, but, for some reason, she hasn't yet got round to it.

In response to her questions, the lab said that the matter of how Iron-Mine Man met his death may, after so long, be impossible to determine. They found no obvious signs of violence on the skeletal remains, so Marylen has to face the possibility that she may never know how he died. It is natural to want answers, but sometimes you can't have them, and perhaps, in the end, it doesn't matter.

Forty-two

After the memorial, I tell Odd Emil I'll see him at home. He wants to spend a bit more time with Maria and the grandchildren.

'Don't stay out too late,' I tell him, but only because he has to take his medication at a certain time and the bottle is in my bathroom cabinet. Just reminding, not nagging.

As I'm walking away from the beach, I hear running footsteps behind me.

'*Bestemor!*'

Elin is panting and, despite the gravity of the occasion, her eyes sparkle and her cheeks are flushed. She looks animated and . . . happy, I suppose.

'Are you going home?' She squats down to pet Asta, who reacts with unseemly barks, bounding around like a puppy.

'Shh, you! Yes. I think it's time we cleared out and left the beach to you young people. Odd Emil is staying a bit longer, with Maria.'

Earlier, I introduced Elin and Odd Emil to each other. I said he was a friend who was staying at my house for a while. Which is true. Odd Emil surprised me by folding Elin in his arms and telling her how lovely it was to meet her, both as a friend of Daniel's and as my

315

granddaughter. I think Elin was surprised by it too, but she emerged from the bear hug without looking too shocked.

'It was nice to meet him, *Bestemor*,' she says, with a decided smirk. 'So, are you two living together, now?'

'No. As I said earlier, he is staying with me for a while.'

'Oh. Okay.'

'And you can wipe that smirk off your face. Isn't the point of your whole . . . being genderfluid and so on, that you don't make assumptions about what people are doing, or who they are?'

'Yes. But asking people is fine, when you don't know.'

'Hm. But I don't have to answer.'

'No, you don't.'

Elin stands up. She is wearing a strange, complicated garment – a combination of narrow trousers with a sort of asymmetric kilt over the top. Very odd. Presumably it expresses all parts of her identity. Apparently, Klara bought it for her in Bodø. I'm happy that they seem to be getting on.

'Well . . . I'm glad, anyway. I'll see you soon, *Bestemor*.'

'Yes. All right.'

She gives me the flash of a smile and scampers back to the gathering on the beach. A long-legged gambol, before she meets and melts into the crowd of teenagers.

Later, we're sitting in silence in the conservatory, which is lit up by the midnight sun. Odd Emil doesn't want to go to bed, on this night of all nights. I think he'd have quite liked to stay on the beach, only Maria took the kids home, and he was embarrassed to be fifty years older than anyone else there. I have got out the remains of the bottle of malt whisky, untouched since our wake in the café, and we are sipping it slowly. I'm so tired I can hardly keep my eyes open, but I'm also so tired I can't make the effort to get out of my chair.

'I saw you talking to Lorentz Jentoft earlier. That was nice of you.'

Odd Emil shakes his head. 'I feel sorry for them. They were so stupid, but I can see why they did it. They're just kids.' After another few moments, he says, 'We all make mistakes when we're young.'

Even through my tiredness, I notice a subtle change in the quality of the silence between us. I can feel that he's looking at me, that there is something else going on, and, if I'm being honest, I suppose I've been waiting for it.

He says, 'I can't feel angry with them. Not that angry, anyway. I can't swear that I would have done differently, in that situation.'

I say, 'Have you ever taken ecstasy?'

'What? No, of course not . . . Have you? Although, it wouldn't surprise me if you had.'

'No, I haven't. Maybe if it had been around earlier . . .'

A pause, in which I close my eyes again. It's almost as though I am asleep and awake at the same time.

'Svea?'

'Yeah?'

'You saw the thing about Iron-Mine Man? That they think they've identified him.'

'Yes, I saw that.'

'I remember Jens Gulbrandsen from Gammelsøy. You must, too – growing up there.'

'I do. A nasty piece of work.'

'Yes. He was. Probably not a great loss to the world.'

'Perhaps not.'

Another pause. This one is a bit longer.

'I don't think I would blame anyone if they had something to do with it.'

My eyes open properly. The sun has wheeled right around to the other side of the conservatory; it must be late, or early, depending on how you look at it.

'Is this your idea of being subtle?' I seem to have woken up again, and glare at him. 'Why don't you just ask me? I suppose Nordis told you what he did to me? When you two were going out? You've always known!'

The whisky runs hotly in my veins, making me feel twenty years younger.

Odd Emil has the grace to look embarrassed. 'No. It wasn't Nordis. My brother told me. He felt so guilty about his part in it.'

A hiss of air escapes my mouth. Immediately, I think: And how many other people knew? Has everyone been whispering and laughing about it all my life? *Do you know what that Svea Hustoft has under her hair? My God . . . a swastika!?*

He says, 'I never told anyone. I don't think Trygve did either. He was too ashamed. And I never discussed it with Nordis, because . . . it wouldn't have seemed fair.'

'Fair? No, it wasn't *fair*! And now you're sitting there asking me if I had something to do with his death? Is that *fair*?'

'I'm not asking you, Svea. I am not. I don't care. And I will never tell anyone else what I know.'

I am breathing as hard as if I've just got up and danced a hornpipe.

'What you *know*? Just what do you think you *know*?'

318

'You're angry with me . . . I'm sorry. I just meant what he did to you when you were a child. You know . . .' He gestures vaguely at his own forehead.

'So, you've been pitying me, all this time?'

'No! Of course not. You're not someone . . . I don't think of you and pity in the same thought. But it must have been horrible. I can only imagine – no, probably not even that.'

'No, I shouldn't think you could.'

'I'm sorry. Forgive me. I shouldn't have said anything. It's the whisky, and . . .'

'It's all right. I suppose I have to let you off . . . at the moment.'

Asta's tail flaps against the floor. She seems to be dreaming – twitching and uttering little excited noises in her sleep.

I take another fiery, golden sip.

'I didn't kill him, Odd Emil.'

'No. I mean, I believe you. I will never do anything to hurt you, Svea.'

You're thinking it too, aren't you? Come on, admit it – you think that my old, but arguably justified, crime is about to be uncovered. So, how did I do it?

From being trapped in the office with Jens Gulbrandsen, I chased him out of the party, and somehow we got up to Nilsbakken, and then I chased him into a mine – all this in my high heels and tight skirt, remember, and then I . . . hit him over the head with a pickaxe? Come on, how likely is that?

Well, maybe I had help. It happened right there in the office. I stabbed him in the stomach with a pair of scissors that were lying on the desk, and then my secret lover – probably my boss – and I managed

319

to bundle his corpse out of there and put it in the boot of his car, and we – or he – drove up to Nilsbakken and hid it in the decommissioned mine, and no one ever noticed.

Sorry to disappoint you, but the last time I saw Jens Gulbrandsen was on that night, during the company party, where he had forced me up against the office door, and he was regrettably very much alive. In those days, I lacquered my hair in place with so much hair spray it never moved, so I had to yank my fringe off my forehead with a crisp sound to show him the scar. When his eyes finally focused, it was as though something had cut his strings. His face went slack, his hands dropped away, he looked aghast. He staggered backwards. At least, I thought, he does remember. But, for good measure, I switched on the overhead light and it fell on us like a blow.

'You can hardly see your knife scars now, but, if you look closely, they're still visible. When I was thirteen, I burned my forehead with hydrochloric acid, to make it go away, but it didn't entirely work.'

His mouth fell open. He looked appalled. Disgusted.

'It hurt like hell. It hurt so much. If anyone ever sees it, I say I was in a motorbike accident. But I wasn't, was I?'

He didn't seem to have anything to say. The adrenaline that was fuelling me like a nuclear reactor started to fade, and it occurred to me that he might kill me – actually kill me. He was undoubtedly capable. So, before he could think about that, while he was still slack and horrified and . . . whatever, I wrenched open the door and fled, tugging my skirt down, back to the party and the other secretaries, and I stuck to them until it was time to go home. I didn't dare go to the bathroom all night. I don't know if Jens came back to the party, but I didn't see him there.

After that night, I knew I had to leave. I figured I'd survived worse. I even made a kind of joke about it, to myself. I'd scared him good and proper. He ran away because he was frightened that I would tell everyone what he'd done to me. The evidence was right there, carved into my face. I don't know why I didn't. Yes, I do. You don't show anyone that kind of thing. Not voluntarily. Not ever.

The only people I told about the events at the party were my sisters, when we met up the following week in the hotel in Fauske. They could tell that something was wrong.

'What's up with you?' asked Magny, who had been scrutinising me.

'What? Nothing,' I said. 'I'm fine.'

'Svea,' said Nordis. 'We can tell you're not.'

I wanted to get up and run out of there, but they were the only people who really knew me, and knew what I had been through, because we had shared so much of it. Who else could I tell? And so I, who never cried, began sobbing and gasping in the bar of the hotel, tears and snot running down my face. That old place, the Northern Lights Hotel, doesn't exist anymore; I was glad when they knocked it down to make room for new offices. It was the place where I bawled in public and didn't care that everyone was looking. I told my sisters about my encounter with Jens Gulbrandsen . . . No. Not 'encounter' . . . Why is it so hard to say it? I told them about the assault, and I can't think about that night without a vivid sensory flashback of the scratchy upholstery prickling my legs through my tights, of the brown carpet that had a staticky kick, the smell of smoke and stale beer.

Nordis held my hand throughout, even though I was gripping her hand so hard it left marks.

321

Sensible, practical Magny said, 'We'll go to the police, Svea. He won't get away with it this time. He should have been locked up a long time ago.'

I said, 'But he didn't really do anything.'

Magny hissed, 'He did that!' and pointed to my forehead.

'That was years ago. I can't prove that it was him. And you can hardly see the . . . one underneath.'

Nordis took my other hand and leant towards me. There was something wild and intense about her face, fire behind her eyes, an avenging fury.

'The police are useless. But don't worry. We'll make him pay.'

Then . . . what? I know Nordis sent him anonymous letters, because she told us. Letters where she let her imagination rip – and, my goodness, she imagined some pretty macabre things. I can guess at the effect they might have had on someone uneducated and superstitious and – maybe, even – feeling some guilt. She was gleeful about it. She could be implacable when she wanted. Whether she went further than that – laid some trap for him; lured him up to the mine and then . . . Who am I to say? It's not as though I was there.

Surely that's absurd. Nordis was eighteen years old, for heaven's sake, a young girl, enjoying her first relationship – with the old man now sitting next to me. Although, come to think of it, she finished with Odd Emil around that time. Never explained. Just Magny to go, then, to complete his collection of the Øvergaard sisters – although, I'd have to say, in her case, that ship sailed a long time ago.

Where was I? Oh, yes, in 1968, Nordis was eighteen, Magny was nineteen and I was twenty-three. The three of us: our years on earth adding up to sixty – a good, round number. A powerful number. In numerology, the sixty represents great love of family, and doing things for others, sometimes selflessly, and sometimes to an unbalanced, damaging degree.

Acknowledgements

Thanks, as always, to my agents, Diana Tyler and Susan Smith at MBA, and to all at Quercus, for commissioning a book they knew nothing about: above all to my editor, Jane Wood. Also thanks to Elizabeth Masters and Ana McLaughlin, Flo Hare and everyone who worked on the book, or who read and commented on the first draft. To my beta readers, thanks for reading so quickly and providing your invaluable feedback: Clare Mockridge, Paul Holman, Bridget Penney and Steve Roser. Thanks, and more, as always, to Marco van Welzen. *Heart emoji*

Massive thanks are due to the people of Bodø in Nordland, and specifically, Marie Peyre and Henrik Sand Dagfinrud of Bodø2024, without whom, quite literally, this book would not exist. They gave me total freedom to write what I wanted, without knowing where the project was going to end up – for that I am immensely grateful. Thanks to them and to the following people, the characters, story and settings somehow crystallised into a book.

Special thanks to the following for answering my questions, providing masses of helpful detail and for rinsing the manuscript of Norwegian idiocies – any that remain are my choice alone: Steinar Aas, Inger Simonsen, Jude Lian and those who wish to remain anonymous.

For taking part in remote writing workshops, for teaching me about the russ celebrations, about their grandparents' experiences during the war and, in general, about being a teenager in the Norwegian Arctic, huge thanks to Leah Sofie Myhre, Kristine flem Willassen, Luna Kjelstrup Ertzaas, Guro Nordskog, Sunniva Elenjord, Emma Kristianne Dragsten, Leo Megård Wiik Wikse, Mina Eiterjord, Tuva, Mathea Strøm, Emrik Nøvik Jensen, Emma Kleven and Johanna Elida Haslerud. I was and remain humbled by your eloquence in a second language.

For writing in with personal and family histories, anecdotes and stories via the Bodø2024 website, thanks to Hildegunn Pettersen, Sven Erik Aaslid, Frank Marstokk, Dag Brygfjell, Kristin Vikjord, Are Andreassen, Vanja Bjørklund, Kenn-Ole Moen and Rita Jørgensdatter.

For expert advice on forensic and familial DNA, thanks to Cristina Coman.

Finally, to those Nordland-dwellers who volunteered their own names or those of loved ones for characters in the book, my thanks go to: Eva Kristine Jentoft, Johnny Skarstein, Helene Albrigtsen Lyngseth, Anne Linn Fjordholm, Odd Emil Ingebrigtsen, Cecilie Haugseth, Marylen Sundfær, Siri Antonsen Haubakk, Renate Torstensen, Stina Kristiansen, Maria Elisabeth Hustoft Fu, Karl Lorentz Kleve, Merete Nordheim, Solgunn Solli, Birk Bodøgaard, Merethe Kathrin Iversen Lindqvist and Hanne Duli Olsen. I hope you like the results!